SERAPH

THE GUARDIAN ANGEL

I dedicate this story
to my best friend and lovely wife, Anastashia Hicks,
a light in this dark world;
and to our little ones that sleep,
Jordan and Skylar.

SERAPH

THE GUARDIAN ANGEL

JAMES HICKS

NEW YORK

SERAPH
THE GUARDIAN ANGEL

Published in New York, New York, by Morgan James Publishing. Morgan James and The Entrepreneurial Publisher are trademarks of Morgan James, LLC.
www.MorganJamesPublishing.com

The Morgan James Speakers Group can bring authors to your live event. For more information or to book an event visit The Morgan James Speakers Group at www.TheMorganJamesSpeakersGroup.com.

A **free** eBook edition is available with the purchase of this print book.

CLEARLY PRINT YOUR NAME ABOVE IN UPPER CASE

Instructions to claim your free eBook edition:
1. Download the BitLit app for Android or iOS
2. Write your name in **UPPER CASE** on the line
3. Use the BitLit app to submit a photo
4. Download your eBook to any device

ISBN 978-1-63047-428-7 paperback
ISBN 978-1-63047-430-0 eBook
ISBN 978-1-63047-429-4 hardcover
Library of Congress Control Number:
2014915720

Cover Design by:
Rachel Lopez
www.r2cdesign.com

Interior Design by:
Bonnie Bushman
bonnie@caboodlegraphics.com

In an effort to support local communities, raise awareness and funds, Morgan James Publishing donates a percentage of all book sales for the life of each book to Habitat for Humanity Peninsula and Greater Williamsburg.

Get involved today, visit
www.MorganJamesBuilds.com

Habitat
for Humanity®
Peninsula and
Greater Williamsburg
Building Partner

But as the days of Noah were,
so shall also the coming of the Son of Man be.
Matthew 24:37

CHAPTER 1

John Summers sat at his computer in his cubicle and looked at the time. He hated his job but it was Friday, so he was eager to get out of work and go home. Five o'clock was quitting time, but he still had forty-five minutes left. He closed his eyes and tried to take a small nap because he had finished his work early. Even though he felt like fifteen minutes had gone by, when he looked at his clock again it was only 4:17. He frowned and sighed. He worked as an entry-level accountant for one of the largest accounting firms in New York City. He had only been there for two years, but he knew this wasn't what he wanted to be doing with his life. Today, though, he had decided that nothing was going to get him down because it was his birthday.

Turning thirty is a big deal for anyone, even for a man with few friends and no girlfriend. John tried to waste time by going to the bathroom, even though he didn't have to go. He ran the water and cupped it in his hands, splashed it on his face, and looked in the mirror. What he saw was a very short African American man with short, black hair sprinkled with a little bit of gray that came from his father's side of the family. He wasn't very athletic, and he was a bit scrawny; he also wore thick glasses, and he wasn't exactly being chased by women to get married. John wasn't an ugly man; in fact he would be quite handsome if he only chose to wear contacts and dressed a little nicer, and he was most attractive when he showed off his charming smile. All in all, John was still grateful to God for his job and for his folks, who were currently living as missionaries in South Africa. John felt most grateful for his best friend, Camilla Adams.

Thirty minutes had gone by, and he figured now was a good enough time to escape this dreary work week. He took the elevator down, climbed on his nine-year-old bike, and rode it home as was his routine for two years now. It was his attempt at killing two birds with one stone, saving the environment and keeping in shape. He arrived at his small studio apartment and greeted Mrs. Roundtree, the old widow who lived on his floor. He took out her garbage whenever he was able because he was a "nice young man," as she put it, and she was a "sweet old lady," as he put it. Just outside his door was a package from his parents for his thirtieth birthday with a card attached. It read: "Happy Thirtieth Birthday, John. Sorry we couldn't be there, but God is really moving down here. We love you so very much. Let's video chat tonight if you can. To: Our favorite son, From: Your favorite parents."

I'm your only son he thought and smiled. On this unusually hot spring day inside his drab one-bedroom apartment, he stripped down and put on the AC. He tried to video chat with his parents to no avail so he watched TV for three hours and had decided he was going to call it a night, when his smart phone rang. It was Camilla Adams.

"Hey, Cammy, what's up?"

"Happy Birthday to you, Happy Birthday to you, Happy Birthday, dear Johnny," she sang, which made him giggle. "What are you doing tonight?"

"Ah, I just got in and I was going to relax here for the night," he responded.

"Yeah right, you were probably watching old reruns." She caught him in his lie. "Why don't you come out and meet me at O'Riley's? We'll have a drink or five and celebrate. You just turned thirty . . . that's a big deal."

"Gosh, ya know I would, but I just, it's been such a long day, and I'm really tired maybe tomorrow or something."

"Jonathan Michael Gabriel Summers," she scolded.

"Wow, my whole name?" He was completely stunned.

"If you don't get your lazy tail out of bed right now, I'm going to come over there and drag you out myself, and it's not going to be pretty," she reprimanded.

"Alright, alright, give me a minute. I'm coming."

Satisfied with his answer, she let him go so he could get ready for his birthday night. He rummaged through his closet to find something, anything, to wear, maybe something that might even impress the young woman. He chose to wear a plaid shirt buttoned all the way to the top, white sneakers, and the cargo pants and jacket he wore to work earlier. He wasn't impressed with his wardrobe, but it was the best combination he could come up with.

He rode his bike and by the time he arrived at O'Riley's, it was close to nine o'clock. He walked in and looked for his friend, who was already on the dance floor. The music got louder as he walked closer to the center of the dance floor, and he had to scream just to get her attention.

"CAMILLA!"

"OH HEY, YOU MADE IT. YOU WANNA DANCE?" she yelled back and hugged him.

"NO, THEY'RE OLD PANTS BUT THANKS," John screamed.

"WHAT?" she screamed back.

"THE MUSIC IS REALLY LOUD."

"YEAH, ISN'T IT GREAT?"

"YOU WANNA GO?"

"KNOW WHAT?"

"NO, GO."

"WHAT'S A NO GO?"

"WE SHOULD GO TO THE BAR," he shouted.

"YA KNOW I CAN'T HEAR YOU. LET'S GO TO THE BAR," she shouted back.

They finally left the dance floor, where the music was eardrum shattering, for the bar, where two people could have a normal conversation.

"Happy Birthday, John, I'm so glad you decided to come out," Camilla exclaimed.

John looked at her and tried to not say anything stupid. He looked at his best friend of twenty years. She was taller than he was by two inches, four inches when she wore heels, like she had decided to do tonight. She was a very beautiful woman in her late twenties. Camilla was athletic and toned, with almond-shaped hazel eyes, and big, black and brown, curly hair that flowed around her face and shoulders. Her caramel skin was a gift given to her by her Caucasian American father and South African mother. Her father, Dr. Richard Adams, was a medical missionary who traveled to South Africa, where he met Abri Kagiso. They were married, and Abri traveled back to New York with him, where she gave birth to their daughter. Camilla worked for her parents in their private medical practice in New York City and was currently a medical student at NYU. She was obsessed with living a healthy lifestyle, both physically and socially, which is why she urged John to join her and was pleased to see him sitting next to her at O'Riley's Pub. He was absolutely smitten with her and she knew it.

"Yeah, I'm glad I came out too. You look really nice today."

"As opposed to other days?" she added with an incredulous look.

John quickly backtracked and tried to recover from his poor choice of words. "Yes, I mean, no, you look great other days too, it's just you—"

"John, relax I was only kidding," she interrupted. "I got you something . . ."

She pulled out a brochure for a brand-new McFadden folding bicycle. The one every cyclist was riding in the city.

"What is this?"

"What does it look like?"

"It looks like you got me a new bike."

"Not just any bike, It's a brand-new McFadden. The one that folds, it's—"

"The best bike in the city . . . you did this for me?"

"Yeah . . . you're my best friend."

John stared into her big, mahogany eyes and fell even more in love with her than he already was.

"Wow . . . thanks."

She gave him a big hug and the brightest smile.

"You're welcome . . . now let's drink."

"Cola is fine."

"Rum and Cola? Got it."

"No, please no rum."

"Don't be such a wimp, Johnny, it's your birthday. Bartender, can I have a rum and cola for the lady, and I'll have a Green Apple Martini please," Camilla said.

In about twenty minutes John was on top of the bar, dancing like a wild man, and having a great night, even though it was still very early. He simply wasn't used to hanging out at bars or partying. He was a homebody and most times when he hung out with Camilla they were either at each other's apartments, special events for their parents, or at church. Camilla had never seen John act this way but was happy to see her friend let loose. She often told him that he was going to "explode" if he didn't find a way to let off some steam. When he fell from the bar, she laughed so hard and helped him up. This was clearly way too much for him to handle, and she decided now was as good a time as any to get him home. She helped him out of the bar as he was high-fiving new "friends" and "happy birthday" well-wishers.

"John, how did you get here?" she asked.

"I rode my bike and I locked it up riiiight . . . hey, where is it?" he slurred.

"Right here? Where this broken chain is?" Camilla asked.

"Aww man . . . somebody biked my stole," John answered, clearly intoxicated.

"Well, good riddance to that old busted thing. Your present is at my place. You'll get it tomorrow, okay?"

"This is the best birthday ever . . . and you're so hot . . . like a hot . . . potato."

Camilla laughed out loud at his response and fielded questions from other drunken strangers asking if he was okay. She offered to pay for a cab ride home but he refused, insisting that the walk home was just through Central Park and that he'd be fine and would call her as soon as he got home. She gave him a hug and kissed him on the cheek, hailed a cab for herself, and went home. John began his long walk from Central Park East to Central Park West, walking slowly through the majestic park that could be quite dangerous at night. John grew up in the great city of New York so he wasn't afraid, just cautious, as he made his way.

Ahadiel had been investigating Ornias for six months per his orders from the archangel Michael. Those orders were handed down from The One personally to Michael, who in turn chose the low-ranking, heavenly peace-keeping officer to find the demon and bring him into custody. Ahadiel had tracked Ornias from continent to continent and was hot on his trail when the demon entered into the United States. He finally caught up with Ornias over New York.

Ahadiel stood nine feet tall with blond hair and blue eyes. He was extremely beautiful, and he was very muscular with a ten-foot wingspan that resembled white eagle wings. He was shirtless with a big golden belt that held up his whiter than snow pants. The gold belt housed a sheath for his massive double-edged sword with a gold-plated and jewel-studded handle. He was a warrior angel that was always ready for battle. He rarely questioned his tasks, even if he felt one was beneath him. He was just happy to be in the service of The One. His only complaint was that he felt underutilized, but here was a chance for him to possibly earn a promotion and be useful in bringing in a fugitive demon. He didn't know Ornias personally before the Great Rebellion. To him this was just another demon that "came across his desk," and he was more than happy to bring him in.

Ornias was also a spiritual being of low rank. He wasn't given the "privilege" of torturing the guilty in hell. In fact the demoness that he worked for thought it was beneath her and thus it was beneath him. He was charged with a simple mission: Find a woman who wants a child but has none. It was these menial jobs that Ornias had to perform at the discretion of his master. He was short by demon standards, just over six feet tall and with gaunt features. He wore a tattered black robe with black bat-like wings protruding from it.

He was completing the mission given to him by his master, but Ahadiel tracked him down in Kansas, and he had been running from the angel for four days now. When Ahadiel finally caught up to the demon, he tackled him in midair and they both fell, tumbling to the ground. Falling through the clouds, Ahadiel managed to direct them away from any buildings to a small clearing in Central Park, where they landed in a grassy area. Ornias was in pain from the long fall and could barely get up, let alone fight Ahadiel— an angel that he couldn't beat on his best day or the angel's worst day. Before the Great Rebellion, Ornias was a messenger angel under the leadership of the archangel Gabriel; physical confrontation was simply not his strong suit.

Ahadiel, being the warrior angel that he was, landed softly on his feet with his wings spread to brace for the impact. Once he landed he was instantly on top of Ornias, not giving the speedy, shape-shifting demon a chance to recover.

"Who are you working for?" Ahadiel said in an easy tone, which sounded like he was singing, but as if there were three other voices speaking with him at the same time, each at a different pitch.

Ornias, fearful of what would happen to him if he didn't speak up, was more terrified at what would happen if he did, so he spoke in circles.

"Please, why are you following me? Is it the time of my torment?" he asked.

"Don't play coy with me," retorted Ahadiel. "I have observed you stalking women who are barren. What do you want with them? What is the connection?"

"Sir, I have no recollection of what you are talking about. I'm but a lowly demon going to and from earth . . . is that a crime?"

"You would do well to not consider me a fool, demon," Ahadiel warned him. "I'm placing you under arrest. I will get to the bottom of this."

As John walked through Central Park he saw something falling from the sky, bright white and red lights. He wondered if anyone else had seen what he saw, but there was no one around to ask, which was odd considering it was slightly after ten o'clock at night. Usually there were late- night joggers or pedestrians walking their dogs, maybe a passing car in the streets that cut through the park, or maybe even a horse and buggy with a dating couple kissing or holding hands. He looked around and saw none of the busy activity that he was accustomed to seeing in this beautiful park, so he slowly continued in the direction which the object, or objects, had fallen. Being a little inebriated, he wasn't really sure if he was imagining things or if he really had seen two lights fall in the middle of the park.

He jogged across the street and stopped just behind some bushes where he was just far enough out of view but close enough to hear bits and pieces of a conversation. When he thought about what he was seeing, he was surprised he could hear the lights speaking at all. They were bright in and of themselves but not bright enough to light up the surrounding area, not enough to draw much attention anyway.

He could tell the bigger, white light was the aggressor and was dominating the smaller, red light. Beyond that he could not tell what they were or what the confrontation was about. So he decided to gain a better vantage point, and the nearby tree provided a perfect view. The last time John made any attempt to climb anything was in high school approximately thirteen years ago. He needed a physical education class to graduate, and to pass the class, he had to climb the rope and "ring the bell," which was rough for him because of his irrational fear of heights. Yet John's curiosity ruled over his fear, and he summoned the courage and began climbing the tree.

He couldn't have picked an easier tree to climb. There were grooves and steps on the tree that seemed to encourage him to press onward. He made his way up the tree very awkwardly, slipping several times and even being rewarded with a splinter for his efforts. In fact, had the tree not been an easy one, he would have never made it up there at all.

He finally reached a branch that grew in the direction of the lights and decided it was the best limb to climb. As he continued onto the branch he could hardly believe his eyes. It looked almost as if the lights were people. At least they looked like people to him. Not aliens with big bug eyes or four fingers who spoke in a strange dialect, but people. He knew they weren't American because they weren't speaking English, and as he continued to look upon them he noticed that they had wings. One had what appeared to be very large white eagle wings, and the other had smaller bat wings, though they were large in their own right. He also noticed that the white being on top had a large sword adorned in gold, was shirtless, very handsome, and very well built, almost as if he was a part of some sort of royal brigade. The red being on the bottom looked nothing like the white being; he wore shabby, disgusting, black garments and appeared to be a sick old man.

John carried 150 pounds on his 5'5" frame, but it was just enough weight on the particularly weak tree limb to snap under him. He tried to make his way back but before he could, the limb gave way and he fell some twenty feet straight to the grass and had the wind knocked out of him.

Ornias was trying to talk his way out of the predicament he was in, but nothing seemed to be working and the weight of Ahadiel was causing him to become short of breath.

"How . . . can I give you . . . answers . . . with your knees in my chest?" Ornias said, gasping for air.

"You will do plenty of—" before Ahadiel could finish his sentence, he heard a noise that distracted him long enough to lose focus on his prisoner. "OOOOOW, MY LEG!!!" Then Ahadiel saw the human who made the pitiful yelp.

Ornias heard the noise too and seized the opportunity to get away from his captor. He kicked Ahadiel in the chest, which did little to hurt the enormous angel. Instead it actually annoyed him. Ornias got up to run off, but Ahadiel grabbed him by one of his legs. Ornias was hopping on his free leg while the angel had the other. What happened next both shocked and infuriated Ahadiel. Ornias grew his black fingernails into talons and scratched Ahadiel in a backhanded swiping motion across his face and eyes, causing the angel to howl and let go of the leg to attend to his injured face. Ornias ran straight toward John, and just as John saw him coming, he raised his arms in a blocking motion to protect himself, but it didn't help in the slightest as the demon jumped right into the poor soul who had unwittingly stepped into a spiritual confrontation with no sort of spiritual protection. John fell and became paralyzed as his body no longer belonged to him. Another entity had taken control. Ornias possessed John Summers.

Ahadiel finally recovered, removed his hands from his eyes, and saw lines of blood on them. Although he was already healing, this made the angel extremely angry. Angry that he was bleeding, angry at the human who distracted him, angry at Ornias for scratching him, but angrier at himself for becoming distracted, which led to the events unfolding the way they did. He looked for the demon but couldn't find him. He closed his eyes and concentrated on smelling where the demon went. If his eyes hadn't been slightly damaged, he would have used his spiritual vision to track the essence of the demonic spirit to actually see where the demon traveled, but he was forced to rely on his nose. As he searched the air for the foul scent that all demons leave behind, he noticed the scent got stronger once he approached the invalid human. He was hoping that the demon hadn't entered the young man, but his fears were confirmed when he smelled the tainted mixture of human and demon odors, a scent he hadn't smelled since the days Jesus and the Disciples cast demons out of humans. According to him, those were the "good ole days."

Ahadiel knelt down in front of John and didn't know what to do. He had never attempted to cast a demon out of a human before. He could call for assistance from an angel that specialized in exorcisms, but the protocol to get the necessary clearance would take entirely too long. And if he left John to get help, Ornias could very well have total possession and be gone by the time he returned. The only other option he had was to enter John and evict the demon personally. Ahadiel decided upon the latter and positioned himself on top of John and fused into the human.

When Ahadiel entered John's body, he could see many things—some good, some bad, neither impressed nor disgusted him. To Ahadiel, he was just another human. He had seen many humans like him throughout his many millennia of existence. His only goal for being there was to find Ornias before he could set up a permanent hold on John, which would make it immensely more difficult to remove him. He searched throughout John's world and thought aloud, "If I were a demon, where would I be?" He assumed that the demon would probably go to the deepest, darkest part of John's soul and that's where he would find them both.

He took flight and traveled from where the skies were serene and peaceful to where the skies darkened, and the turbulence in the air made it too difficult to fly. He had obviously traveled to an area where John struggled terribly in his life, resulting in the storm that Ahadiel found himself in the middle of. This area of a person's life is a perfect breeding ground for a demon to erect a stronghold and attempt to control it for his own demonic purposes.

Ahadiel landed and scanned the area. All he could see were the various idols built by none other than John himself. These idols were in the shape of women in suggestive poses, indicating what John struggled with most in his life. For other humans these idols might be in the shape of different things, such as cars, money, foreign gods, and even statues of themselves, for those who struggled with pride. They took lifetimes to create and no one but that person, in this case John, could have built them.

Ahadiel saw idols as far as his angelic eyes could see. As he weathered the storm, he used his wings for protection from the poisonous rain. Thunder thundered and lightning illuminated the surrounding region, emitting enough light that Ahadiel could see a dark figure at the edge of what looked like a cliff. He approached until the figure called out to him.

"That is far enough," shouted Ornias with his talons across a young man's throat. "Any closer and I will open his neck."

"The moment you do, I will destroy you, Ornias," Ahadiel responded.

"Would you rather this sinful soul be damned to the fires of hell? Huh? Would you like to explain how you lost one of The One's precious souls?"

"BUT I'M A BELIEVER!" shouted John.

"Shut up you worthless human," Ornias screamed. "You really think The One would accept you? Look at this place! You have destroyed your own temple, and you think The One will forgive you for this?" Ornias tightened his grip on John's neck, making him cry out in pain.

"I didn't put these here . . . well, it was me but not really me." John tried to explain.

"Oh so you're a liar too? Yes, yes, The One will be most proud of you." Ornias scoffed.

"John, don't worry. I will get you out of this." Ahadiel tried to comfort John.

"Worried? Who's worried? HELP ME!" John was beginning to panic.

"Don't make promises you can't keep, angel," Ornias warned.

Then suddenly there was a fourth voice that no one recognized except for John, and he knew the situation had gotten significantly worse.

"Let. Me. Go," said the fourth voice.

"Oh, no, no, NO, WE HAVE TO GET OUT OF HERE NOW!" John was terrified.

"Who said that?" asked Ornias.

And then suddenly the demon was attacked. A figure climbed on top of Ornias's back and bit a huge piece of flesh from the demon's neck. John fell to the floor and scrambled toward the angel. They both watched as Ornias was attacked by the hooded figure. It wasn't the attack of a seasoned warrior; it was the attack of an undisciplined madman. A positively insane man who was full of the venomous rage that consumed him.

"We have got to get out of here. This is his part of the body and he will kill us both after he's through with Ornias," John warned and tried to encourage Ahadiel to leave.

"What is that?" asked the angel.

"It's not what, it's who. He is me or I am him."

"What?" Ahadiel was truly confused.

"I'll explain later, just know that this is his territory and we must leave NOW!" John responded.

"Not without Ornias," Ahadiel said.

"What? Leave him."

"I can't. If he stays here, he will eventually find a way to subdue him . . . you . . . and take control of this vessel permanently."

With that said, Ahadiel advanced on the being and the demon. The other John was quite smaller than the larger demon but had maintained the upper hand and continued to brutally attack the demon. Ornias was seriously injured from the confrontation. Whatever this thing was, it was clearly very dangerous. Ahadiel reached to grab the menace, but it looked at him with blood red eyes filled with hatred and malice, and ran off before the angel could get ahold of him. Ahadiel was stunned at how fast he was but decided not to give chase. He knelt down to carry Ornias, but before he could, the being ran and scratched Ahadiel in the face and ran off again. It came back for a second assault, but Ahadiel grabbed him by the neck in mid-run and looked at him as he struggled in his arms. The other John was unkempt and dirty with dirty hair, filthy yellow sharp teeth, and bloodshot eyes. He cursed the angel, himself, and God. This person was undoubtedly demented. Ahadiel walked the creature to the edge of the precipice and dropped him. He picked Ornias off the ground and walked back toward John.

"If you don't mind, could you hurry up," shouted John, trying to be heard over the thunder and lightning.

"I don't see the need to rush. I have the demon and the other you is over the cliff." Ahadiel said with confidence in his voice.

"You don't understand, you can't kill me here. This is my body. You've only slowed . . ."

And then a hand reached up onto the gravel over the edge, and both John and the angel looked toward the cliff.

" . . . him . . ."

And the madman pulled himself up to where all that could be seen of him were his terrifying red eyes.

" . . . down."

And the other John pulled himself completely up the cliff and started to run toward the three intruders on his land. John and Ahadiel, carrying the bruised demon, began to run as fast as they could. They ran past the female idols that the other John built and noticed that he was gaining on them, until Ahadiel grabbed John by his shirt and flapped his majestic wings and flew straight into the air. He almost made a clean get away, but the other John grabbed the angel's foot. Ahadiel looked at him and simply kicked him off, and the tortured soul careened to the ground, crashing into a few idols. The other John shook off the fall and watched as they escaped. Ahadiel traveled battling the wind and rain until the skies began to change from black to twilight and then to a very calm, peaceful, and beautiful blue. Ahadiel saw a paradise that could almost rival heaven. Its beauty was truly captivating, and then he heard John speak.

"This is my region; you can set us down here."

It was a gorgeous meadow with flowers of all kinds, small trees, large trees, and even rivers. It was an amazing place for any soul to make a home.

"You built this place, John?" asked the angel, setting Ornias down on the grass. The demon had lost an eye, a big chunk of his neck, and part of his wing in the confrontation with the other John, but even now he was slowly but surely beginning to heal.

"Yes, I did," John said with righteous pride.

"This place is wonderful. It's almost as beautiful as heaven itself." Ahadiel complimented. "I must ask you, what happened back there? What is this place?"

"I don't know much. All I can tell you is that ever since I've been here, he's been here"

"The other you?"

"Yes, and he is exceptionally evil. All he wants to do is destroy . . . everything."

"And what about you?" asked Ahadiel.

"I don't want to destroy anything. I only want to do what is good and see it prevail. We are inside the spiritual world of John, which is his inner body. We have been fighting for years, trying to control the body. Sometimes I win, sometimes he wins, but we always fight."

"Why was he so strong?" Ahadiel questioned.

"We were deep, too deep in his control of the body. He derives his strength from his territory, like I do mine. Here, I am strong enough to imprison him, but only here. That's why he never comes here and I never go there . . . if and when we do fight, it's always on neutral ground." John tried to explain as best he could. "But now I have questions for you. Who are you?"

"I am Ahadiel; Peace Keeper of the Heavenly Order of the Most High Elohim." Ahadiel proclaimed.

"Elo-who?"

"Elohim . . . means 'God' and I am in his service."

"Oh wow, YOU work for The Most High?

"Yes, I do."

"That is great, just great . . . what in the world are you doing here?" John said, shrugging the angel off.

"My mission was to track down this . . . WHERE DID HE GO?" Ahadiel looked frantically and scanned for any sign of where the demon had gone, but there was no trail that he could see. The only thing that he could see was demonic residue where Ornias had lain, and then the vapor disappeared into a portal that was there but was gone.

"Did you not see him escape?" asked the angel in a loud tone, but he did not scream at the human soul.

"No, I was . . . I didn't see anything," John answered.

"I must leave at once." Ahadiel tried to open a portal but couldn't. He tried again and it still didn't work. He concentrated harder and focused his mind on creating a third portal, and it actually held for a second before it collapsed again. Then suddenly a three-foot-long, black chain appeared and clasped onto John and Ahadiel. The manacles seared themselves onto the wrists of John and Ahadiel, and neither could hide how painful it was. The cuffs had barbs on the inside and dug into the flesh of the two individuals. Both began to bleed and the slightest tug or pull only made their small injuries worse.

Ahadiel realized he was trapped with John, stuck as a foreigner in a strange country with no way to return home. Neither John nor Ahadiel was pleased with the situation that had befallen them. Ahadiel took out his sword and was trying to figure out the best angle to swing that would cut the chains but not injure John or himself. However, John didn't feel comfortable with the angel making any sort of attempt, so Ahadiel decided he would seek The One's help, but finding a way to "gate out" of the body was the dilemma.

John woke up in pain with a leaf in his hair. He took it out and lay on the green Central Park grass in the middle of the cool night sky. A massive headache erupted and he clutched his head. His back hurt as well when he realized he was tangled in a fallen tree limb. He placed his hands under the tree to procure a better grip as he lightly pushed the tree limb off, but the tree flew forty feet into the air and landed across the street over seventy feet away. John was shocked at what happened and jumped to his feet, but his jump landed him at the very top of the tree that he fell from. He was now afraid and shouted, "What is happening to me?"

John looked down from his perch, and what he saw blew his mind. Not only could he see individual blades of grass, but he could see an earthworm slithering through the grass and trying to burrow its way into the soil. He could not only see the worm, he could also hear him. He heard the grass being moved by the sliding worm, but suddenly he heard a car horn outside the park and fell out of the tree again. On the way down John hit the broken tree limb that stuck out of the tree and landed on the ground. He cried out when the branch bore into his leg and protruded out the other side. John called for help twice but no one came, and he decided to try to pull it out himself, something that he had only seen in movies. He thought he was crazy for trying it himself. But he reached down and grabbed one end of the branch and pulled it out of his leg. He winced from the pain and even let out a small whimper. The tree limb was covered in his blood, and he put his finger through his cargo pant leg and looked to see how bad the wound was. It looked very bad but almost instantly began healing itself right in front of his eyes, until it was whole again with no trace of a scar. The blood that remained was the only clue to a rupture in his flesh. "My God," John said as he stood up very slowly and began walking out of the park. The cacophony of sounds, from the honking horns, the screeching tires, even people having conversations on their cellphones, pounded his head and made his headache that much worse.

He came to a crosswalk and waited for the image of the "white walking man" to appear in the pedestrian traffic light before he crossed. When he had the right of way he stepped into the middle of the street, but a taxicab driver overeager to catch a new rider ran the red light and was about to hit John. When John realized he was about to get hit, he tried to brace himself for the impact with his outstretched arms. His hands met the hood of the car and dented it; he applied so much force to the front of the car that the back of the taxi went five feet into the air before it slammed back down. People looked at John with shock and awe. Although New Yorkers are used to seeing many things, they had never seen a man stop a speeding car with his bare hands. For at that moment the world stopped, and all eyes were on him, something he had never experienced before. Before anyone could ask him if he was alright, he ran off, and in a blink of an eye, he was gone.

John arrived at his apartment and opened the door with two fingers and closed it with his pinky so he didn't cause further damage to anything else. He was tired from the day and exhausted from the ordeal he just had, promising himself that he would find out what was happening to him, tomorrow. It would be best to figure it all out on a full night's sleep and fully sober. He took his clothes off and lay in his bed. Sleep not only came, it overtook him in a matter of seconds.

Ahadiel had been working on making portals for about an hour and most of his attempts ended in defeat, but he could tell with each passing moment that making them was becoming a little easier. A few of the portals were stable for more than a few seconds but not long enough for him to pass through, let alone with two beings. And when he wondered why, he realized that his portals were attempts to exit the body, but they weren't attempts to go to another dimension, say heaven or even hell. When Ahadiel grasped that concept he decided to try another way. He opened a beautiful, stable, blue starry portal that led directly to heaven. Pleased with his accomplishment, he woke up the resting soul.

"Why are the skies darkening," Ahadiel asked John.

"The body is resting; most vital operations are shutting down," he replied.

"Do you rest with the body?"

"Not usually, we never sleep and we are rarely ever tired . . . but after tonight's events I am very weary," John explained.

"Well, there will be no rest tonight. We are going to see The One," Ahadiel said.

"The One?" John asked. "Do you mean God? Like God, God?"

"Does this surprise you? Yes, we are going to see them," Ahadiel countered.

"Them? We're going to see Jesus and the Father both?" John inquired.

"Yes and no."

"Why do you call them The One?" asked John.

"We address them by many titles. We call them by their Name or the Creator, Father, Son and sometimes we call them The One. Only they can help us, but we will not see them separately," Ahadiel answered.

"I . . . don't understand . . ." John was completely puzzled.

"It may become clearer in a moment. Hold on." Ahadiel assured.

Before John had a chance to react, Ahadiel opened a magnificent gateway and walked through, taking John with him. Traveling through the portal, John felt a sense of euphoria, peace, and tranquility. He also felt love echoing through the cloudy, sky blue, starry portal. He could hardly believe his eyes or his feelings. He just kept thinking that this had to be a dream of some kind. The last thing he remembered was lying down on his bed, but everything seemed much sharper than being awake, which is incongruous with dream worlds. They walked only a few steps and then John saw a light in the distance. A white light. It appeared when he finally stepped out of the portal. He arrived in a great, white hall, and there was a man on the other side looking at him. John knew instantly that this man was The One.

CHAPTER 2

She sat in her dimly lit chambers and waited for her lackey to arrive. According to her, she was waiting entirely too long. She sat patiently nonetheless, with her feet on her rock table.   Her cavernous abode with its faint red glow she had sculpted out of the mountains herself, far from the reach and jurisdiction of the Evil One. Here she was able to be, to dictate, and to control without any interference from Satan. She was not a servant of his, but in hell everything and everyone belong to him in one way or another. Lilith lived in a mountainous, desert range far from the cries of the billions of the guilty that inhabited hell. There were millions of these poor souls where she called home, but they were buried deep in the sands of the Ottocom Desert, being afflicted by whatever they deserved. She didn't participate in dealing punishment to the guilty in hell like her demonic counterparts, but neither did she feel sorrow, only apathy, believing that it served anyone right for rejecting The One and consequently making this place their eternal home, like she once did. No, Lilith was above that.

She was astonishingly beautiful. She chose to take the appearance of a young woman, olive-skinned with dark hair that made her red eyes stand out, similar to how she was originally created in the Garden of Eden; it was her way of staying connected to the Creator. She was a strong, liberated spirit that conformed to no one's will but her own. However in order to advance, even in this dimension, she knew she had to rub shoulders with the elite demons in this realm. So she set a series of events in motion, and her slave, Ornias, had an essential role to play.

Just when she thought she couldn't wait any longer, a deep auburn portal opened before her. She hated portals in her private chambers because she never knew who would walk through them. Usually when a portal opened in her private chambers it meant trouble, and although it did not happen often, high-ranking demons, or even Satan himself, opened gates without announcing their arrival, which always made her uncomfortable.

This is why she requested of some, and demanded from those beneath her, that they walk through the mouth of her cave if they sought an audience. She stood and waited for the being that would step forth and when it did she was both angered and relieved.

"Ornias! Haven't I told you to never portal jump into my chambers?" Lilith yelled and began hurling fireballs at him.

"Yes, mistress." He cowered and dodged as best he could, "but I had no choice. Please believe me."

"You are an imbecile and I should feed you to Shaziel."

"NO, PLEASE, mistress, I beg of you no. I can explain . . ."

"I'm waiting," Lilith said impatiently

"You'll never believe what I've just been through."

"Try me." She hurled another fireball in his direction and nailed him.

He yelped with pain but continued as best he could. "Ahadiel has been hunting me down . . . and he finally caught me. . . . He was going to bring me before The One . . ."

"Go on." She threw another fireball that intentionally missed.

"Well, he almost had me but I managed to escape. . . . I possessed a young man . . . and the angel did something that I didn't think was possible. He too possessed the young man."

"Get to the point."

"Well, I got away because I jumped out and trapped him in the man." He began laughing, marveling at his plan.

"You did what?" She began working a big ball of fire between her hands.

"I imprisoned the angel inside the man so I could escape."

"The depths of your stupidity know no limits." And she let the big ball of fire go and it burned him immensely.

"Mistress, my apologies but I fail to understand," he said as he begged for his existence, writhing in pain on the floor.

"Clearly," Lilith reprimanded. "You trapped an angel inside of a HUMAN!" She hit him with yet another fireball. "You imprisoned heavenly power inside a mere human? If he has a spiritual awakening, he will have power to cause serious problems, not only for us but the entire kingdom. And what's worse . . . what if Satan finds out what you've done? He will see us both to the Sea of Fire." She shuddered. "Find him and release him at once!"

"Mistress, I can't. He is surely long gone by now, and even if I can find him, the moment the angel is set free, he will surely overpower me and arrest me. Either way, we have no choice but—"

"—to continue as planned," Lilith finished his sentence. "You idiot. You had better hope that your little mistake doesn't become a big one or you will have hell to pay."

"Y-yes, mistress."

"Did you at least find what you were looking for?"

"Mistress, I did. Her name is Andrea Lewis-Rose," Ornias said with a wide smile.

John looked at The One and could hardly move, let alone speak, as he was gently tugged forward by the hulking angel that had accompanied him on this strange journey. A journey that led them into a beautiful, great white hall that had pillars that went up to the sky, which was deep space with a multitude of stars in the great expanse, with the occasional shooting star and super nova. John was beyond words as he divided his time between gazing at The One and space. He had never seen anything so beautiful, so amazing. Any doubts that this omnipotent and benevolent being had created the universe were erased when he saw The One face-to-face for the first time. Ahadiel approached The One with a sense of familiarity, as if he knew this being since his creation, and knelt down before him. John was too shocked to comprehend anything as he stood there looking at The One with wide-eyed amazement until his chain was yanked down and he fell on both knees before him. John looked up and could see him looking back with a smile. His hair and his beard were white like wool, as white as snow; and his eyes were like a flame of fire; and his body like unto fine brass, as if it burned in a furnace; and his voice was loud and deep. He also wore a white robe with a golden lapel, and on it were the words "King of Kings and Lord of Lords." John looked up and smiled faintly, and he could hardly believe that He, the Creator, God, The One, was smiling back at him.

"Rise," The One said.

Ahadiel rose to his feet gingerly, but John was still in too much awe to even hear the word, and then The One spoke again in a soft, gentle voice that seemed to make everything instantly better.

"Rise, John, give me a hug."

John rose to his feet and greeted the man who died on a cross for his sins and rose from the grave in three days so that he may one day meet him and call heaven his home. He rose and hugged the Supreme Being and spoke his name.

"Jesus . . . ," John said. "Am I dead?"

Jesus laughed aloud with genuine laughter. Each of the Father's children always had a different reaction to him when they met, but Jesus' favorite reaction was when he encountered the living who thought they had died.

"No, you are not dead, but you are really here."

"Here? Is this place heaven?"

"A part of it, yes. This isn't where the saints come once they have passed from earth and are ready to enter their reward. But this is heaven."

"Am I not allowed? Am I being rejected?"

"No, no of course not, child, you are here because you are not ready for heaven. You still have much work left to do on earth before you can come home."

"Where is the Father?" John asked.

"He and I are one. You cannot see Him. My Father is far too holy to be seen by any man—you would be destroyed instantly. Man is too sinful to see My Father's face and live, so that is why I address you. But always know that anyone who has seen me has seen the Father also because—"

"You and the Father are one." John answered, trying his best to understand.

"Exactly, John," Jesus assured him.

"My Lord," Ahadiel interjected. "We have a small problem." And he raised his arms to reveal the manacles that he and John shared.

"Yes, I see. I suppose you'd like to be free."

"Yes, my Lord, so that I may finish pursuing Ornias and bring him into custody. I almost had him and—"

Jesus raised his hands before Ahadiel could continue his statement. "Ahadiel, relax." He examined the manacles and saw how disgusting and dirty they were. The One could see the blood around their wrists and the barbs that caused them. He took the chains in his hands and when he touched them, the cuffs became gold and comfortable to wear. Gold from the cuffs to the chains that connected them. Ahadiel looked stunned and confused.

"My Lord?" Ahadiel questioned. "You, you did not remove them . . . why?"

"Yeah, I thought you said he was going to free us," John added.

"I will, just not yet. Walk with me," said The One.

As the two beings began walking with The One, they went from the great, white hall. Within a few steps they went through a misty fog and ended up walking on an ocean. John immediately panicked and began sinking. Ahadiel tried to pick him up, but The One held up his hand to test John's faith. The One never spoke to John, and John never asked for help. He simply remembered the story of old Peter, and amidst his drowning he looked to The One and instantly found solid footing on the calm waters. Jesus smiled when he saw his faith and knew he was ready for the task that was about to be placed on his shoulders.

"My return is near. . . . I do not know when, only the Father knows, but it is very near. I have watched the earth suffer under the curse of man, and it is crying out to me from the dust to the seas, from the heavens to the animals. Even my people who are called by my name are beginning to awaken, anxiously awaiting for me to return, to set them in their own land and set up the Kingdom of Heaven on earth. I have heard their prayers and I will answer them soon. However, the demons have sensed that their time is coming, and they are beginning to manifest themselves in physical form like the days when I once graced the earth's soil. Some have possessed, others are showing mankind their true natures. Some people have taken to working for them, others have begun worshiping them.

The wrath and reign of the Beast and the False Prophet are coming upon an earth that is ripe for their harvesting. I would rather that many more would turn to the truth first so that when I crack the skies, more of the beloved children would meet me in the air. You can help me. Fight for me! Face these demons head on! Loosen their footholds around the world so that my creation will have a spiritual awakening and turn to me. Will you help me?"

Ahadiel was the first to bow low and respond with a resounding yes; John was a bit more tentative. He said nothing; he just stood there and looked upon The One.

Jesus continued, "John, I know that you are afraid because you feel inadequate, you feel that you will fail, you feel you are unworthy of me to use you, but I will equip you with everything you need if you just say yes. Don't be afraid because you don't understand—Nicodemus didn't. Don't be afraid because you are young—Timothy was. And don't be afraid because of your short stature, or that you are the least in your own family, or even if you struggle with lusts of the flesh; David struggled with all of those and I still used him greatly. . . . What do you say?"

"Yes," John whispered with tears in his eyes.

"It is good," was Jesus' response and He touched John on his forehead and a blue inscription appeared, imprinting him with a burning sensation. The mysterious letters burned a bright, fiery blue, and the flame started at his head and then began to consume his whole body. From his head to his torso, neck to his arms, legs to his feet until he and Ahadiel were both engulfed. The fire burned brightly and fused the human and the angel into one entity. When the fire was extinguished he was covered head to toe in a white, blue, and black body armor suit. His whole body was protected and the ancient blue inscription was engraved on his forehead and disappeared. The helmet protected his whole face, and his eyes glowed bright bluish white. Two angels approached from the skies carrying two objects on two very small clouds. They landed on the water next to The One. Jesus took the first object from the first angel and placed it on John's left forearm. It was a blue light shield to protect him. When John activated it, he swung it around to try to get a feel for it. It wasn't heavy, but he was assured that it would protect him from anything. When John deactivated the shield, Jesus took the second item and placed it in his hands. It was a handle without a blade attached to the end.

"What is it?" John asked.

"It's a sword. Well, it's just a handle," Jesus answered.

"How do I turn it on?" John responded.

"By staying close to me. This sword is connected to my Father's Holy Spirit, the source of all power here in heaven. You stay connected to me and it will be your most powerful weapon. The suit has no power by itself; it only serves as your protection from the elements and from injury that you would otherwise sustain without it. Ahadiel will help you harness your new supernatural abilities. Take care of him and he will take care of you. It is important for you to be what I'm calling you to be, that you two learn to coexist. You are my guardian angel on earth and I will give you a new name. From now on your name is Seraph," Jesus said.

When Jesus said those words the sword powered up, and an erratic beam of orange fire shot out until it stabilized and extended about forty-two inches from the handle. The bright, burning, orange glow reverberated with energy, making it feel like the sword itself was alive. John could feel the warmth emanating from the weapon as he stared at it. The sword slowly began to cool and the double-edged blade made from blue-angel steel replaced the burning fire. The sword's edges were extremely sharp and surrounded white-angel steel that had two words on either side written in the angelic tongue.

"What does it say?"

"'Living,' and on the other side, 'Powerful.' I have written the Name of my Father on your forehead. You have been sealed to do His will just as I do His will."

The sword deactivated and when it did so, John placed it in his sheath on his right thigh, then the entire suit powered down.

"What do you want us to do now, Lord?" John questioned, not knowing if they should get started on a task right away or wait until they were issued a formal assignment. But Jesus didn't answer his question; instead, he only asked that John close his eyes. John closed his eyes tightly and waited for something mysterious to happen. After he thought he had waited long enough, he opened his eyes and found himself lying in his bed. John looked around and could see that his alarm clock read 8:54 a.m.

The sun was shining in his eyes through the blinds in his studio apartment. He felt a little bit of soreness on his forehead. Jumping out of bed he ran into his bathroom and looked into the mirror, he could see the writing on his head but knew not how to read it. He only knew that it was the Name of his Father in Heaven, assuring him that whatever he dreamt actually happened. But before he could examine the mark that was emblazoned on his head further, he heard a knock at the door.

※

Camilla Adams stood on the other side of John's door, banging loudly. She had a bad feeling about letting him walk home by himself as intoxicated as he was. She had sent him over twenty-seven text messages and called thirteen times, until she finally fell asleep at 4:00 a.m. She even called 911 to file a missing person's report, but they told her she couldn't file a claim unless he had been missing for twenty-four hours. So she decided she would try and get as much sleep as she could and check on John first thing in the morning.

She continued banging on the door until she heard a voice tell her that he was on his way. She breathed a sigh of relief and thanked God that John was okay.

When the door opened, it wasn't who she expected. She saw a tall, very handsome young man with bulging muscles and indented abs under a white T-shirt that was obviously too small for him. She looked down at the young man's sturdy athletic legs—his strong, robust thighs were covered by a pair of high school gym shorts that began ripping from the new body wearing them.

His suddenly handsome face sported a well-trimmed goatee and he had a buzz cut with a perfect hairline. Had she not been so attracted to the stranger, she would have screamed immediately. But then the man said, "Hey, Cammy, what are you doing here?" She screamed, simultaneously taking out the fresh pepper spray she kept in her purse, spraying the young man right in the eyes. John hollered, rubbed his eyes, and tried to remedy the burning sting. Camilla ran past him screaming to John that she was here to rescue him and telling him that he could come out now.

"JOHN! JOHN! WHERE ARE YOU?" Camilla yelled.

"Cammy, I'm over here," John said.

"WHERE OVER HERE?" Camilla yelled again.

And then the strange man appeared before her, using his T-shirt to wipe his face. But Camilla didn't recognize him and hadn't seen him talking to calm her down.

"STAY AWAY, I KNOW KARATE AND OTHER DANGEROUS WORDS!!! JOHN, WHERE ARE YOU?" Camilla screamed and ran into the kitchen to get a knife.

"Cammy, I'm right here . . . put the knife down," John said laughing.

"What . . . what are you talking about? John is short, scrawny, and wears glasses. You are far from either. Now where is he?"

"Cammy, yesterday was my birthday and I got drunk, did some dancing on tables, and you let me walk home by myself, remember?"

"Yeah, whatever. You could have been stalking him at the bar and followed him home. You could be some thug that beat him up and kidnapped him. Please just tell me what you've done with him . . . Please . . . he's my best friend . . . ," she cried.

John thought real hard about his next move. He clearly looked so different than what he used to look like that he couldn't convince a woman who had been his best friend for twenty years otherwise. So John thought a moment and told her a story that only they would know.

"Do you remember the day we became best friends? I do. We were at Lake George in upstate New York. You were a spoiled little eight-year-old brat, and I followed you around because you were the only other kid there for me to hang out with at a Fourth of July barbeque.

"Anyway, I chased you to the end of the dock, and you stopped right before the edge. You said, '*Na nana boo bee, you got the cooties!*'"

He laughed at that last comment before he continued. At this point Camilla sat down in a chair and put the knife down to listen to the rest of John's story. "When I turned to leave, I don't know perhaps the dock was wet, I heard a splash and when I turned around, you were flailing around in the water. I called out for help, but no one could hear me over the music so I jumped in, caught you, and swam back to the docks with your arms around my neck . . . nearly choking me . . . but by the time we got back to the dock, everybody was there to pull you out."

"I wasn't a spoiled brat," Camilla said.

John laughed hysterically at the comment and Camilla ran over to hug him.

"John . . . what happened to you?"

"That's a long story . . . and I'll tell you over breakfast," John said.

Andrea Lewis-Rose was just getting off work at the Second National Bank in Wilsonton, Kansas, where she had worked as a teller for over twenty years. It wasn't her dream job by any stretch of the imagination, but it was all she had. She longed for the glamorous life—expensive cars, big homes, lavish jewelry, and paradise getaways. When she was in high school, she wanted to become a model and an actress because she was very beautiful back then and could have been both.

A tall, leggy blond, with dazzling blue eyes, Andrea was the most beautiful girl in her county. This was confirmed by the blue ribbons she won twice at a state fair, and she was also homecoming queen her senior year. Her king was her boyfriend, senior and starting quarterback Kenneth Rose. She seemed to have the perfect life and opportunity to achieve her dreams, but things weren't always what they seemed.

Kenneth had a really rocky home life, watching his father beat on his mother and feeling his wrath as well. Abuse was a natural way of life in the Rose home.

Kenneth's father was an alcoholic and tortured him until he got big enough to fight back. Kenneth often fought other kids at school and was very angry; the only one who could calm him down was Andrea. She was the one bright spot in his life, but that didn't stop him from lashing out at her in screaming fits every now and then.

Andrea had hopes of going to New York or Los Angeles to pursue her dreams, but that was dependent on where Kenneth went to college. Wherever he went, she decided to follow so they could maintain their relationship. She loved him very much. Kenneth didn't get accepted into *any* college because his grades were horrible.

Sensing he was going to lose her, he begged Andrea not to leave Kansas without him. They made a plan: Kenny would go to Wilsonton Community College and play for the football team there, work on getting a good GPA, and then transfer to a major university. That way they would stay together and she could still chase her dreams, but in the meantime she would work at the bank and go to college.

None of those plans came to pass. Kenny began partying and drinking at the local parties, skipping classes, and eventually was cut from the team. Andrea was slowly dragged down between having good, but mostly bad, times with Kenny and keeping up with her classes, until she unexpectedly found herself pregnant as a sophomore. Not coming from a family who believed in abortion, she decided to keep the baby.

Kenny didn't want the baby but supported her decision to keep it, and proposed to her. With the support of her family, she accepted and they were married before she began to show. Slowly but surely she felt her dreams slipping away.

The more Kenneth drank, the worse their fights became and the more he became like his father. He even hit her a few times, but never hard enough to leave a visible mark. On one particular night, after a day of heavy drinking, Kenny and Andrea got into a violent fight about her frustrations. Angry because she was trapped in her small town, Andrea said very hurtful things to Kenny and in his rage he kicked her down a flight of stairs. Before Kenny realized what he had done, Andrea was unconscious at the bottom of the staircase in their home.

He called an ambulance and they rushed Andrea to the hospital, but it was too late. She lost the baby in her second trimester. When she was questioned by the police, she lied about the incident, claiming a dizzy spell had caused the fall.

She stayed with Kenny after he promised to never hurt her again, but he broke that promise over and over again, by continuing the verbal and physical abuse. In between the abuse they tried to have other children, but each pregnancy ended in a miscarriage. This cycle continued until Kenny got behind the wheel of his car after drinking at the bar and drove off a bridge.

Thirty-eight-year-old Andrea was a sad woman who never realized her potential and hated herself because of it. She looked for any bright spots in her dark world, but found none. Eventually, depression set in. Anxiety attacks and insomnia became a daily and nightly routine. She didn't feel beautiful anymore, even though she was still quite an attractive woman in her late thirties. She still had a nice figure and lovely hair with a small touch of gray, but her eyes that once sparkled told a different story. They told a story of a sad woman who never achieved her dreams, never bore children, and who had attempted suicide on more than one occasion.

Once she was rushed to the hospital by her father who found her on the floor with her prescription pills spilled next to her. Another time her neighbor baked a homemade pie for Andrea's birthday and found her on her living room floor with her wrists slit. And yet another time, her best friend Sally stopped her from driving home from the bar after getting way too drunk.

This was all Kenny's fault for trapping her in this small town, for keeping her from her goals, for beating her, and for taking away her chance to be a mother.

After much counseling, however, she gained a little bit of peace in her life and even went to church a few times, mostly on the holidays. She hadn't committed to Jesus, nor did she feel she was ready to, but at least she stopped drinking so much. She took her pills responsibly, and the urge to commit suicide began to fade. She decided to try to make the most of the life she had and went home from her job every day just happy to be alive.

In the murky, faintly lit cave that served both as protection and home for Ornias and herself, Lilith began devising a plan to attain a better position of power in hell. She sat on her small throne made from the bones of angels and demons from wars past. She learned from war that demon and angel spirit beings could be blasted to mere particles, and although they would eventually be made whole again, that process could take years or even decades until the spirit fully recovered from "death."

No angel or demon truly dies but whenever they fight, limbs may be lost and need to be regrown with proper rest; Lilith took the limbs of her fallen adversaries whether they were human, angel, or even demon and added their bones to her throne. She spoke to Ornias from this throne while he played in the dirt like a child.

"I hate it here. I hate having to submit to demons who are beneath me in every way. I am superior or at the very least equal to all of Satan's generals. Yet I am confined to this cave, an outcast, accosted at every opportunity. Shown no respect when I could kill or outwit them all in combat and strategy. But that isn't even what I want. I do not wish to command an army or torture the guilty. All I want is to own my own territory and live in peace, be seen as equal. If only Satan had the weakness of men this would be so much easier. But he doesn't trust me . . . no one does. If I'm ever going to realize my full potential in this desolate place then I need to make a gesture to Satan that says we are on the same team," Lilith thought aloud.

"Mistress, are you talking to me?" Ornias asked.

Lilith threw a skull and hit Ornias in the head. "Who else could I be speaking to, moron?"

"My apologies, mistress," Ornias whimpered. "Do you have an idea of how to go about it?"

"No, but I thought *you* had a plan. Don't you? Otherwise, what was the sense of you finding some human wench?" Lilith pondered.

"Yes, of course, mistress. My plan is to give him something he doesn't yet have," Ornias said.

"What do you mean?" Lilith questioned.

"Well . . . no, I'm sorry — it's stupid of me to even think it."

"Ornias, if you do not speak up I will singe you with a fireball till you begin to smell your insides burning," she said as her hands began to glow a bright orange.

"Yes, mistress, my apologies. It's just, well, do you remember before the Great Rebellion and the Fall?" Ornias asked her.

"No, I do not. Has it escaped your memory that I was a human woman once?"

"Yes," he smiled slightly. "Sometimes it does. Well, before the Fall, Satan was once an angel named Lucifer. He had the grandest position in all of heaven. Even greater than archangels Michael and Gabriel. Well, there came a day when The One left his heavenly throne to create the universe. The Father and Son left Lucifer in charge of the heavens until they returned. The One had only been gone for six days and returned by the seventh day to rest. However, they returned to civil unrest. Many angels, me included, did not understand and were upset that The One had abandoned us for so long. "

"Seven days isn't a long time," Lilith interjected.

Ornias continued. "To you it isn't, but to us our whole lives were dedicated to pleasing and worshiping The One. Anyway, by the time The One came back Lucifer had moved his throne into the throne room, and they were very angry to see what he had done. This was not when Lucifer was banished from heaven.

"In the days following, Lucifer was overcome by pride unlike any he displayed before. He was always a bit prideful because of his title and position, but this new display was extreme—even for him. He wanted to be like the Most High God. I remember that day like it was yesterday because it forever changed who we were as spirits. I foolishly supported the idea that Lucifer should keep his seat in the throne room because of the wonderful job he did running heaven in the absence of The One.

"As you know, the Great Rebellion and the subsequent Fall led us here. A place without the spirit of The One. Here Lucifer became Satan, and here he still desires to be like God."

"That's a great story. What does that have to do with me getting a better position in hell?" Lilith asked.

"Everything, mistress. Satan still desires to be like The One—the Father and the Son, but what is the one thing he doesn't have?"

"A son . . ." Lilith exclaimed.

"Exactly, mistress. This is why I went searching for women on earth. I think that we can give him a son, and he will gladly promote you and make you master over many."

"And you thought of all this by yourself?" Lilith said. Surprised that a demon that she held in such little regard had come up with such a brilliant plan.

"Yes, mistress," he said shyly. "This is where Andrea Lewis-Rose comes in. She has never borne a child and would welcome any opportunity to have one. The hard part is convincing Satan to impregnate her."

"You had me and then you lost me." Lilith shook her head. "He would never be with a human. He despises them. Why do you think he commands his minions to torture them so gruesomely? No, that would never work . . . however . . . you could be the one to do it."

"Anything for you miss—wait . . . What?" said a shocked Ornias.

"Yes, *you*. You should be the one to bring forth this son for him. I can present it as a gift and I will be welcomed and considered the same as any of the other demons in hell," Lilith said confidently. "Tell me about this Andrea Lewis-Rose."

"Mistress, I *don't* want to do this."

"You do not have a choice in the matter."

"But—"

"YOU DO NOT HAVE A CHOICE! . . . Now tell me about this woman."

" . . . Very well then . . . you already know her name. She is thirty-eight earth years old; she had tried for many years to have a baby with her husband but was unsuccessful." He sighed.

"Is she still married now?" Lilith asked.

"No, mistress, her husband is dead."

"Really? Was he saved or is he guilty?"

"Guilty. His name is Kenneth Rose."

"Then we must find him and give him a reprieve from his torments, he could be . . . useful." And a sly grin came over Lilith's face. "You must go to the hall of records and find him in the chronicles. He will tell us the best way to seduce this Andrea."

"Mistress, it is not so easy. There is protocol and clearance that I must obtain. Other demons will ask me why I need the chronicles, and they know that you are my master; if my answers don't satisfy them, then they will bring me before generals and maybe before the Evil One himself. It will not be good if I am caught."

"Well then you best not be caught," Lilith commanded. "Now go find his chronicles and bring its knowledge to me."

Once the command left her lips, Ornias was compelled to obey and opened a dark red, vapid portal and stepped inside. Walking out in mere moments, he walked from the portal and appeared at the gates to the city of Sheol. The first city built in hell since the fall, it also served as the capital. When Satan was first cast into outer darkness, hell was the only planet in the dimension orbiting a dull orange sun very closely.

When hell was first created, it was mostly mountain ranges and desert with few rivers and one gigantic ocean made of boiling, slick black oil—no life existed inside of it, no life could because it consumed and fed on any living thing that fell into it. Engulfing the unfortunate being that fell into its calamity, reproducing and multiplying around it in order to completely devour its prey, it was almost as if the Sea of Fire was alive. That is how it acquired the name the Sea of Fire. This planet was the home of Satan and all of the angels that followed him, and they began to shape the planet to better suit their needs as demons.

Yet that wasn't the first transformation to hell. During a cataclysmic event on earth called the flood, humans poured into outer darkness in the tens of millions. The demons even called this incident the flood because of the flood of human souls that occupied the city of Sheol. This occurrence marked a turning point for Satan as a sadistic oppressor. He decided to turn hell into his torturous playground, assessing how a human lived his or her life on earth and doling out punishment to fit the crimes they committed.

They were always evil, horrible, and worse than anything any human mind could conceive. The demonic holy city Sheol became a place where human souls passed through to be judged and given their eternal punishment. This is when the humans became known as the guilty. Sheol held no human prisoners other than new arrivals waiting to be sentenced, but it held a hall of records, living quarters for demons, and Satan's palace.

The hall of records was located just a few blocks from Satan's palace, which was naturally in the center of Sheol. As Ornias made his way through the city and toward the hall, he saw many demons, male and female, some that were about their business and others that were just trying to exist in a world outside the love of The One. Some greeted him with evil looks, while others ignored him completely.

Upon his arrival, he did not have trouble gaining entry. Any demon had access to the hall of records. It was the section that was dedicated to humans that required clearance. Although there were no guards watching the entrance into that area, lieutenants, captains, and generals frequented this sector to keep tabs on their human prisoners. Here they acquired information on current prisoners and new arrivals, so it was quite busy.

Ornias focused his mind on locating Kenneth Rose's chronicles in the hall of records. As he concentrated on finding it, he realized that the book was on the third floor, the eleventh column, in the twenty-seventh row of the human souls sector, and he instantly gated to the location of Ken's book. Luckily there were no demons in the vicinity and when he finally found the correct Kenneth Rose chronicle, he grabbed the black book and opened it. From the outside, Ornias appeared to be reading a book, however from Ornias's point of view he had just entered Kenneth Rose's life.

The whole world became pitch black, and he could see a small cell reacting to metaphysical changes. It began multiplying by twos, then fours, then eights, then sixteens, and Ornias realized he was looking at Kenneth's conception. He quickly fast-forwarded and stopped at Kenneth meeting Andrea Lewis in the fourth grade.

In the middle of an elementary school cafeteria he watched as a friendly and innocent Andrea Lewis shared her lunch with a bruised Kenneth Rose. He skipped ahead a few more years and stopped at a place where a 17-year-old Kenneth Rose finally had the courage and strength to fight his abusive father, sending him to the hospital, nearly beating him to death, and earning his first run-in with the law. He skipped past Ken's college years and even the Lewis-Rose wedding.

He did, however, stop at the point when Andrea was pregnant and Kenneth kicked her down the stairs. He watched Kenneth become an alcoholic, and he finally arrived at the day Kenny died by driving off the bridge. He saw Ken drown in the river below and then saw his soul swim to the top and grab onto the snowy river bank.

He watched as four demons appeared in an electric, deep purple vortex and dragged Kenny, kicking and screaming, into the great white judgment hall in heaven. Ornias saw Kenneth watch in horror as the angel was unable to find his name in the Book of Life. He saw Kenneth plead for his soul yelling, "There MUST be some mistake," and saw him being dragged by the four demons that escorted him into the great hall. He skipped ahead to see Kenny brought before Satan himself; he saw Kenny's fear as he gazed upon the devil and was sentenced. This is what he was looking for, the sentencing.

"Kenneth Rose, I've been waiting for you," Satan said.

"Where the hell am I? Who the hell are you?" Kenneth cried, his voice full of fear.

"Where? Why, you are in hell of course. Your home for the foreseeable . . . eternity." Satan laughed. "And if you are in hell then I must be . . . ?" Satan asked.

"No, no, nooo you can't be," Kenneth cried.

"Oh, come now, who am I?" Satan asked again.

"The devil?" Kenny whispered.

"Close, the devil is *what* I am, *who* I am is Satan. And your new lord," Satan gladly corrected the prisoner. "Anzu, you did a marvelous job bringing yet another soul into the fold. Please enlighten me about Kenneth Rose's crimes."

"Who is he?" Kenneth looked on in confusion.

The demon greeted Kenneth with a backhand to the face for speaking when he wasn't being spoken to.

"I am Anzu," said a tall, menacing, and extremely aggressive demon with the face of a raven and the body of a man, with big black feathery wings. He was a particularly evil and powerful demon. "I was assigned to you upon your conception to keep you away from the love of The One and to tempt you into all types of wickedness and I succeeded. With your help, I was able to defeat the many angels that were assigned to you on a daily basis. You made my job easy and I thank you." And then turning to address Satan he continued. "My lord, Kenneth Rose is guilty of fornication, adultery, and idol worship, but his major crimes are drunkenness, the physical and verbal abuse of his wife, Andrea Lewis-Rose, and the murder of his unborn child when he kicked his wife down a flight of stairs."

Satan was thrilled because he had so many punishments in mind for Kenneth. "There are so many crimes here. I truthfully don't know which one to pick." He laughed aloud and said, "Truthfully, that is something you don't see every day. Should I have you sent to our forest where my demons spend hours building their strength by hacking away at human trees? Or perhaps I should send you into the Lake of Fire. Although I would like to, I pride myself on judging fairly, and you do not deserve that. I reserve that for the truly wicked or if I get lucky enough to judge one that has fallen away from the truth. No, you should not be sent there.

"Ah, yes, I have it. I will send you to the Ottocom Desert. I send most humans who are guilty of abuse to this place. Since you have beaten and abused your wife in the privacy of your own home, there you shall suffer in the privacy of your own coffin. You will be locked in a coffin lined with spikes on the interior. For company you will be abused by our chemaworm, named *chema* from our tongue meaning wrath. These worms originate from this planet, not unlike your leeches but way more deadly. Razor-sharp teeth that secrete a toxin that paralyzes their victims and also causes an intense burn once injected into the bloodstream. They live beneath the dirt of the entire surface of this planet and you will never see a more venomous creature."

Kenneth Rose wept bitterly, he cried so profusely that he could barely put words together to form a coherent sentence.

"How . . . can . . . I . . . survive . . . that?" Kenneth asked as he continued to cry uncontrollably.

"What? What did he say? Did anybody catch that?" Satan asked the horde of demons that laughed at the suffering soul.

"I think he wants to know how he's going to survive," Anzu spoke up.

Satan continued, "Oh simple. When you stood before The One you were granted a glorious body and you didn't even know it. These bodies are vastly superior to your body on earth. There, depending on the severity of your injury, it may take a few days to a few months for you to heal. You can also die from almost anything there. But in heaven and hell, you cannot die again. When you get hurt here you will heal within a matter of seconds or hours. On earth if you lose a limb, you will never get it back. However, here, Anzu . . ."

And a demon grabbed Ken's arm and held it out as Anzu took out his axe and came down with such a devastating force that he cleanly severed Ken's right forearm. Ken hollered in a way that he never had on earth. The scream seemed to come from deep within.

"Kenny, stop your screaming. It will grow back eventually. Take him away," Satan said as Kenny fainted before the congregation of demons.

Ornias had the location of the damned soul but watched to see how the sentencing played out. He skipped ahead until he came to the Ottocom Desert. There he saw two demons chain Kenneth and kick him into his coffin. He watched as Ken yelled in pain, and he saw one of the demons pick up a jug and dump it on Kenneth. The worms spilled out and fell on Kenneth and quickly began eating him.

Ornias watched as Kenneth screamed in horror, and he even saw one of the chemaworms enter Kenneth's mouth as he opened it to scream. The coffin was closed and the screams became more muffled, and then the coffin was lifted telekinetically by one of the demons and placed into a deep hole, where sand was shoveled onto the casket telekinetically.

The screams became muffled until they disappeared completely, either because Kenneth lost the ability to scream or perhaps he was too far down to be heard. Either way, Ornias had his location. He closed the book and put it back on the shelf where he found it. He was instantly brought out of Kenneth's world and back in the hall of records where he had started his journey.

"What are you doing here?" asked a deep dark voice.

"Anzu . . . what are the chances of meeting you here?" Ornias said.

"What are you doing here, whelp?" Anzu asked again.

"Nothing. I was just looking around. What are you doing here?"

"Sometimes I like to check up on souls that I have imprisoned. . . . What business do you have with the Kenneth Rose chronicles?"

"Research, sir. I was just interested in what happens to a human soul once they enter our world. . . . I've never witnessed a sentencing before."

"Really? Do you know what I think? Your mistress, Lilith, is forbidden in the city and she makes you do her dirty work."

"No, sir," Ornias answered, "I'm doing research for myself out of pure curiosity."

"Do I look like a fool to you?" Anzu squawked.

"Well . . . ," Ornias said.

Anzu grabbed the small demon by his cloak and lifted him into the air

"Take care how you answer," Anzu seethed. "Your master, Lilith, is refused entrance into our city because she is a human-demon hybrid. What need does she have for a lost soul's chronicles?"

"She is more committed to the kingdom of darkness than you think," Ornias said trying to ease the growing tension. "Please, sir, if you are not arresting me, then may I leave to attend the rest of my business?"

Anzu thought while he still had Ornias in the air. He knew that if he brought Ornias before his ranking officers, they would consider him wasting their time. And even though his loyalty was without question, Anzu knew that his overzealous nature earned him a reputation as a troublemaker in the kingdom. Even though Lilith wasn't regarded in great esteem, one couldn't, and wouldn't, bring an accusation against her without just cause. She was deceptive, intelligent, beautiful, and extremely dangerous.

Every spirit, demonic and angelic, knew of her throne of bones. They knew she collected the bones of those that tried to oppose her, and Anzu was unwilling to risk his being added to her collection. If he was going to accuse Ornias and Lilith of anything, he needed concrete evidence that they were up to something. So he threw Ornias down.

"I will be keeping a watchful eye on you and your mistress. If I find you two planning sedition, I will bring you before Satan myself," Anzu threatened.

Ornias stood up, dusted himself off, and bowed before exiting the hall of records. As soon as he was outside of the city he gated out and appeared at the mouth of Lilith's cave in the Ottocom Desert — where she sat admiring the view of the eerily beautiful red sand and mountain ranges as far as her captivating eyes could see. He bowed low and addressed her. She was eager to hear the news he brought.

"Mistress, I have good news and bad news," Ornias began. "The good news is I have found Kenneth Rose, and I know exactly where he is."

"Well, don't just stand there tell me where he is," Lilith demanded.

"He is here in the Ottocom Desert. Approximately seventy-eight miles south of our current location. Next to the Sea of Fire. "

"What are the odds that he'd be buried in my province?"

"It is good fortune, mistress," Ornias said, "Every now and then luck is needed to accomplish anything."

"Then what is the bad news?" Lilith asked.

"Anzu found me in the hall of records looking at Kenneth Rose's chronicles. He was the demon assigned to Kenneth in his time on earth."

"Anzu?" Lilith groaned. "He is one of the demons that I hate the most; his hatred for humans knows no limits. He still sees me as human, but nevertheless if Anzu gets in my way, I will add his bones to my throne."

CHAPTER 3

The table was filled with all kinds of food—bacon, waffles, Italian sausage, three cheese omelets, and even cereal—that John had prepared for breakfast. It was positively the best breakfast Camilla had ever had and the best meal John had ever cooked. Camilla ate to her heart's content, but John had the lion's share. His new appetite came as a surprise to Camilla because she had never seen him eat that much. In fact, she never even remembered John as a cook. The last time he made breakfast for her was over four years ago when he nearly burned down his apartment. It was also John's first attempt to impress her in a romantic way and after it backfired, he never tried again. Even though today's breakfast was no such attempt, Camilla couldn't help but notice that John was never going to be the same frail little man she once knew. She sat on the sofa with her coffee and inconspicuously admired him as they spoke.

"So, you're telling me there is an angel living inside of your body right now?" Camilla asked.

"Yeah, his name is Ahadiel. He's huge but nice," John added.

"What does it feel like?" she questioned.

"Well, everything is sharper and clearer than before. Not like putting on a pair of glasses though—it's more like looking at things through a microscope or telescope. And I can hear and smell everything too, and everything tastes so much better! It's actually pretty weird," John answered.

"Can you read minds? Ooh, what color am I thinking of?" Camilla joked.

"Blue," he said as Camilla looked at him in wide-eyed amazement.

"Oh my goodness!" she exclaimed.

"Cammy, I can't read your mind. I knew that because it's your favorite color," he said with a laugh.

"Ha-ha very funny, but seriously what can you do?" Camilla asked.

"You know, I honestly don't know. The One never told me."

"The One?" she inquired.

"Oh, it's what they call him . . . them, Jesus and the Father. The angels call them The One."

"Makes sense," she stated.

"You understood that?" he queried.

"Yeah, sure I did. I've been going to Bible study on Wednesdays."

"Nice," he said with a genuine smile.

"All kidding aside, this is the most unbelievable story I've ever heard."

"But you believe me, right?"

"How could I not? I mean, look at you . . ."

She admired his new physique. In her mind it was like he had been cut from black stone.

"Hey, I have an idea," Camilla said. "When was your last physical?"

"What?" responded a bewildered John.

"I want to run some tests to see exactly what you're capable of. Come on, let's go," she exclaimed. She waited for John to get dressed in clothes that were clearly too small for him and hurried him out the apartment.

They arrived at her parents' medical office, which was closed on weekends, except for emergencies; she had John wait in the patient waiting room. When she was ready for him, she called him back to the examination room while donning a white lab coat and a stethoscope. John chuckled at seeing his friend in a doctor's coat that obviously belonged to her father, because it was too big for her.

"Don't laugh, it's for effect," she said as she laughed with him.

"No, it looks good," he replied.

"Okay . . . now take off your shirt."

John looked at her dubiously and gave into her wishes. As he took off his shirt, she observed every newly acquired abdominal muscle that he possessed, making his stomach look like hills and valleys on a chocolate-skinned meadow. She ogled his pecks that were perfectly symmetrical—not bulky like a massive body builder.

His body now resembled a finely tuned athlete who was in peak physical condition. She kept staring until John cleared his throat and looked at her, which snapped her back to the reason she brought him here in the first place.

"First, I'm going to measure your new height and weight. Step on the scale." She insisted and John obliged her because he was eager to see what his measurements were. "Okay, you are now 6'2"."

"Whoa," John said smiling.

"'Whoa' is right." And you now weigh 223 pounds," Camilla responded.

"Good lord, so I've grown almost a foot and gained over 100 pounds in one night. That's got to be some kind of record." John stated.

"I . . . I don't know, John," she said in disbelief.

Camilla applied the stethoscope to his chest to monitor his breathing and heart rate and noticed that both were normal. She measured his blood pressure and it was perfect. Next she gave him an eye exam and told him to step back and read the smallest line he could. So he walked down the long corridor as far as he could, which was about sixty feet from the Snellen Eye Chart and read the smallest line he could see.

"Snellen chart. Copyright 2013. Made in China," John read aloud.

Camilla looked at the chart and wondered what line he was reading until she saw the tiny words written in a size smaller than the 20/10 line on the chart. She was stunned at his newly acquired visual acuity and whispered to herself how crazy she thought it was, to which John responded from sixty feet away, "Yeah, it is crazy isn't it?" Which meant that John could also hear decibels that would barely cause a blip on a decibel measuring device.

Finally Camilla decided she should assess John's stamina and strength, so she drove him to an abandoned junkyard in Jersey. Once there, John began lifting old cars and tried to find heavier ones that would push him to his limits. He never found one, so they moved on. He lifted cars and buses with one hand and tractor-trailers and trains with two.

Camilla was in complete awe as she watched him lift tons with the greatest of ease. She was more shocked that he said the heaviest objects felt like he was lifting no more than 100 pounds. His new senses and abilities were truly supernatural, and even though she couldn't measure or discover all of his abilities, she knew that he had become something special and was destined for greatness.

John had wowed Camilla, albeit with his newfound supernatural abilities, but day was turning to twilight and they were close to ending their day of tests.

"I gotta say, John, you can do things that people only see in the movies . . . It's really freaking me out."

"Really?"

"Yeah . . . it's just so hard to believe because . . . this is real life and people aren't supposed to do what you can do. . . . And we haven't even discovered if you can fly?"

"Only one way to find out"

"I don't know, John"

"Well, I have an angel living inside me."

"Yeah."

"Well, angels can fly so maybe I can too."

"But what if you can't? It's dangerous. You can get hurt."

"No worries. I have superfast healing too," he said climbing to the top of a junk pile.

"Yeah but you can't heal if you're dead . . . seriously this is reckless."

Once John was at the top, the drop was much scarier than he had anticipated. Suddenly he was apprehensive. Then Camilla started making chicken noises.

"I thought you didn't want me to jump."

"Yeah . . . but you're up there now!" she yelled back

Camilla only made louder chicken noises. John rolled his eyes playfully and climbed to the top of the pile. He looked down from the forty-foot pile and Camilla egged him on.

"JUMP, JOHNNY!"

John bent his legs and leapt from the pile and floated downward before falling really hard on the junkyard ground. John scraped his arms and hands and skinned his knees. Camilla rushed to his aide to check on his cuts, but his body was healing instantly. Camilla was in awe.

"Told ya."

John shot up the pile again.

"Look, John, you don't have to keep doing this. Maybe you can't."

"I can," John said with a determination that she never knew he possessed.

John tried jumping into the air. He landed back on his feet and tried again. He jumped a little higher but came right back down until he heard a voice tell him to simply "think" fly. John stilled his heart and mind and thought about flying, and he slowly began rising into the air. He flew around the junkyard, trying not to bump into the crane and other objects. He was quickly becoming accustomed to the idea of flying.

Camilla looked up at him flying around, hardly believing what she was seeing. John made his way to where she stood and hovered above her. Camilla tried to say something, but nothing came out, however John found his voice.

"Don't wait up."

And he took off.

Pitch black darkness and endless, excruciating pain had become his reality for what seemed to be an eternity. Kenneth Rose couldn't even think of a time when he wasn't in perpetual anguish and darkness. Hell had transformed from a figment of imagination for people he considered to be weak and feeble to a place that was physical, with a foundation and rules. With each passing moment, the worms ate at whatever flesh they could find; when there was none, they sought bone. Even after they devoured his bones, they hungered still and ate at his soul. He wept, screamed, tried to sleep when the worms hunger seemed to be sated, and he even prayed when the worms began eating again.

He prayed for solace, for a reprieve, but mostly he prayed that Andrea, the wife he mistreated almost the entire time he knew her, wouldn't find her way here. Maybe, just maybe, if God was listening he would find a way to reveal himself to her so that she would find him and be saved.

At least someone would be because he knew there was no one coming to save him, until one day he felt something that he hadn't felt for a long time—movement on the outside of his coffin. He felt sand falling around it. He also began to feel the sensation of something being raised or dropped, but he couldn't tell in which direction. Kenneth's fear began to overtake the pain and the eternal darkness that lived with him in the coffin.

Before he was thrown into the casket the demons told him that his coffin was close to the Sea of Fire and that it had already claimed thousands of coffins and carried them off to sea. Dread gripped his heart, knowing that there were that many coffins filled with living souls dealing with the horror inside the coffins, coupled with being subjected to the worst torment that hell offered, the Sea of Fire. The thought that his coffin was next to suffer the same fate was unbearable.

With the movement of his coffin, he certainly knew that he was next and there was nothing he could do about it. Suddenly the movement stopped and he could hear voices outside. A strong, feminine voice dictated orders and another weak, masculine voice obeyed. He had not heard voices other than his own for quite some time. Soon the voices grew louder, clearer, and he heard a loud crack as the casket was opened.

Lilith and Ornias looked upon the unfortunate soul and what they saw was an all too familiar sight of a withered and tormented being. Kenneth was mostly all soul with very little bone and little to no flesh on his body. Though the hellish sun beat down on the desert, it felt like cool air after being trapped inside the coffin for so long. Lilith and Ornias spoke among themselves, but Kenneth only heard muffled voices because his ears hadn't grown back. The full and lethargic chemaworms poured out of the coffin. Ornias picked some of the creatures up and tossed them aside, but one got away and slithered close to Lilith. She crushed its head.

"I can't look," Lilith said. "The sight of a tortured soul is always a disturbing one."

"Really? I kind of like it. How come it doesn't bother you when you disfigure others?" Ornias asked.

"Simple. I'm the one doing the disfiguring and I love to admire my handiwork, but enough talk. Can we move him?"

"No, he isn't well enough. If we take him through a gate in this state, then he may be lost inside the portal. But if you're desperate to move him, we can carry him," Ornias replied.

But when Lilith gave a look that signified her disgust, he corrected himself.

"I mean I can carry him . . ."

"How long will it take for him to completely heal from his injuries?"

"With this amount of damage, it will take at least a full day or two."

"A DAY?!" she yelled. "Surely demons on their routine patrol will discover what we've done."

She thought for a bit and decided on their next move.

"Place the coffin back into the sands, cover it, make something to carry him, and let us begin walking before a patrol spots us," Lilith commanded.

"Yes, mistress," Ornias responded.

Ornias followed his orders and began crafting a gurney out of thin air using the power of his mind to create it. He crafted the wooden frames and even a cloth material to form a bed. He placed Kenneth on top of the gurney and Ornias used his mind to lift it. The three were ready to travel. Most demons in hell had not mastered this trick that came to them as second nature when they were angels. In heaven, crafting things from the mind was a power made possible by drawing power from the Holy Spirit to create. Anything that one could imagine could be crafted with practice; however in hell, the Holy Spirit was absent.

Creating anything took more practice, more patience, and more time because it required that a demon draw the power from their own spirit. Lilith mastered the technique eons ago, but what was the sense of having a slave if one didn't take advantage of their presence? They hadn't walked but 100 yards before Raum and Nicor, two demons on patrol, landed before them and accosted them.

"Well, what do we have here?" Raum asked.

"Lilith, how interesting it is to see you and your slave outside of your cave," Nicor said.

"Hello, boys," Lilith greeted the two ruggedly handsome human-looking spirits. They were tan-skinned with black hair. Raum sported a neat beard, but Nicor chose no facial hair. Both were strong and menacing, donning swords, and they worked well as a team. Their duties were to ferry souls to the Ottocom Desert to begin their eternal punishment. They frequently kept accurate counts of the guilty and could tell when a grave was disturbed. When they noticed a disturbed grave, they looked around and noticed two spirits traveling north and flew in to interrogate.

Both wore black robes with black bat wings to identify themselves as demons, differentiating themselves from the fallen angels that wore gray robes and black-feathered wings resembling those of a crow. Upon meeting the two demons, Ornias simply bowed low and tried to hide their precious cargo. However, Kenneth Rose was oblivious to what was happening and moaned and groaned periodically as his body was slowly but surely healing itself.

"Do you know that Raum and I keep an accurate count of the guilty in this desert?" Nicor said.

"And we can always tell when there is a disturbance in a grave site," Raum followed.

"Do you know anything about a disrupted grave less than 100 yards south of here?" Nicor questioned.

"No, I do not. My slave and I were just admiring the view of the Sea of Fire. It's actually quite beautiful until you realize that souls are being eaten alive by it every day," Lilith answered.

"If you are going to play stupid, perhaps you should try it several miles away from where you just committed the crime," Nicor said.

"Crime?"

"You should assume that we already know the truth of the matter," Raum added.

"And that would be?" Lilith asked.

"THAT YOU STOLE FROM US. KENNETH ROSE IS OURS!" Nicor yelled and drew his sword and pointed it at Lilith.

"I've seen bigger," Lilith smirked.

"If you give him back, then we will not tell General Deviat of your treacherous thievery," Raum said hoping to avoid a confrontation.

Lilith sought an altercation from the moment they landed and was the first to attack. She drew her short sword and met Nicor's weapon; she attempted a roundhouse kick in Raum's direction, but he ducked and drew his sword. Ornias took the gurney and tried to move away from the fray. Lilith was graceful and deadly as she easily parried their advances and began to take control of the fight.

Nicor raised his arms to deliver a killing blow, but Lilith caught his arm and stabbed him in his chest twice before he knew what happened. Nicor fell to the sand, clearly hurt. Then she turned her attention to Raum, and as they fought she began pushing him toward the sea, hitting him in the face and body with elbows and knees while blocking every attempt he made.

Nicor rose slowly to help his partner and made his way toward the melee. Raum made a slashing attempt, but Lilith ducked and stabbed him in the neck; her sword went clean through to the other side. She removed it and her next strike landed in Raum's eye. He screamed and Lilith let out a blood thirsty roar as the demon fell to the desert floor with her sword still in his eye socket.

Nicor's war cry gave away how close he was, and Lilith turned around weaponless. She leaned to the side to dodge a stabbing attempt and then another. Nicor made a high-arching stabbing motion with his right arm and Lilith turned into him, grabbed his right wrist with her right hand, and in one continuous motion used his own momentum against him, plunging the sword deep into his chest as she moved away from his devastating blow.

Lilith grabbed his waist with her left hand and rushed him to edge of the Sea of Fire and threw him in. Nicor fell screaming into the beyond boiling liquid oil, sword sticking in his torso and out of his back as he swiftly submerged. She watched him until he vanished into the blackness and dusted her hands. She returned to finish what she started with Raum, who was now up and limping toward Ornias and Kenneth with the sword still in his eye. Before he could reach them, he suddenly burst into flames.

He screamed so loud that others would have heard, if he hadn't been in the Ottocom Desert. He kept burning until his skin melted, then his muscles, next his bones, and then the rest of him until he was nothing but ashes that blew away in the desert wind. Lilith had finished Raum until he was a spirit floating without a body, and there was no telling how long it would take for his spirit to even begin building a new one.

With both witnesses dealt with, the only thing that was left from the battle was her sword in Raum's eye socket lying in the sand. She grabbed the sword and the skull, and the three of them continued on the journey back to Lilith's cave without further incident.

Early Sunday morning, John was ironing his shirt for church. Adjusting to his new body and powers was taking some getting used to, but he felt more and more comfortable every day, even though it had only been two days since his change. The knock on the door was none other than Camilla, and he was elated about seeing her for a third day in a row. They were going to accompany each other to church.

Breakfast wasn't quite as lavish as yesterday's, but it was still quite good. Camilla sat down and enjoyed it and turned on the news. The big story was the grand opening of the Freedom Tower. New York City had been constructing a new building since the September 11, 2001, terrorist attacks. They watched as the news showed footage from the ground and the air, including reactions from ecstatic New Yorkers celebrating the opening of a new landmark.

"I can't tell you how good it is to see that building finally completed," Camilla said.

"Yeah, I remember the attack like it was yesterday, but like New Yorkers, we always pull through."

"So . . . are you going to tell me about it?"

"About what?"

"Flying! How was it?"

"In a word? It was incredible, exhilarating."

"That was two . . ." She smirked halfheartedly. "I called you late last night but you didn't pick up so I figured flying must really be something special."

"It is."

"Where'd you go?"

"If I told you, you wouldn't believe me."

"Tell me anyway."

" . . . I went to Dubai, then Rome, China, Hawaii, Mexico, and then I came home."

"Impossible."

"I can fly fast . . . I mean really fast."

"How long did it take you?"

"Well, I left you late afternoon and didn't get back home till three this morning."

"You traveled the globe in under ten hours?"

" . . . Yeah . . ."

Camilla was at a total loss for words.

"Hey, I'll be right back; nature calls."

"Yeah, sure."

Camilla continued to follow the live coverage as John answered nature's call. Then one of the news helicopters showed a military tanker traveling down the West Side Highway. She called out to John who also came to watch. They both thought it was odd but assumed it was a part of the grand opening. The same news helicopter also picked up what appeared to be a military helicopter off in the distance.

Suddenly a missile was fired from the military chopper. It hit another news helicopter, and the whole sequence was captured on video! Simultaneously, the tanker also began firing on civilian cars. John and Camilla knew then that this was another well-planned terrorist attack on the city. The M1A/2 Abrams Battle Tank began riding over civilian cars. Some people were able to escape but others couldn't. The AH-64 Apache also kept shooting missiles at nearby buildings and cars.

John knew that this was his first test. He didn't really know what he was supposed to do, but he knew that he couldn't, nor wouldn't, just sit back and let whatever was happening continue to happen without his interference. He felt a tug in his heart and heard a calm still voice tell him to go to the roof of his building. When he ran out of his apartment and raced upstairs, Camilla followed him. Once there, he felt the strange inscription on his forehead begin to pulsate and glow.

Camilla was right behind him, wondering what was about to transpire. What she saw next left her astounded. The burning sensation was intense and John thought about his armor. Instantly the suit powered up and began growing on him almost robotically. It started at his chest and progressively covered his torso, waist, thighs, legs, and feet. His head and face were last. Then it was complete.

"Amazing," Camilla whispered. She had never witnessed an event like this, and it was all very surreal.

John settled down and thought about flying and began to rise off the roof. Suddenly he was off. He looked back at Camilla who was getting smaller by the second as she waved good-bye before leaving the roof. John could see the Apache helicopter and noticed that it was on a trajectory course for the newly opened Freedom Tower. He didn't know if that was the pilot's intended course, but he slowly put two and two together, and it made the most logical sense to him.

He was next to the pilot's window within seconds and knocked on the window of the helicopter and pointed downward, trying to give the terrorists a chance to end their madness. The pilot was completely astonished that there was a man outside his window. Of all of the terrorists' contingency plans, none included dealing with a flying man. The pilot took out his pistol and emptied the clip in John's face. John fell back toward the tail and punched a hole in the fuel tank.

The Apache began to plummet. As it did, he was caught by the rear spinning blades. There was a mini explosion at the collision, and he was thrown a bit. The pilot managed to steady the AH-64 and fired a final missile. The entire time John was busy trying to stop the craft, the pilot had locked onto the Freedom Tower and waited for a perfect moment to fire.

John looked at the rocket and followed its projected course. His assumption was confirmed. He also noticed that the pilot jumped from the chopper without a parachute. Obviously this was a suicide attack by both the pilot and the driver of the tank. John didn't hesitate and flew straight down to the pilot and caught him about twenty feet from the ground.

The Apache crashed to the street just a moment later, crushing abandoned cars. John slowed his momentum very awkwardly but gathered himself and flew toward the missile. He followed the smoke trail and could see the distance was closing both on the collision and how close he was to catching it. He reached out to grab it and wrapped his hand around it.

Success!

He stopped the missile within fifty feet of the Freedom Tower and landed on the street, missile in hand. Most drivers with operational vehicles drove out of harm's way, but there were still a bevy of destroyed cars lying in the middle of the street. John gave the terrorist to the NYPD officers on hand and dropped the missile at their feet. They watched without moving or saying a word. They were utterly amazed at what was happening in their city before their very eyes. And then John spoke to them.

"You guys got him?" John asked.

No answer.

"Hey . . . cop? Take him. I gotta go."

Stunned faces. But the police sergeant did try to formulate words.

"Oookaaay," and John walked off to deal with the Battle Tank. Just then the officer found his voice.

"Fr-Fr-Freeze!" But John had already left, leaving the terrorist and officers in wonder.

The police scattered and watched as this heroic, incredible, godlike being walked into imminent danger with an Abrams Battle Tank bearing down on him. The tank approached John and stopped about 40 feet in front of him. The main gun on the tank took aim at John and fired a direct shot. John dug his heels into the street and took the shot directly to the body, and the explosion surrounded him. The dust rose and set and the smoke began to clear.

John was standing tall. He did not even take a knee. He advanced on the tank and punched the front end and completely smashed it in. He then climbed onto the tank, grabbed the main gun along with the turret ring, and separated it from the hull. He softly tossed the main gun and grabbed the front of the tank and flew into the air about fifteen feet. John held the driver's hatch upside down, and the driver fell out of the tank—shaken but relatively unharmed. John grabbed him and flew him to the police officer, where his accomplice sat in handcuffs with an array of guns trained on him.

When the whole ordeal was over, news reporters, pedestrians, and even police officers surrounded him. John was swamped by the flashing lights of the cameras, video cameramen rolling their continuous live feed, and reporters asking him 100 questions at once.

"Who are you?" asked one female reporter.

"Seraph," was his answer. And then he bent his knees and flew into the sky, leaving the crowd of people shocked and awed by what they had all just witnessed.

Kenneth healed nicely over thirty-six hours. Bone grew; flesh, muscle, sinew, and other tissue grew around it. His skin had completely regenerated, and he even had hair on his head and chest. He appeared to be a young, fit athlete, as he was in his college days, instead of the overweight middle-aged man he was when he died. Although he had physically recovered, the mental, emotional, and spiritual toll on his psyche was significant due to the never-ending torment he endured during his time in hell.

His ordeal left him exhausted, and he slept peacefully without torture and pain for the entire time he was rescued. He didn't know that his rescue was almost short-lived, had Lilith not been able to dispatch Nicor and Raum. But they were dispatched and Kenneth was sleeping like a baby.

Ornias watched over him, but not out of love or care. He was simply protecting their investment until Lilith got back. Suddenly a bright red glare appeared from around the rocks, coming from the mouth of the cave, and Ornias could hear footsteps. This was either going to be a good thing or a bad thing. He reached over to grab an old rusted sword Lilith left lying around and prepared for whoever was coming. When he finally saw who it was, his heart stopped racing. The beautiful Lilith had come around the corner.

"And what do you intend to do with that?" Lilith asked glaring at Ornias who was standing there with sword in hand.

"I'm sorry, mistress. I thought it might be someone else." Ornias answered letting the sword down.

"How is he doing?" Lilith inquired.

"Well, he's been sleeping the entire time you've been gone . . . Where did you go?" Ornias probed.

"I don't see how any of that is your business."

Ornias looked dejected by her response.

"I've been to and fro, on earth and heaven, if you must know," Lilith responded.

"Heaven?"

"Yes . . . I went to see The One."

"Why?"

" . . . Because sometimes I like to see my Father," Lilith snapped. " . . . wake him."

"Yes, mistress." Ornias obeyed and woke the slumbering man.

When Kenneth Rose awoke he saw the two demons and screamed loudly. Ornias tried covering his mouth with his hand but Kenneth bit him. Ornias struck the man's face with his talons out of anger, and Kenneth screamed again and tried to get away. Kenneth looked at Lilith, and his attraction to her stopped him dead in his tracks. Ornias moved in to punish Kenneth, but Lilith raised her hand, and he made no further advances.

"Kenneth Rose. Do you know where you are?" Lilith spoke.

Kenneth looked around and all he could see was the faint red glare of the candles and rock. He appeared to be in a cave of some kind and he answered her accordingly.

"Yes, but do you know *where*?" She pressed further.

Which led Kenneth to shake his head no, she then instructed him to sit and he acquiesced. Ornias was also commanded to sit and he obeyed his mistress while keeping a watchful eye on Kenneth.

"Where am I?" Kenneth asked.

"This is hell. You are presently under my protection as long as you remain inside my cave and prove your usefulness to me," Lilith said getting right down to business.

"Who are you?"

"This is my slave Ornias, and I am Lilith, your mother."

"My mother? My mother's name is Diane Middleton," he responded.

"Of course it is, and I am her mother too. I am mother to every man, woman, and child on earth for I was the first woman," she answered.

"What? Wait, I thought it was some chick named Eve," Kenneth asked skeptically.

"That is what many would have you believe. But I was the first created woman, and I gave birth to the first human child," Lilith countered.

"Okay . . . why are you telling me this?" he queried.

"Because I love my children. All of them, and one in particular, are in great danger."

"What does that have to do with me? I'm stuck in hell. How can I help anyone? Furthermore, why would I help anyone?"

"Considering who it is and how harshly you treated them, it would behoove you to help me or I'll personally find a punishment worse than the one you've endured for so long," Lilith threatened with fire brewing in her hands.

"Alright, I'll help; please don't hurt me," Kenneth cowered.

"That is more like it, coward," she responded.

"Who is it?"

"Andrea Lewis-Rose."

"My wife?" he asked shaken.

"She is no longer your wife, swine," Ornias interrupted.

"Relax, Ornias," Lilith said with a grin.

"What's wrong with her?" Kenneth asked.

"Some very evil demons have conspired against her, and they seek to kill her and drag her down to hell."

"WHAT? NO! SHE CAN'T COME HERE!" he yelled.

"She most certainly will be brought down here if you cannot help us convince her to leave Wilsonton, Kansas."

"Wait, how can you help when you're here in hell with me? Aren't you demons?"

"You impudent human," Ornias exclaimed. "How dare you speak to Lilith, your rescuer, in such a manner?" Ornias rose to strike him.

"Ornias, keep calm and sit down. It is a fair question. We are here as secret angels. I believe they are called spies where you are from. We saved you from your torturous coffin; would a demon save you from anything here?" Lilith spoke with assurance.

"I suppose not," he said and believed.

"If Satan ever found out what we've done, we would have to escape back to heaven where we are from. But we came here to rescue you so that you could tell us how to best save Andrea. And in return, I was assured that you'd be given a reprieve from your punishment and allowed to enter heaven," Lilith said confidently.

"REALLY? I COULD GO TO HEAVEN?" Kenneth hoped.

"Yes . . . so will you help us?" she responded.

"What do you need me to do?" he asked.

"Excellent, all you must do is tell us about Andrea. What would make her want to leave Kansas so the demons cannot find her?" Lilith pressed.

"I'll do anything to protect my wife, I mean Andrea," Kenneth replied.

"That is good, very good," Lilith said smiling.

"Okay, when she was younger she wanted to be a model and an actress, and she could've been; she was very beautiful. She still was, even when I died. . . . She likes luxury, cars, homes, money. She loves kids and her favorite color is yellow. Do you need to know more?"

"No, my son, I'm so very proud of you. You have done more than enough. This will be so very helpful and I will definitely tell The One about your complete cooperation in helping us protect Andrea. Ornias prepare to leave at once."

"Wait, is that all?" Kenneth questioned.

"For now. Yes," Lilith said.

"Is there any way I can give her a message?" he wondered.

After thinking about whether she would allow him to contact Andrea, she had Ornias give him an orb. "This is a messaging orb," Ornias said. "Simply hold it and speak to it, and it will record your message. I will show it to Andrea."

"Thank you . . . May I have some privacy?" he apprehensively asked.

"You may use my private bedroom chamber," Lilith replied. "Come out when you are done."

Kenneth entered Lilith's private chamber. It was enormous, beautiful, and elegant, yet dark and reminded him of earth. Many things she had in her chamber were things that reminded her of her short time on earth as a human. The massive room, just through the door, was a deep chasm where an assortment of creatures lived. Some flew, others grazed, and a few played, but most rested.

Her chamber had the feel of a dark jungle. Flowers, plants, bushes, and small trees thrived under a fireball that spun in the ceiling of the fissure. He marveled how something so beautiful could exist in a place inhabited by billions of tortured souls. Then he remembered why he was in the chamber in the first place and began recording.

"Andrea, it's me, Kenneth. The first thing I want to say is sorry. I'm sorry for the way I treated you and for how long I treated you that way when the only thing you wanted to do was love me. I'm sorry for keeping you from your dreams and for killing our unborn child. I was wrong in so many ways, and I'll never be able to make it up to you, but at least I am going to try.

"Lilith and Ornias are angels, and you should trust them. They can guarantee your safety if you go with them. You are in a lot of danger and demons are trying to kill you and bring you down to hell where I am. . . . I don't want you to come here. It is the worst place imaginable. I am being tortured day and night. It never ends. Just constant pain and anguish." He began crying. "There have got to be millions, no, billions of people being tortured here even as I speak to you. We're all crying and filled with dread.

"THERE IS NO HOPE HERE. . . . NO HOPE. PLEASE DON'T BE FOOLED INTO COMING HERE. THE DEVIL IS REAL, I'VE SEEN HIM,

AND HE WAITS FOR ANY SOUL FOOLISH ENOUGH TO REJECT GOD," he screamed. "But I've also seen Jesus. He is real too. And he wants to love us. He died for us and rose from the grave. I believe that now, but it is far too late for me. Far too late. But it is not too late for you. . . . Please listen to Lilith and Ornias and escape my fate. I'm sorry and I love you. God bless you and good-bye."

Kenneth finished his message and gave the orb to Ornias, who lied about giving it to Andrea. Lilith told him to stay in her private chamber because no one knew of its existence, and it would offer him protection. She also told him not to venture outside the cave under any circumstances. After he promised her he wouldn't, she made a gate to earth and they stepped inside. Kenneth was left in Lilith's cave all alone.

Camilla sat glued to the six o'clock news as continuous footage of the attack and the mysterious hero was shown by every major network. Seraph had instantly become a global phenomenon. The news showed the attack over and over again, and there was more video rumored to be synonymous with the new hero. The news began showing a video that was captured by a smartphone and placed on a very popular video site. The video had gone viral and it was of man stopping a taxi cab with his bare hands and then running off before anyone could identify him. John watched as well, but he wasn't as interested as Camilla was. The news story brought assumptions of the origin of this new hero.

Pedestrians were questioned and offered their opinions. Some thought he was an alien; others believed he was a guardian angel. And a small number of people believed he was a government science experiment and that the whole attack was staged by the government as part of a conspiracy—especially when the apprehended terrorists happened to be Americans.

Camilla and Seraph got a kick out of the assumptions people made, but it was clear from a pedestrian poll that ninety-one percent of the people loved him. Seven percent were on the fence, and the other two percent either were apathetic or disliked him altogether.

Camilla loved Seraph, and the things he was able to do, and couldn't wait to see him do more. As she watched the news from John's cramped apartment, she noticed some things that she hadn't before. His brown eyes, his broad shoulders, his ripped muscles, his New York accent, and even his scent were suddenly attractive to her. She was amazed that despite having the same scent he always had, it smelled better than ever. While she was always quite fond of his personality, she never loved him romantically and was never drawn to him sexually. This enabled their friendship to blossom easily. But now, she found herself feeling in ways she had never felt about her best friend. She was falling in love with him and she knew it.

CHAPTER 4

Andrea was finishing up by counting her teller drawer. It was perfectly even as usual. If she actually had become a model, she would have been an exception to the rule because she had a very sharp mind. She was excellent with numbers, a result of her twenty plus years of working at the bank. Her mathematical superiority helped her earn promotions, become a senior bank teller, and eventually assistant manager. Today was a normal day without highs or lows. She left work without any hiccups and was going home to spruce up for the local bar scene. It wasn't anything spectacular; it was the same old bar with the same old people in the same old town.

Andrea arrived home, took a shower, dressed in a beautiful yellow sundress, fed her dog, and left for the bar. She drove her 1979 Chevy Blazer into the parking lot and pulled up beside a yellow 2014 Chevy Stingray. She thought the car was absolutely stunning and was intrigued at the thought of a high roller in town. Strangers didn't frequent the town, let alone the bar where everyone knew everyone.

Wilsonton was so small that everybody even knew each other's cars, and sometimes Andrea would drive to the bar only to drive back home when she recognized a car of someone she disliked. So to see a new car in the lot was very surprising unless someone recently hit the lottery, but in such a small town, everyone would've known anyway. After she was done admiring the Stingray, she went inside.

She scanned the bar to see if there was indeed someone new inside the old bar, but there was no one there who she didn't recognize. She sat at the bar and waited for the bartender, her best friend from high school, Sally.

"Hey, Sal, how's it going?"

"Same old crap just a different day."

"Are you feeling any better?"

"Some days are worse than others . . . this is one of those 'worse' days, but I'll manage."

"Is there anything I can do for you right now?"

"No, hon, don't you worry your pretty little head about it. You've already did more than enough when you took me to the doctor's."

"Sal, you know that was nothing for me. . . . You're like my—"

"Sister. I know and I love you for it." Sally gave a wide smile and continued. "But really I'm fine for now . . . so will it be the usual, honey?"

"Yeah, thanks."

Sally made Andrea's favorite drink—Kahlua, lemon juice, Scotch, and Triple Sec mixed together—a Blackjack. Andrea could drink that all night. The first time she had it was on Sally's first day at the bar. Andrea didn't know what to order and Sally surprised her with it and she'd been drinking it ever since.

"Here ya go, honey, one Blackjack."

"Thanks." After taking a swig she continued, "Hey, Sal, did you see that gorgeous yellow Corvette parked out front?"

"What?" Sally asked.

"Go ahead, take a look," Andrea urged.

Sally did.

"Oh, wow, there really is. I wonder who it belongs to."

"It's mine," said a man at the door. He looked as if he had just stepped out of a Brooks Brothers catalog. Wearing comfortable navy blue pants and a tailored yellow shirt with a white collar, two buttons were left undone at the top. He sported a white tweed blazer and white buck shoes to match. The tan-skinned man had a perfect smile, a dark beard, trimmed neatly to the sideburns that connected to the hair on top of his head. He approached the bar and sat next to Andrea and introduced himself.

"Hello, the name's Oscar. And you are?"

Andrea's heart raced. She had never in all of her adult life met a man like this. She was instantly attracted to him and even if she tried to hide the fact, her eyes were dead giveaways. She smiled and introduced herself.

"Andrea." She giggled.

"That is a beautiful smile you have there, Andrea."

Andrea hadn't heard words like that from a man in such a long time. Kenneth never spoke to her like that when he was alive, and no other man would dare compliment her beauty because Kenneth had a dangerous temper. In fact, it was part of the reason she was still single three years after his death.

"Wow, uh thank you," she said blushing.

"Bartender, do you have any Scotch?" Oscar asked.

"Do I? Honey, I got everything."

"Well then I will take a Scotch on the rocks and if you have lemon juice, Triple Sec, and Kahlua; mix them together."

"One Blackjack coming up," Sally said.

"Okay, hold on. This is crazy. Who are you?" Andrea asked.

"What do you mean?" Oscar replied.

"Well, for one, you come in here, out of nowhere, wearing my favorite color, ordering my favorite drink . . . Am I getting punk'd? Cuz it's a good one." She laughed nervously.

"Here's yer drink, hon," Sally interrupted.

"Sal, do you know this guy?" Andrea quipped. "Are you trying to set me up with someone? You did good, girl." Andrea kept laughing.

"No, honey, I don't know him, but I'd like too." Sally joked.

"Ladies, I'm sitting right here," Oscar said.

"You sure are, and if you play your cards right, you could be sittin' somewhere else," Sally replied.

"Sally!?" Andrea laughed hysterically now.

"Honey, gorgeous is gorgeous. Kinda man that could make me go back to the other side."

Even Oscar joined in the laughter.

"I'm just kiddin', honey," Sally said, wiping off the bar and leaving.

"So who are you?" Andrea asked again.

"I told you my name is Oscar," he answered.

"Yes, but where are you from? What is an obviously big city slicker doing out in the middle of nowhere?" Andrea pressed.

"Right, of course . . . Well, I'll give you the short version. I'm from California, LA. And I work as a talent scout for a big modeling and acting agency. I was heading out to visit a potential client in Kansas City. But when I went to the young woman's address, it didn't exist. I called her and she told me she lived in Kansas City, Missouri. Stupid me. I booked the flight to the wrong state. I was pleasantly surprised that I could drive to Missouri from Kansas, so I bought the Corvette at a dealership and headed down I-70 and three hours later I ended up here."

"Wait, you bought an eighty-thousand-dollar car for a three-hour drive?" She asked.

"Yeah. I needed a car and it was just sitting there looking like the sun on wheels. So I said, 'what the hell' and bought it."

"Wow, that's quite a story."

"Yes, I feel like a complete idiot for landing in the wrong state, though."

"Oh don't. People confuse Kansas City, Kansas, with Kansas City, Missouri, all the time. And as strange as it is, Kansas City, Missouri, is the Kansas City that everyone talks about."

"Yeah, just imagine how I feel," Oscar replied. "So now I'm looking for a bed and breakfast for the night, and I'm going to head back sometime tomorrow." After taking a swig of his drink, he continued, "Andrea, has anyone told you how beautiful you are?"

"Stop . . ." as she blushed again.

"No really, I'm serious; you are stunning. How old are you, if you don't mind me asking? Twenty-nine, thirty?"

"Oh come on, I don't look that young." She looked at him in disbelief.

"Actually, you do. I'm many things but I am not a flatterer," he said seriously. "It's so obvious and disingenuous."

"I'm thirty-eight."

"Have you ever been interested in doing some modeling or acting?"

"Yeah, when I was a kid, but those days are so far in my rearview mirror."

"Who says they are?"

"Well, just look at me."

"Yeah, I'm looking and I see a gorgeous woman with an amazing figure and a dazzling white smile. Your skin is flawless, even your hair is in good health, and anybody could be held captive by those big, beautiful blue eyes." As he said this he stared directly into her eyes. She felt as if he was speaking to the creature that existed inside her physical body. She was drawn into his brown eyes, falling into a deeper attraction with each kind word he spoke.

"Our clients range from four to fifty-two years old," Oscar continued. "You are never too old to chase your dreams. There are all kinds of models out there."

"Really? I thought it was a young woman's game," she confessed.

"It is but if you are driven and determined, my company can find all kinds of work for you."

"And what is this company anyway?"

"LOTAS, Lillian & Oscar's Talent Agency and Scouting, named after my partner and me," he replied, taking another sip.

"Oh, okay. I've never heard of your company. Who do you represent?"

"Well, we've only been in business six years, but we represent all kinds of talent. Kelli Brisbane, Matt Kingsley, and Bali Mora, to name a few."

"Wow, those are some really high profile clients." Andrea was impressed.

"Listen, it is getting late and I must get going or I'll be sleeping in my car. I'll be leaving tomorrow to meet the client I told you about earlier. You don't strike me as the kind of person who will let a once in a lifetime opportunity pass her by. Here is my card. Call me if you seriously want to follow your dreams." Oscar started for the door.

"Uh, okay, I'll think about it," Andrea replied looking hard at the business card.

"Don't think too hard." And then he left.

Oscar walked out of the bar and Andrea watched him through the doors, following him with her eyes as he passed by the window and to his yellow Stingray. He climbed in and the sports car roared like a big cat. He pulled off and she watched as the dust settled. He was gone for the night.

"So what are you gonna do, hon?" Sally said as she washed her glasses and got ready to shut down for the night.

"You know, I honestly don't know. I'm just not so sure about him."

"What's to be sure of? He's handsome, drives an awesome car, and dresses better than anyone I've ever seen in person . . . You know what I think? You're just scared of following your dreams. You've been stuck in this humdrum town for so long, you're like an animal that's been caged and when the cage is finally open, it's afraid to escape.

"Don't be like me. I haven't even left the town, let alone the state, except for that time you took me to see Dr. Jacobs. I'm on my last few months, and I wasn't good enough to be something special, and to be totally honest, most of us ain't good enough to become anything special, but *you* . . . you are the most special person to be born in this town in a long time.

"If this guy can do half of what he says, then you'll be doing ten times better than everyone here put together. Get out of this town. Chase your dreams."

After a pause Andrea said, "What about Max? I can't leave my dog behind."

"I'll take care of him," Sally replied, "and when you settle down, we'll both fly out to LA. Deal?"

Andrea thought, came to a conclusion, and smiled brightly.

Sally smiled back at her.

"Call him, honey."

Andrea left the bar, climbed into her Blazer, and drove home thinking about everything both Oscar and Sally had said. When she arrived home, she hopped into bed and studied the card. After a moment of pondering, she reached for her cell phone and dialed the number on the card. She was about to hang up when the phone was answered on the sixth ring.

"Oscar here."

"Hey, Oscar . . . it's Andrea."

"Andrea, I didn't expect to hear from you tonight, but I assume you have made a decision?"

"Yes, yes, I have. I want to go with you tomorrow," she said.

"That is wonderful news. Simply wonderful," he exclaimed. "Your life is about to be changed forever. Tomorrow I will pick you up at the bar at eight o'clock sharp."

"Great. . . . What should I pack?"

"Nothing. I'll take care of everything."

"Okay, good-night."

"Night."

The next morning, Andrea was more excited than she'd ever been in her life. She felt like a teenager again. Tonight, her life was going to change. She met a man by sheer luck who wanted to help her change her life. She prepared for what was apparently going to be her last day. She went to the bank and submitted her resignation letter, which was a surprise to her manager, but once she explained why, he was more than happy and wished her luck.

When the news made its way around the bank, her fellow coworkers pooled their money and bought her a farewell cake from the local baker. Once the baker knew, he obviously told the butcher and the news spread like wild fire. The cake was so good and she was so happy that she cried.

When the work day finally came to an end, she hugged everyone and said that she would miss them all, and would try to keep in touch with everyone as much as possible. They asked her not to forget about the "little people" when she became a big star, and she promised that she never would.

She raced home and was pulled over by Tommy, the police officer, another one of her lifetime friends who she graduated high school with. Even he knew the good news. He wrote her a speeding ticket, for old times' sake, with no intention of filing it. She hugged him and was sent on her way.

Once home, she showered and put on her best smelling perfume and tried to wait as long as she could. She was so excited that she only waited twenty minutes before leaving for the bar, arriving ninety minutes early. Sally gave her a big hug and a kiss and told her that the drinks were on the house. Those that were there also offered their well-wishes. It seemed that everyone in the town knew. In a town of less than 900 people, news traveled fast. Andrea sat at a table and waited for the handsome and eccentric Oscar to walk into the bar and rescue her from her dreary existence.

Andrea looked at her watch and it was fifteen minutes to eight and her heart began pounding. She fought hard to control her breathing and remain calm. Suddenly, the doors opened and Andrea looked toward the entrance thinking it was Oscar, but it wasn't.

A woman walked in, an unfamiliar one. It was clear that the stranger was new in town, but she wasn't dressed fancy like Oscar was last night. She was dressed simply. She wore a white flower dress, a dark denim jacket, and opened-toed sandals. She looked nice but not unlike any other woman you'd see in a big city. The very beautiful red-haired woman walked up to the bar and sat down.

Andrea noticed the stranger and wondered who she was, until her curiosity got the better of her and she struck up a conversation.

"You're not from around here are you?" Andrea asked.

"Is it that obvious?" the stranger responded.

"Yeah, it is. We don't get a lot of strangers around here."

"Sophia."

"Andrea."

"Now we aren't strangers," Sophia said.

"I guess not."

"What can I get you to drink, honey?" Sally asked.

"Water is fine," Sophia answered.

"Water? Ha! What are you a nun?" Andrea questioned.

"Ha-ha, no I can drink like a fish, but I'm driving to Missouri."

"Oh, what part?"

"KC."

"Oh, really. I'm actually supposed to be heading there tonight."

"No kidding. By yourself?" Sophia wondered.

"No, I met a guy yesterday, but it's not what you think."

"I didn't think anything . . . What's out there?"

"I feel kind of silly telling you this," Andrea confessed.

"Here ya go, honey." Sally interrupted with the water. "And take this Blackjack over to your new BFF."

"Thanks." She took her drink, left the bar to sit next to Andrea, and handed her the Blackjack.

"Do you mind?"

"No, not at all."

"Okay, so tell me why you're headed out there," Sophia continued as she sat.

"Well, yesterday I met this guy, a talent agent, and somehow he gets lost and he ended up in Wilsonton. Anyway, he strikes up a conversation with me and thinks I have potential to be a model and wants me to travel with him to Missouri and eventually California. I know it sounds strange and maybe even naïve but . . . I'm going to take a chance," Andrea said.

"It doesn't sound naïve to me. I'm sure Oscar told you a pretty convincing story," Sophia said.

"How do you know his name? Who are you?" Andrea stood from the table and when she did, she bumped into a barmaid and made her spill her order of drinks. But Sophia stood up and the entire bar froze in time, except for her and Andrea. Andrea looked around and then looked at the woman who was a couple inches shorter than her.

"Okay, what the hell is going on?" Andrea yelled with panic in her voice.

"Keep calm, Andrea Lewis-Rose. I'm a friend. My name is Sophia and I'm here to warn you about Oscar."

"Warn me?"

"Yes, he is not who he claims to be. Do not trust him. The kingdom of darkness has conspired against you. I don't know what they are planning, but it will be terrible, I assure you."

"The kingdom of darkness? Do I look stupid to you? I don't believe you. I don't even know you."

"But I know you. I know about your abusive husband. I know that he is dead now from drunk driving. He is suffering in hell right now as we speak."

"So what, everybody in this town knew about my abusive husband . . . and if he *is* burning in hell, the drunken bastard deserves every second he's there," Andrea said clearly unimpressed.

" . . . I know your son."

"Well, see that's where you're wrong because I've never had a child. Let alone a son," Andrea refuted.

"No, you *do* have a son. His name is David Lewis-Rose. He came to heaven as a six-month-old baby the night he died. He died when you were kicked down the stairs, and he and I are great friends. He asked me to come down to warn you. He's been keeping a close eye on your chronicles ever since he grew up and learned about you. He loves you so very much and wants you to be with him in heaven. He is bright, strong, and courageous. Most importantly, he loves The One, our Creator, very much."

"David?" she said as a tear fell from her eyes. She was crying because this was the name that she chose for her son. She never told anyone the name she picked, not even Kenneth. "If you're telling the truth then, he should be eighteen now?"

"Yes," Sophia confirmed.

"How do you know all this? What are you?" Andrea asked.

At this question, Sophia decided on a big risk and transformed into a beautiful angel in front of Andrea's eyes. Sophia was gorgeous; she wore a pristine white sleeveless robe. The bottom part of the robe ended at mid-thigh, and she looked much like the ginger woman who met Andrea in the bar, except her hair was made of actual fire.

Her eyes were stunning, reddish orange and positively amazing. Her white feathery wings resembled those of a majestic eagle, and her wingspan was seven-feet long. Andrea could hardly believe what she was seeing. She felt serenity, love, and strength but also fear and disorientation, and her heart rate elevated. This state of euphoria left Andrea fixated, and she stared at the angel that was undeniably spectacular and terrifying at the same time. She couldn't say a word as she looked up to the being that now stood taller than she was.

"Oh my god. Are you an angel?" Andrea asked in astonishment.

"Yes, I am. And the man you know as Oscar is really a demon named Ornias. He is very dangerous and you must flee this place. Drive west to the next town. I will meet you there and take you the rest of the way to the West Coast. I must leave now."

"Wait, tell me more."

Sophia transformed back to a human woman and fixed the barmaid's food and drinks as she talked to Andrea.

"No, there isn't any time. Just do as I say and everything will work out fine." Sophia left the bar and when she did, time unfroze and the barmaid steadied her tray as Andrea backed away, wondering what she had truly just witnessed.

"Whoops, almost made a mess there, sorry Andrea," said the barmaid.

Andrea halfheartedly acknowledged her and ran into the bathroom to pull herself together.

There were too many people outside of the bar for Sophia to simply gate back to heaven, so she got into a car and started it without a key and began driving west to the next town where she would later meet Andrea. Once the bar disappeared from her rearview mirror, a man appeared in the middle of the road. She swerved and hit a light pole. Sophia was dazed and had a gash on her forehead right above her eye. Had she been in heaven or in her angelic body, she would have healed almost instantaneously. However, since she wasn't in her natural element or state, she didn't.

She opened the car door, unfastened her seatbelt, and stumbled out of the car. She called out to the man and asked if he was okay, but all she could see were two eerie bloodred eyes staring at her. Then she knew it was a demon. She just didn't know who it was. Sophia summoned all of her remaining strength and transformed into the magnificent being that appeared before Andrea. She began healing, but it didn't change two facts.

The first was that she was tired from the crash she just endured and the other was that she wasn't a warrior. She was a messenger. However, every angel is equipped with heavenly armor. Whether they are warrior class angels or not, all angels prepare for battle because whenever they enter earth's atmosphere, they can be attacked at any moment. Nevertheless, before things escalated, she would attempt to communicate with the demon that stood in the shadows—out of the light of the remaining light pole.

"Who are you demon?" Sophia called out.

The demon said nothing.

"Answer me, maybe we can come to a resolution," Sophia called out again.

"There will be no resolution," the demon responded.

Sophia recognized the voice and summoned her armor by the power of her mind and a gold chest plate, helmet, shin guards, boots, gauntlets, shield, and sword suddenly appeared. Even the top and bottom of her wings were covered with some sort of gold protective plating, but the middle of the wings were left exposed; they weren't indestructible, only protected.

"Ornias," Sophia said taking a defensive posture.

Ornias stepped out from the shadows prepared for battle. Donning the same armor as Sophia, except it was blackened with rough edges.

"Did you think I would not see you talking to Andrea? I saw everything through the window. I even watched you reveal yourself to that worthless wench," Ornias seethed.

"What do you want with her?"

"If I just told you, you'd never know the satisfaction of earning it. How about we fight for it?" Ornias suggested and then continued, "If you win I will tell you our plans for Andrea. If I win, then I will keep you alive just long enough to find out what those plans are. Fair enough?"

"I do not wish to fight you," Sophia admitted in a last ditch effort to dissuade him from a melee.

"At this point, what you wish is irrelevant," Ornias declared.

Ornias attacked Sophia. She tried to hold her ground, parrying when possible and blocking other flurries. Ornias swung his dark sword as demonic and angelic steel met. Although Sophia wasn't a warrior, she was no slouch either, having taken lessons from the great archangel Michael. She tried her best to dodge as many of the attacks as she could but Ornias's strength, combined with the fact that he was well rested, gave him a distinct advantage in the confrontation. When he finally saw an opening in Sophia's defense, he exploited it.

Ornias elbowed Sophia in the face. He dodged a back roundhouse kick and hit her with the handle of his sword. Sophia stumbled back, gathered her footing, and lunged forward in a straight stabbing motion. Ornias swiftly evaded her attempt and kneed her in the midsection, which knocked the wind out of her. He spun around and swung his shield in a backhanded motion and it collided with her face.

Sophia landed on her back from the strong blow and her armor vanished. She was abruptly left dangerously vulnerable. When Ornias noticed the battle was nearing its end he powered down his armor, but his assault on Sophia took a ruthless turn.

Ornias jumped a defenseless Sophia and punched her repeatedly, lacerating her face. Angelic blood spilled from her nose and mouth. He then lifted Sophia above his head and slammed her into the car. She lay still, clearly battered from the fight. Ornias approached Sophia and peeled her from the car, which was now totally destroyed after the angel was body-slammed into it.

He threw the helpless angel onto the road and put his foot into her back, pulling at her left wing as hard as he could and ripping it from her body. Then he did the same to the right. Sophia cried out in pain. The deafening shriek shattered the lightbulb. Her flaming hair extinguished and then she blacked out. The road was completely dark. The only light came from the faint red and white glows their spiritual bodies emanated.

Ornias carried Sophia and materialized the yellow Stingray, morphed into Oscar, put the bloody and brutalized angelic body in the trunk, and drove back toward the bar. Once he pulled into the bar he saw Andrea walking out. He pulled up beside her and got out of his car to talk to her.

"Hey, Andrea, I'm so sorry I'm late. I had to take care of some business. Where are you going?" Oscar asked.

"Well, I uh . . . I changed my mind and don't want to go with you," Andrea answered.

"What? You don't want to follow your dreams? What happened to the beautiful and precocious woman I met yesterday?" Oscar asked.

"Nothing, I just changed my mind."

"Or someone changed your mind."

"Huh? No!"

"Relax, Andrea, everything is okay. Did you meet a young woman named Sophia tonight?"

"How do you know that?"

"I was afraid of that. Sophia is a woman who couldn't cut it in the entertainment business. She's been following me and trying to ruin my recruitments. I have a restraining order against her . . . She's not even supposed to leave the state of California."

"No, that can't be true! She turned into an angel! I saw her with my own two eyes, and she told me things that I've never told anyone. She said you were lying to me and that you were a demon!"

"A demon?" he cried condescendingly. "Don't tell me you're one of those whackos who believe in angels and demons, heaven and hell, and that heebie-jeebie, superstitious mumbo jumbo? Did you have anything to drink tonight?"

"Yeah, I had a Blackjack. One Blackjack."

"Did she give it to you or did you get it from the bartender?"

"She gave it to me," Andrea answered.

"She's done this before. . . . You were given a hallucinogenic drug called Lysergic Acid Diethylamide. Also known as—"

"LSD."

"You know the drug?" he asked.

"I experimented some in college."

"Well, Sophia has met many of my potential clients in the past, slipped them this drug in a drink, and you won't believe the stories that some of her victims told. But she is arrested and on her way to a jail in the next county. I saw her in the bar talking to you and I called the cops. With the restraining order, they were more than happy to arrest her and did so just down the road . . . I came back to meet you before you disappeared."

"Show me the police report," she said skeptically

"I don't have one."

"If you want me to go anywhere with you, you better show me something."

"Okay, okay. Hold on." Oscar turned around and headed into his yellow sports car and acted like he was looking through the glove compartment.

What he really did was use whatever energy he had left to materialize a piece of paper that looked like an official restraining order from the state of California and a mug shot with the image of Sophia for good measure. When he exited the car with the papers, he showed Andrea—who was flabbergasted.

"I don't get it . . . How did she know about my miscarriage and my abuse? How did she know about my son?" Andrea asked as things began making less and less sense.

"I don't know . . . But before I discovered her, she was a computer genius and she has been known to hack into people's backgrounds. I assume that she did the same to you. If there is personal information about you anywhere online, then she'll find it and use it against you. She is a crazy woman, and you aren't the first person she's done this to. All of this because I refused to work with her. She is a very sick and insane person. Trust me."

Andrea looked at Oscar. Looked into his eyes and tried to find a trace of deceit, but she found none. She looked over the restraining order and there was Sophia's name. Sophia Llamas, plain as day.

"I didn't know she was a Latina," Andrea said.

"She's Spanish to be exact."

"Jesus . . . I'm such an idiot."

When Andrea said the name of the Son of God, Ornias had to use every ounce of the strength he had left not to be exposed. His cover was almost blown at the mere mention of Jesus' name. Had Andrea called upon the name for help instead of using it in vain, Ornias would have been forced to flee. However, he held his composure.

"No, you were almost just another victim. Look, I understand if you don't want to go with me anymore, but after everything that happened, I feel like I owed you the truth," he said as he turned to his car.

"No, wait . . . I want to go with you."

"Really? After everything?"

"Yeah, I do and I don't care if I never see this godforsaken town ever again. Let's get out of here."

"Fantastic. You will not regret this. Let's go."

Andrea got into Oscar's car, and the inhibitions she had had were now quelled. She was ready to begin her new life. She felt so confident in what Oscar told her—that her experience really did come from a hallucinogenic drug. She felt ashamed, hurt, and lied too. She couldn't believe that someone would stoop so low as to use extremely personal information to hurt someone they'd never met before. But she believed Oscar. She believed he had her best interests at heart and really wanted her to succeed. As they drove, Andrea fell into a deep slumber from her long day, even though it was not yet ten o'clock—she had experienced a spiritual and emotional high and low in a matter of sixty minutes.

Oscar arrived in Kansas City, Missouri, at about one o'clock in the morning. He checked into the nicest hotel and booked a gorgeous suite for both of them on the top floor. Andrea sleepwalked from the car, to the front desk, to the elevator. From there, Oscar carried her the rest of the way. The elevator opened to the suite, and he laid her on the bed without undressing her. He left Andrea in the comfy bed and closed the door. Then he left the extravagant suite and headed to the roof.

Once there, a woman was waiting for him, sitting on the edge of the skyscraping hotel without fear that the edge didn't have a protective gate. Lilith sat waiting for Ornias dressed as a stunning woman in a sexy red dress, crossing her legs with Italian red leather shoes, and sipping a glass of red wine. Her hair was a deep red, which matched her alluring lips tonight. She lived for the night scene earth offered and spent her nights seducing men for many millennia. She heard Ornias arrive on the roof but hadn't turned around to greet him.

"You're late," Lilith said.

"Please forgive me, mistress," he apologized, "it took a little longer than I anticipated."

"Where is Andrea?"

"She is resting for the night in the suite below."

"Perfect. Did you run into any trouble?" Lilith asked.

"As a matter of fact, I did. Sophia showed up at the bar tonight. That is why I took longer than I intended," Oscar confirmed.

"What happened?"

"She met Andrea before I got there. When I pulled in, I could see her sitting there already talking to her. She told her things and even revealed her supernatural nature to Andrea." When Lilith heard the news she turned around and crushed the wine glass in her hand, blood trickled from the wound.

"And then?" Lilith asked.

"When Sophia left the bar I followed her and appeared before her in the road ahead as a human. She predictably swerved out of control and crashed. After a brief heart-to-heart, we fought and I defeated her in battle," he recounted the story.

"Interesting. Does she know of our plan?"

"No, mistress, she asked but I told her nothing. Afterward, I went back to the bar and convinced Andrea to come with me."

"Really? How did you accomplish that?"

"I spun a marvelous lie. Satan himself would be proud."

"Impressive. Where is Sophia?" Lilith wondered.

"She is in the trunk of the yellow Stingray in the parking garage."

"Good. Now listen carefully. You have one chance to accomplish your mission. Show her a wonderful day tomorrow and buy her whatever she asks," she instructed.

"Make her feel special and take her to a very expensive dinner at night. Make her desire you and then seducing her should be easy tomorrow night. Stay the course and remember the endgame."

"Yes, mistress."

"You did well, I truly am impressed, Ornias, or should I say . . . Oscar," Lilith praised him.

"Thank you, mistress," Ornias said with a wide smile and a bow. He watched as Lilith left him before returning to the suite.

Lilith walked off the roof and jumped to the ground and once she landed, she walked out of the alley and onto the main street. She walked into the garage and located the yellow Stingray. She went right to the trunk, opened it, and just as Ornias had stated, Sophia was there—still beaten and bruised.

She was so badly injured that she could hardly move, and her eyes were still swollen shut. She wasn't healing, she wasn't speaking. Her fiery hair was still out and she just lay there, barely moving her head in the direction of the noise of the opening trunk. Lilith looked at her and spoke.

"Sophia, darling, you look a mess. And what happened to your beautiful hair? Yes, you must have been beaten nearly half to death. Luckily, you didn't run into me because I would have surely killed you. I would kill you now, but I take no pleasure in killing someone who cannot defend herself. But since I know you can hear me, I'm only going to say this once. Our plan, that you so desperately seek to know, is this: Andrea is going to bear a son for Lord Satan, and the child will be raised to rule and conquer the earth and the new earth to come. He will be a conduit that leads millions upon millions of souls to worship Satan. And while Satan and his son rule on earth, I will rule in hell."

Lilith finished her small soliloquy and slammed the trunk once again. She climbed into the driver's side of the yellow Corvette and turned it on. Once again the Stingray came alive with a loud roar, except this time when it started it changed from yellow to red. Lilith grinned and drove off with her prisoner in the trunk.

CHAPTER 5

The sun was just beginning to rise when Camilla woke up in John's cramped apartment. She had fallen asleep on the sofa after watching news about Seraph, which had dominated the news for the whole day and night. Camilla actually fell asleep with the TV on and when she woke, there was still new speculation about who Seraph was and what he was.

She still had a couple of hours until she had to be at her parents' private medical practice and then to NYU later in the evening. She sat up and performed her morning prayers and devotions, but her mind was elsewhere. While the whole world was fascinated with Seraph, she was fascinated with the man underneath the mask. She went to sleep thinking about him, she dreamt about him, and she woke up thinking about him.

If truth were told, John was exactly what she wanted in a man. He was smart, funny, and quirky, but he could be charming as well. She just wasn't physically attracted to him; she didn't think herself shallow because she believed everyone was shallow to a degree.

However with John's recent physical transformation, she found that she was undeniably drawn to him. He remained the same person she loved, but now he had exceeded even her physical desires in a man. Camilla thought about John and before she knew what she was doing, she was staring at him from his door while he slept, wondering if his feelings for her were any different now.

John slept soundly, peacefully. The warm summer air had him sleeping shirtless with an open window so fresh air could breeze over his body. His new abilities made it difficult to sleep. His sense of smell and hearing were particularly sensitive at night. Any slight scent in the air would hit his nostrils as if he had inhaled it with his nose touching the object. An ant crawling across the floor sounded like someone knocking at the door. A fly's buzzing sounded like a motorbike, and a spider spinning its web sounded like a guitarist tuning his instrument for a performance.

For the first few nights with his new abilities, he stayed awake just listening to the sounds, but by this night he had learned to control his senses to some degree and was able to get a decent night's rest. This morning John noticed the subtle change in the air and the shuffle of socked feet lightly walking on the tile floor and his eyes opened.

"Camilla?" John asked in an early morning raspy tone.

"Yeah. How'd you know I was here?"

"I could hear you . . . and smell you."

"Wow, that says a lot about this deodorant," she joked.

"What are you doing up?"

"I don't know. I suppose maybe to head home. I have to work in a few hours."

"Sure, of course."

"Okay . . . so . . . I guess I'll be seeing you," she said.

"Yeah sure . . . I'll see you around."

Camilla started to leave, frustrated at herself for not saying what she really wanted to say. John was equally upset with himself, wondering why he didn't speak what was in his heart. Why did he just let her walk out like that? Even though he had physically changed, a small part of him still saw himself as the unattractive man he had been just four days ago. Camilla grabbed her jacket and headed toward the door. She opened it but swiftly shut it again and ran back into John's room.

"Hey . . . did you forget something?" John asked.

"Yeah, I did. We should go out tonight."

"You're sure after three straight days that you want to make it four?" he joked.

"Yes, I'm sure . . . but tonight will be different," she said.

"Different?"

"Goodness, John, do I have to spell it out?"

"Oh, wow. You mean a date?" John said truthfully surprised.

Camilla only shyly smiled at him.

"Yeah, yeah, we . . . I'd like that," he stammered.

After that short exchange Camilla headed out of the apartment with a huge smile on her face. John lay back in bed, smiling ear to ear. Both were excited, and even though they'd hung out plenty in their lives, they both knew that tonight was going to be different. Tonight was going to change their relationship in a negative or a positive way. Either way, things weren't going to be the same.

<hr>

Andrea woke in a strange bed that was more comfortable than anything she'd ever slept in in her entire life. The white satin curtains were open wide and the beautiful sun with all its glory shone in. Oscar was on the balcony having a glass of orange juice, waiting for Andrea to rise. When he heard a commotion he turned around to see the woman who was even stunning in the morning.

"Good morning, sleepy face," Oscar said.

"Sleepy face? Do you mean 'Sleepyhead'?" Andrea corrected him.

"My apologies," he laughed.

"Where are you from that they didn't teach you how to say sleepyhead?" she joked.

"I'm not from around here," he laughed.

"Where are you from?"

"Did you sleep well?" he asked deflecting the question.

"I did; it was amazing."

"Good because we have a big day ahead of us."

"We're not going to see your recruit?"

"No, she will keep for one more day. Today, I'd like to treat you like a princess."

"Is that so?" She smiled.

"Yes, we are going to start with a big breakfast, a helicopter ride, and the rest of the day is a surprise."

Andrea was excited about the events of the day. She wasn't sure what Oscar's plans were, but she didn't mind because she was attracted to him. He was tall, dark, and handsome. Everything a woman could want. He had broad shoulders, was over six feet tall, and apparently very successful. She felt that she had hit the jackpot, and although he hadn't confessed having feelings for her, she knew he also found her attractive.

The day began as planned and after their massive breakfast, they made their way to the helicopter tours. Oscar was the epitome of a gentleman. He opened doors, held out her chair for her, and even held her hand. There was a rush of different emotions flooding through her mind. He looked at her as if she were the only woman in Missouri and she felt like it. Once they were done with the tour, they walked in a local park and stopped at a bridge with a peaceful stream underneath.

"This is the best day I've had in a very long time," she said.

"Me too. I've not been on many dates before."

"Oh, this is a date?" She laughed.

"No, I mean, yeah. We can call it that?" he asked nervously.

"Yeah, we can call it that."

He stared into her eyes and grinned.

"Why are you looking at me like that?" she coyly asked.

"You're just so beautiful . . . ," he answered.

"Is that all that you see when you see me?" Andrea responded.

"No, not at all." He looked deep into her eyes as if he was peering into her soul.

"I see a woman who is tired of being hurt, who wants to be loved," he softly replied. "You are brilliant, courageous, kind, and gentle. You are a bright star shinning in the midnight sky, and you deserve someone who will work hard to reach you."

Andrea heard those words and her heart was putty in his hands. She leaned in to kiss him, but just then a remote-control car hit Oscar's leg and the moment fled. The young man apologized, and Andrea didn't make a big deal of it, but Oscar showed the young man a terrifying glare that made him run off screaming, leaving his car behind. Andrea didn't see the exchange, but called out to the young man to retrieve his toy. But the young man didn't even so much as look back; he ran as fast as he could away from the couple.

"Well, that was strange. I wonder why he didn't come back," Andrea said picking up the small car.

"Never mind that. Tonight is going to be an amazing night. I must go to prepare, but I want you to go and buy the sexiest dress you can find and anything else you want. Money is no object because tonight is going to be unforgettable," Oscar said, taking the car away from her and dumping it in the stream under the bridge.

"How did I get so lucky to meet someone like you?" Andrea asked. And then she took his credit card and left to find the sexiest dress in Missouri.

Oscar watched Andrea leave. Lust was in his eyes as the shapely figure seemed to glide out of sight. Oscar really did have to set plans in place to make the night a truly memorable night for her, but first he had another order of business to attend to. He walked off the bridge to the stream and found the remote-control car. He intended to return it to its owner. By simply touching the car, he could see in his mind's eye who the owner was and where he lived. Timothy Fitzgerald lived just a few blocks from the park, and Oscar began walking in that direction.

Once he arrived at the young man's residence, he could hear loud heavy metal music blasting through the door. Even if he had knocked, there would have been no way for Timothy to hear him. Oscar concentrated as hard as he could and walked through the locked door. He walked around the young man's tiny studio apartment and searched for him.

The loud music came from the bedroom and that is where he went. He opened the door to the room and saw Timothy with his back to the door. The loud MP3 stereo was next to the door and Oscar smashed it to bits with his bare hands.

"Timothy Fitzgerald!" Oscar screamed.

"Holy crap!" Timothy shouted, wiping a white powdery substance from his nose. "How the hell did you get in here?"

Oscar didn't answer so Timothy asked again.

"Who are you? What do you want?"

"I want you, Timothy Fitzgerald."

"How do you know my name?"

"I know many things about you."

Oscar looked at the white residue on the young man's nose and bed.

"Cocaine," he smirked. "It is amazing how it has proved its usefulness for years."

"What are you talking about?"

"More than six millennia ago I helped teach your ancestors how to grow coca seeds. We taught them to transform the plant into the drug that you use to get high . . . this isn't even a good batch."

Timothy looked at him, his face caked in the substance.

"In those days cocaine wasn't used for recreation. The hallucinations it caused were one of many doorways for a seer to communicate with the spirit world. However, what is about to happen is no hallucination."

"I don't understand."

"Understand this, I know you, Timothy Fitzgerald," Oscar replied. "I know that before you were a user you were a seller. I know that you used to sell this poison to your little sister, Jackie Fitzgerald, which led to her overdose two years ago. I know that you're so dependent on your addiction that you will sell your own body to feed it."

"How do you? That was a long time ago, and I've been drug free for fifteen months. I've changed my life," Timothy cried, sweating.

"And yet the sweat in your pores is oozing with cocaine residue. You are a liar, and most importantly, I know that seven months ago your best friend attempted to tell you about Jesus and you cursed him and rejected your salvation. You see, I know many things about you," Oscar continued.

"How do you . . . ?"

"I know that your time on earth is up and the hour of your judgment is at hand!" he said, transforming into a hideous demon right before Timothy's eyes.

"I BELIEVE! I BELIEVE NOW!" Timothy screamed and fell backward onto his bedroom floor.

"It is too late for you to believe now. Timothy Fitzgerald, you have been weighed on the scales and have been found wanting," Ornias replied, hovering over Timothy before taking his life.

The day flew by for John Summers. He took a personal day and stayed home from work but worked via remote access. He simply didn't know what to do about his new stature, especially at a job he had had for two years. But none of those problems mattered nor deserved a solution at the present. Tonight was a night he had dreamt about most of his life but never actually believed would happen.

To his surprise, he didn't even have to go shopping because his clothes began to grow to fit his new body much like the Israelite clothing grew in the wilderness those forty arduous years. He put on his best suit that snuggly embraced his body. The tan suit and lavender shirt without a tie gave him the look of a model. Even he was surprised at how handsome he looked. He never thought of himself that way, but his reflection proved *that* way of thinking was in the past.

John headed out to pick up his best friend and date for their first romantic night out. He took a cab over, and when she came down, she was the most beautiful thing he'd ever seen. Camilla wore a tight, white and blue dress that hugged her curves like a Formula One car on a Grand Prix race track. Her soft lips were dressed with a tiny hint of gloss, and her beautiful curls bounced around her face. Her white heels offset the leather blue clutch she carried. John's eyes took in every inch of her, and Camilla's eyes did the same.

When they finally arrived at the jazz restaurant, they were ready for a night of eating and dancing. They nervously small-talked, both shy, both wondering what the other was really thinking. Since John and Camilla knew each other so well for many years, there wasn't much to actually converse about. This was simultaneously an advantage and disadvantage.

Most of their communication was through body language. She bit her lip, played with her hair, looked at him, and glanced away smiling. John offered undivided attention, making her believe she was the only girl in the world, smiling at her and staring deep into her round, chestnut eyes. They were both equally shocked that this was the turn that their friendship was taking. However, the awkward moments ended when John asked Camilla to dance.

John pulled her close in the middle of the dance floor, and her sweet smell engulfed him. He took big breaths to soak in every scent of her. Camilla laid her head on his chest and hugged his broad shoulders. The melodic music played in the background and the soulful singer sang songs that pulled at heartstrings that needed no further tugging.

Everything seemed to disappear from their periphery, and the only thing that now existed in their world was each other. They could faintly hear the performers in the distance as they seemed to be a million miles away. While they were lost in the void, John whispered, "I love you." Camilla heard him plain as day, looked him in his big brown eyes, and their lips inevitably collided. From this moment forth, John and Camilla were totally and irrevocably in love, and she confessed her love when their lips parted.

The night was far from over for either of them, but they left the Harlem Jazz Club, hands wrapped together from the door to the cab to John's place. It was unclear what either of them wanted from the night, but it was obvious that if they continued along this road, the night had only one logical outcome.

Camilla kissed John again and was losing herself in the man of her dreams. She was growing less and less concerned about the vow she made and promise ring she wore that signified her abstinence.

John was a bit more conflicted. He found himself trying to fight an urge that was so natural in a situation that seemed so perfect. There was a battle waging inside the man as he fought to control himself, but as he kept kissing her, slowing down was becoming less and less of an option.

Andrea was instructed to meet Oscar at a new restaurant at the top of a skyscraper called Revolving Roma—a five star restaurant that revolved while guests ate, and the most expensive place in Missouri. When Andrea arrived, she was shocked to see that the restaurant was empty, save for Oscar who stood waiting at a table in the middle of the establishment. He looked at the beautiful woman who wore an elegant, formfitting, open back, black maxi dress with a plunging neckline. She spared no expense at Oscar's request to look her absolute finest. She also had found beautiful pear-shaped diamonds to go with her dress. Her blond hair was in an *updo* that accentuated her neck and gorgeous face with limited blush. Oscar was floored when he saw Andrea coming to the table. He expected her to be prettier than usual, but he had not expected her to be drop-dead gorgeous. Seeing her this way aroused him, but not in the way he had expected to be later that night. A small part of him really took a liking to her and for a small moment, he forgot the plan.

"Wow," he said.

"Oh stop . . . ," Andrea said shyly.

"No really . . . I don't know if there are words to express how spectacular you look tonight."

"Thank you . . . You don't look so bad yourself."

"Please, allow me," Oscar said, pulling her chair out for her.

"Thank you."

"You are most welcome," he said with a grin.

Andrea smiled back and then asked, "What is this place?"

"It's a brand-new restaurant called Revolving Roma. The food here is supposed to be fantastic."

"Then why is it empty?" Andrea laughed.

"Good one," he laughed. "I bought it out for the night."

"Oh my goodness, wow! I've heard of people doing that, but I never thought someone would do that for me. . . . You didn't have to."

"Why not? You're more than special enough."

"Oscar . . . I . . . ," she stammered.

"What is it, Andrea?"

"No, never mind; it's silly."

"Nonsense, speak your heart."

"Okay, look I appreciate the kind words, but those kinds of words will only lead to one logical ending."

"And what ending is that?"

"Love, and I don't want to scare you, and I don't want to rush into anything because my ex-husband really broke me down in the worst way imaginable. But I haven't heard anyone speak to me like this in years, and I love it, but those words are only going to make me fall for you so if you don't mean them . . ."

"Andrea, I've already told you that I'm no flatterer. And I don't say things I don't mean. I don't date often and usually the women I do end up going out with are total bimbos. And I don't believe in the cliché of 'love at first sight,' but with that said, there is something about you that is magnetic, and I find myself drawn to you in the most unusual way. In the short time that I've known you, I've actually come to care about you."

Andrea just smiled and let her guard down and opened herself up to the possibility of a new relationship. After all, she'd been single for over three years, hadn't been intimate with a man in nearly two, and if this man really did care about her, it was worth giving him a chance to find happiness.

Staring into Oscar's eyes gave her a sense of security she hadn't felt since she and Kenneth dated as teenagers. His eyes were warm and inviting—they hid any ulterior motives—and the only thing she saw in them was truth and the possibility of romance. She saw a love that would protect and not abuse, abide and not abandon, provide and not deprive—and far be it from Andrea to deny herself the love of a good man.

"You make me feel very safe," Andrea said. "Which is something I haven't felt in years. Since before Kenny was alive."

"Tell me about him."

"Where do I start? In the beginning, he loved me and he took care of me. He came from a rough family, but he was kind to me. He was my first and we had spent one summer just making love anytime we could. But in a town where there isn't much entertainment, what are two kids in love supposed to do? We both had so many big dreams, and they included each other. As you know, I wanted to act and model, but he wanted to be a professional football player, but things didn't quite work out that way, and he became frustrated with life. Things began changing after that. He began caring more about drinking and partying than our relationship.

"I'll never forget the first night he hit me. It was for the stupidest thing too. My best friend Sally—you met her at the bar—well, she's a lesbian and years ago Kenny wanted a threesome, but I didn't want any part of it. Neither did Sally for that matter; we weren't those kinds of friends and instead of understanding that, he accused me of cheating with her behind his back because we were so close. You see Sal and I hung out every chance we got. When I wasn't with Kenny, I was with her. But when I denied him, he beat me for it. I'll never forget that night. I sat up the whole night crying.

"Sally stopped being my friend to protect me from his abuse, and we weren't able to be best friends again until after Kenny died. She hated him for it. After that the abuse got even worse, and it even caused two miscarriages. This led to me distrusting men, even after Kenny died. I wasn't interested in a relationship or romance, that is, until I met you. I don't know what it is about you, but I feel like I can trust you and that's what scares me."

"Wow, after that I understand your hesitance. I would be much the same way if I were ill-treated. With that said, I want you to trust me. I won't hurt you."

"We'll see . . ."

After the conversation, the waitress approached to take their orders, and the rest of the night went smoothly. No more talk about Kenneth and abuse or past lives and mistakes. It switched to happy thoughts and dreams, favorite books, movies, and colors. Andrea was never happier in her life. Oscar enjoyed himself so much that he lost the parameters of the mission and found himself actually enjoying the date. He was conflicted because she was supposed to be a mark, an objective. Get in and get out, but he had lost sight of that and now was developing feelings for her.

He had heard the stories of the fallen angels who fell in love with the daughters of men. He knew that it was possible for a spiritual being to grow romantically interested in a human, but he was shocked that it was happening to *him*. Oscar tried to fight the new feelings, but it was becoming harder the longer he looked into her eyes (or whenever she smiled), which seemed to disarm him.

Even the smell of her body was beginning to make him desire her. Andrea was unaware of the intoxicating effect that she was having on him because she was experiencing the same feelings around Oscar.

When dinner was over, they made their way to the hotel where they were staying, holding hands the entire way. Oscar's heart pounded as they made their way to the elevator and up to their suite. Andrea led Oscar by the hand into the bedroom and looked into his eyes in the candlelit room that Oscar had had the hotel staff prepare.

"Candles? Do you think you're getting lucky tonight?" Andrea asked with a wide smile.

"I . . . uh . . . ," Oscar stuttered.

"Shhh," Andrea said with a finger over his mouth.

She made her way to each candle, blowing them out one by one until the room was dark. The only light came from the full moon shinning into the dark suite. Andrea slid out of her tight seductive dress, sensually crawled into the bed, and waved her finger at Oscar; he approached her, and they consumed each other.

Good John and Ahadiel got to know each other in the days they spent together. They exchanged stories and secrets of their pasts, and both were enthralled with the other's stories. Ahadiel told stories about the creation of the angels, heavenly bodies, the creation of man, and even his own personal history. Good John spoke on the inner workings of the human spirit and body, and told gripping tales of legendary battles between him and bad John. The past three days that they had been stuck together were rather uneventful, but the peace that they enjoyed was coming to a close. Tonight was going to be a much different night.

When John looked into the sky he began seeing red streaks heading south. When John noticed this phenomenon it wasn't strange to him, but Ahadiel had no idea what was happening. Good John then rose and began to lead Ahadiel to the mountains in the distance. The mountain range was the border that separated good John's territory from the neutral zone.

"Where are we going?" Ahadiel asked.

"We're going to the neutral zone," good John replied.

"What's over there?"

"There is something that is happening on the outside. We have to find out what it is."

"How do you know this?"

"Do you see those red streaks in the sky?"

"Yeah, so?"

"So those red streaks are heading south. The red is blood, and it's heading toward the southern part of the physical body."

"I'm afraid I still do not understand."

"Gee whiz, there is something that is arousing the physical body, and we have to investigate it before bad John gets there, if he isn't there already."

"Ah, is this one of the times when you will confront the other you and try to keep him from taking control of the physical body?"

"Yes, exactly. We need to get there and find out what is causing all the commotion, but we'd get there faster if you flew."

Ahadiel carried good John and flapped his majestic wings, flying high into the air. From this view good John was able to see past the mountain ranges and into a region of the body that was in control of John's physical body. A bright white light shone in the sky about ten miles south of their current position. Good John explained to Ahadiel that the white light was from a golden temple at the top of a waterfall surrounded by an ever growing forest.

Good John explained that the trees in the forest were grown from both good and bad choices made by John. He also explained that no matter whether good or bad John won a battle, the ultimate choice was made inside the golden temple where John's free will resided and could override any victory. Ahadiel then understood that good John and bad John didn't really fight for control of the body, they fought for influence.

The white light was a window to the outside world and if it was activated, it meant that bad John was already there and was heavily influencing John's free will. Ahadiel, realizing what was at stake, began flying faster. The light became brighter as they drew closer, and good John had Ahadiel land about forty yards shy of the golden pyramid temple.

"We'll run the rest of the way," good John said. "Just try to keep up."

They both sprinted toward the temple. When they got there, they ran up the side of the temple stairs to the top. Bad John was already there and staring up into the sky. Good John could see Camilla through the window getting very comfortable and undressing. He called out to bad John, who had his hands on top of two waist-high parallel poles that were influential conduits of the will.

These conduits were known as the controllers, simply because whoever managed to maintain a dominant hold would be able to influence the will toward good or evil. This is where most of the confrontations between John's good and sinful natures took place.

When good John made it to the top of the pyramid he tackled bad John who lost his grip on the controllers. The Johns, along with Ahadiel, careened down the temple, hitting every possible step on the way down to the forest floor. Good John managed to fall atop bad John, and Ahadiel, who was still chained to good John, landed about three feet next to them both.

Good John turned to look into the window to see what was happening with John and Camilla, and that small distraction cost him. Bad John reached and grabbed a stone and smashed it on good John's head, which caused him to bleed profusely. The rock smashed into smaller pieces upon impact, and bad John stood over good John and was about to smash his face in, but Ahadiel tackled him to the ground. Ahadiel raised his shackled hand to deliver a decisive blow but couldn't; so he swung with his other hand and brought it down upon bad John. Both Johns hollered in pain. Ahadiel was going to deliver another blow, but good John grabbed his hand to stop him.

"What are you doing, good John?" Ahadiel asked.

"You can't attack him," good John explained. "We'll *both* feel it. These inner battles can only be fought and won by us."

The small respite gave bad John a chance to roll away from his two enemies. He began running away from them toward the waterfall, and they followed him. There was a small clearing at the top of the falls that was an ideal place to settle this fight.

"Good John, why are you fighting this?" bad John asked.

"You know why I must," good John replied.

"This is the first night that we can feel the warm embrace of a woman. . . . Why would you take that away from us?" bad John asked.

"This is not the right way."

"And why isn't it? It feels right to me . . . it even feels right to you."

"Feelings can betray you. Not everything that feels good *is* good."

"The will wants this; you weren't there when I held the controls. You will be fighting a losing battle. Join me, if we both—"

"You are so selfish. Look at the larger picture. You were there when The One told us to remain holy. We are on the verge of something incredible, and when the time is right, we can let this happen, just exercise patience."

"Patience!" bad John screamed. "Your 'patience' kept us from drinking beers in high school with our buddies while they drank and laughed in our face. Your 'patience' made us miss out on a promotion that should have been ours, and your 'patience' will keep us from being with the woman we love. This is the first time she's ever shown any romantic interest in us, and your 'patience' may cause her to move on to someone else. . . . No, your 'patience' will not keep us from something we deserve," bad John yelled, and charged at both good John and the angel.

Bad John drop-kicked good John and he fell to the ground. Ahadiel, who had listened to the argument, was now involved whether he wanted to be or not. Bad John attacked him too kicking him, but the powerful angel just blocked the attacks. Good John got up and punched bad John in his face. He swung with his chained hand, but didn't get a lot of power behind the blow to bad John's midsection.

Bad John grabbed the incoming fist as it made contact and then grabbed the chain, pulling both good John and the angel closer. Bad John kicked both of them in their midsections and then kicked the taller angel's shoulder. He finished by connecting with good John's head, all in one fluid motion.

Good John backed away trying to catch his breath. "We cannot beat him chained like this without working together." Ahadiel only nodded, and bad John charged once more. But this time Ahadiel grabbed his partner and swung him into the air. Good John's feet collided with the charging enemy.

Bad John was stunned, and they took full advantage—charging with an attack of their own and using the chain as a clothesline. Bad John fell limp when the chain collided with his head and got up slowly. When he finally did, Ahadiel and good John used the chain as a sort of bind and wrapped it around the evil entity.

"Grab him; we'll dump him over the falls."

"That won't kill you?"

"No" was the response from good John, and Ahadiel grabbed bad John and carried him to the edge of the falls. However, bad John was clever and once he regained his equilibrium, he waited for the perfect time to strike. When good John unwound his chain from the evil being, it spit a black toxic substance in Ahadiel's face. Ahadiel was temporarily blinded. Bad John began falling but grabbed good John's leg and brought him over the edge of the waterfall. Ahadiel's massive arm was dragged down, but the big angel held firmly atop the falls.

Bad John head-butted good John, and he was knocked unconscious. Bad John then climbed up the chain until he reached the top, grabbing onto a rock for leverage, then he jumped over the hulking angel to the main ground. Ahadiel was still blinded, but was too busy concentrating on calling out to his partner and trying to pull him up. Blinded, Ahadiel began pulling good John up, but then he heard bad John call his name and when he looked toward the direction of the voice, he unexpectedly met with a blow to his huge head by a sturdy tree limb, causing him to fall over the falls. Both he and good John fell into the water below and began drifting down the calming riverbed, unconscious.

Bad John was pleased with the outcome and threw the heavy branch over the falls. He began making his way back toward the golden pyramid temple. Once there, he reactivated the window and looked into the sky to see that John was staring back at himself through a mirror. He grasped the two controllers and began maneuvering John back toward Camilla. Bad John said something, and John opened his mouth and spoke the words.

Kissing led to touching; touching led to Camilla and John traveling faster than a locomotive toward a destination of lust. John and Camilla kissed each other passionately, only stopping to catch their breath. John's heart was racing; he had never been with a woman, let alone a woman whom he was completely in love with. Camilla's heartbeat and intensity matched John's. They both were so far gone that stopping now was nearing impossibility. John was intoxicated by Camilla, her hair, her breath, her eyes, and her aroma. However, he had a moment of clarity amidst his euphoria.

"Wait, we can't do this," he said.

"What's wrong?"

"I don't know. I mean I *want* this. God knows I do, but there's just something inside . . ."

"I don't understand, John. Is this some kind of game to you?"

"No, how could you think that? You know I love you. I've never been in love before, but I know what I feel for you is the truest thing I've ever felt."

"Look, I don't want to rush you into anything. I've never been with anyone before. I'm kind of worried I'll disappoint you."

"You disappoint me? That could never happen. It's not you, it's me."

"You did not just hit me with that stupid line. Whatever, John, I'm out."

"No, no. That came out wrong. Give me a second. I just don't know if I'm ready. Sit down; I'll be right back."

Camilla sat back down on the sofa and John went to his bathroom to try and get a grip on his emotions. He didn't really understand what was happening. He wanted to be with Camilla, but it was like there were two forces fighting for control, and it was making him indecisive. Camilla was everything and more than what he wanted in a partner. She was beyond beautiful, brilliant, and educated, had a good job, great sense of humor, and had a wonderful personality to boot. If there ever was a definition of the total package, Camilla definitely fit the bill. John spent several minutes in the bathroom trying to decide what he would do. And then when he couldn't think anymore, it was almost as if the answer came to him out of thin air.

He was suddenly cool, calm, and collected. He splashed water on his face and dried off with a towel. He smiled at himself in the mirror and thought to himself that this was the moment he had been waiting for his whole life. He was a thirty-year-old virgin, and he had the opportunity to begin a relationship and make love to a woman who he'd seen in his dreams on numerous occasions. He walked out to see Camilla, jacket in hand, heading to the door, but she stopped when she saw him. She only stared into his eyes as he stared back into hers. John walked to his bedroom door smoothly and leaned against the door post.

"Where do you think you're going?" he asked.

Camilla looked at the young man whom she had never seen in a sexier light. Without a word she began walking toward him, dropping her jacket on the living room floor. She fluffed her hair and unzipped the back of her dress and walked into John's bedroom, and he closed the door behind her.

CHAPTER 6

Several weeks went by and John and Camilla spent every night together. It was very intimate; mostly, but not always physical, and at times there was also emotional and mental stimulation. Camilla was happier than she had ever been in her life. John was equally happy, but he was fighting the conviction of the Holy Spirit daily. He knew sleeping with Camilla this way was not the way of a holy Christian man, but he couldn't help himself and neither could Camilla. She felt convicted as well, but not nearly as much as John did. For him, it felt like the weights of his sinful actions were piling on his shoulders the longer he refused to repent to God. The Holy Spirit didn't feel as close to him as it was when he started his new journey. In a strange way he also felt that his abilities were slowly being physically drained. He meant to go to God sooner and repent, but Camilla's beauty and charm were extremely hard to overcome.

Maybe it wasn't such a big deal anyway; they did love each other, and marriage was certainly what they both wanted. Maybe he was blowing this whole thing out of proportion, but it didn't change the fact that he felt like he was moving further from God after becoming closer to Him than he had ever been in his life. He also hadn't received a "special" mission from The One in quite some time, and he thought this might be the way the arrangement would be. He'll call upon John to dispatch a local terrorist or deal with a random demon and then John would go back to his normal life. Not knowing what was expected of him, combined with momentarily taking his eyes off God, John began sinking into the flood of events that life often becomes.

Whatever he meant to do about his new lifestyle with Camilla was going to have to wait because they had planned another romantic night. The beginning of their sex life had been awkward and clumsy; neither of them had any prior experience. But they both loved that about the other. After a few weeks they began to settle into a groove, making it all the more difficult for them to quit each other.

A candlelight dinner and slow music were on tonight's menu followed by dessert: each other. It was another perfect night, and Camilla once again fell asleep in John's arms. They had a peaceful night's sleep until a visitor entered John's room. John sat up, but Camilla remained in a deep sleep.

"Good morning, John," the visitor said.

"Gabriel!" John cried, jumping out of bed. "To what do I owe the honor of *you* being here?"

Gabriel looked at the young lady who remained sound asleep and wished neither to wake her nor scare her. He remained in his supernatural state, a big beautiful angel in a white robe illuminating light that he appropriately dimmed due to the time of morning. If Camilla did wake during their conversation, she would have been terrified almost to death.

"Can we speak outside?" Gabriel asked.

"Whatever you want."

John dressed in pants and a jacket and Gabriel transported them both to the roof where they were alone.

"I'm sorry you had to see that," John said.

"See what?"

"Camilla. I know it's wrong but—"

"I'm not here to judge you. Nor am I here to report on anything that I've seen or not seen. We are not agents seeking to get you in trouble with the almighty God," he said putting his hands in quotation marks and continued. "We are not here to accuse you. That is *Satan's* job. He's your adversary. We are friends to anyone The One sees as friend; you have nothing to fear. The One calls you friend, and there is nothing that you can either do, or not do, that will separate you from the love of The One," Gabriel assured him.

"Thank you. I've been feeling a little distant lately and don't really know what I'm doing," John admitted.

"If you feel distance between you and The One, it is because you've moved. He has not withdrawn himself from you nor will he ever. Draw near to God once again and he will draw near to you."

"Thanks . . ."

"Anytime, but now to the matter that is the nature of my visit," Gabriel continued. "Three earth weeks ago one of the angels under my authority went missing on a mission. She has not come back, and I am beginning to worry about her."

"Do you know what her mission was?"

"Yes, of course. I gave it to her. She was to go and warn a woman about the enemy's plans against her life. The woman's name is Andrea Rose."

"Do you normally intervene in random people's lives every time the enemy plans something?"

"No, that would be an ineffective use of our time," Gabriel answered. "We do help as much as we can, but a lot depends on the choices that an individual person makes. We were focusing our efforts on her specifically because of her son, David, a young man who has been living in heaven since he was approximately six months old. He approached Sophia to help his mother, and I gave her the permission to go. David has been following this story and has notified me that Sophia has not yet returned home; he thinks she may be missing. After reviewing the evidence, I have reason to believe his report."

"Where was she last seen?"

"Wilsonton, Kansas, is her last known location."

"I'll get right on it."

"Thank you."

"Don't mention it."

"Take nothing for your journey. Everything will be provided wherever you go. Just ask for what you need. If someone refuses to help you, shake the dust off of your shoes and move on. Find her. Bring her back."

The sun began coming up when Gabriel flew into the air and vanished before John's eyes. John went downstairs and felt better about his relationship status with The One and knew what he had to do. Now he had to find a way to Kansas, and the skies were looking pretty clear for a flight. When he went back to his apartment, Camilla was already awake.

"Hey ya," she said.

"Hey ya back."

"Where'd you go?"

"I had a visitor," he responded.

"A visitor? Was it an angel? Which one was it?" Her eyes widened at the possibility of John talking to an angel.

"How do you know it was an angel?" John laughed.

"Who else would it be? Mrs. Roundtree?" she joked.

"She has been staring at me when I take out her garbage; I think she thinks I'm kind of hot now." He laughed even harder.

"Babe." She flirtatiously hit him in his bulging shoulder.

"Okay, it was Gabriel," he confessed.

"WHOA! *The* Gabriel? Mary's Gabriel?"

"The one and the same."

"Wow . . . when?"

"He came while you were sleeping."

"Why didn't you wake me?"

"Honey, he would have scared you to death. He didn't want to do that to you; besides it wasn't a social visit."

"No?"

"No. Apparently there's a missing angel somewhere in Kansas, and he wants me to find her. Her name is Sophia."

"Sophia . . . never heard of her."

"Neither have I, but I'm going to find her all the same."

"When are you going?"

"Now."

"Oh . . . okay. Well please be careful," she said a bit surprised at the urgency of the situation.

"I will. I promise. It's just a rescue mission. I'll be in and out." He was turning to leave before she stopped him to ask him a question.

"Sweetie, before you go I found this CD on your nightstand. Who is 'Saint James'?"

"Oh, Saint James? He's an underground Christian rapper. That's his album *True Story: The Saint James LP*," he answered.

"Where'd you get it?"

"It's available everywhere online. Go ahead and give him a listen; he's pretty good."

"Okay, I will . . . look, please be very careful," she said. "I love you so much."

"I love you too," he responded.

With that he kissed Camilla twice and headed to the roof while she remained in bed. He tried to activate his suit with the power of his thoughts, but nothing happened. He thought harder and still nothing happened. No glorious transformation, no burn, no nothing. This worried him, but he knew he didn't have time to worry about why the suit hadn't powered up. Perhaps it would activate when he really needed it. Whatever the reason, he needed to move. He wondered if he'd be able to make it to Kansas without it activating until he remembered that the suit had no power, but only served to offer protection. He bent his knees and flew straight into the air. *Wilsonton, Kansas. Here I come.*

Oscar and Andrea had been spending every waking moment with each other. They'd been going on dates and long walks, but the majority of their time was spent indoors. Andrea had completely fallen for Oscar in this short time, and her infatuation for him was the closest thing she'd felt to being in love since she was a teen. Oscar was no better than she was. He had completely lost focus on the task he had been charged with, all of this was so new to him. Even though he was essentially several millennia old, he had never experienced romance. Neither of them said those three magical words, but to anybody on the outside looking in, they looked as if they'd been together for years instead of for a twenty-six-day-old midsummer fling. He had explained away the supposed potential client as not having the "it" factor, and that was the last Andrea ever worried about it. She was happy, truly happy, making love on warm summer nights with the most devilishly handsome man she'd ever met in her life. Oscar was equally as thrilled until one night his master summoned him and he knew that playtime was over.

Upon waking, Oscar left Andrea sleeping with a note so that she wouldn't get worried, assuring her that he would be back shortly, but a business meeting with his partner Lillian was something unavoidable. He left the suite and took the elevator down to the garage where the yellow Corvette had been waiting for him. He climbed in and drove off.

The drive was peaceful, no radio, no music, just silence. He used his spirit vision to follow his master Lilith's trail to the safe house she'd been using. He drove close to an hour away to a deserted wooden cabin surrounded by pine trees and brush. He hadn't seen or spoken to Lilith since the night he had arrived at the hotel with Andrea and Sophia. He hadn't the slightest clue what kind of mood Lilith would be in, but when one is summoned, one must appear.

When he entered the cabin he saw his master sitting in a big comfy red leather antique chair, wearing a red miniskirt and a red top that showed off her equally impressive figure. She sat in her chair and stared him down as he stood in the doorway, waiting for her to end the deafening silence.

"Have you been having fun?" Lilith asked while Oscar only stood there. "Well, have you? I've been watching you . . . Surely you've been having fun going out, eating steak and shrimp, going to the theaters, courting this woman as if you were an actual human.

"Have you forgotten the mission? The very reason why we are here?" she continued.

Oscar wasn't sure if the questions were rhetorical so he remained mum until she demanded that he speak up.

"No," he finally spoke up.

"THEN WHY HAVEN'T YOU COME TO ME AT THE SAFE HOUSE UNTIL NOW?" she yelled, rising out of the chair, picking up a kitchen knife, and throwing it into his shoulder. Oscar screeched and fell to the floor clutching his injured shoulder.

"DO YOU KNOW HOW LONG IT'S BEEN SINCE YOUR LAST CHECK-IN?"

"Twenty-six days," he murmured.

"Twenty-six days you've been running after that worthless whore and for what? You've gotten your first taste of human flesh, and you've gone off the reservation? You should ask your fallen brothers if chasing after the daughters of men is worth it." After a short pause she continued. "Do you still remember the parameters of your mission? Seduce her, impregnate her, and present the child to Lord Satan. Did I miss the part of the plan that included 'long walks on the beach'?"

"There aren't any beaches here, mistress," he interjected.

When she heard those words exit his lips she walked to him, pulled the knife out of his shoulder, and then dug her six-inch red leather heel into the wound, making Oscar howl.

"You think this is a game?" she asked in a deadly tone.

"Please . . . mistress . . . I didn't mean to be funny."

"You had better not," she said, stepping further into the wound before letting up.

"I hope you made the most of your time with her because you will not see her again, ever. You will remain here until I have the child in my possession, and you will watch Sophia. And if by chance something were to go wrong, Ornias, I will make you wish that I'd thrown you in the burning Sea of Fire. Have you misinterpreted anything I've commanded?"

"No."

"No, what?"

"No, mistress."

Lilith began to leave, but Oscar spoke up.

"Wait, I have a question."

"Speak, swine."

"Sophia . . . Where is she?"

Lilith didn't answer him. She walked to the stone fireplace in the small cabin and pushed a brick; a wall of stone moved in and slid to the side. Another wall slid forward and there was Sophia, shackled to another stone wall in her human form, wet from head to toe. She was totally healed from her battle with Ornias and she was livid. When she saw him she snarled and tried to set herself free. She shook and screamed, but Lilith commanded her in an angelic tongue, "*Gervau gongisa*," which roughly translated is "be still and quiet," and doused her with a nearby bucket of water.

"Do that every hour on the hour. There is a small stream not too far behind the cabin. When her hair is completely dry she will burst into flames and burn this place to the ground," Lilith said.

"I *will* burn this place to the ground," Sophia promised, fury living in every word.

Lilith only smirked at Sophia's prophecy and addressed Oscar. "For your sake, she had better not." She left the two supernatural beings disguised as humans in the cabin and flew off.

John Summers finally arrived in Wilsonton, Kansas, and landed just outside of town. The sun was going down, and he would walk the rest of the way in. He had seen from his bird's eye view that flying into the small town would definitely get him spotted. And he wanted to remain as inconspicuous as possible. He knew he would surely stick out enough as the stranger in town.

He was about a mile outside of the town limits when he heard police sirens behind him. He turned around and there was a Wilsonton Police Department patrol unit pulling up right behind him. The bright lights from the police cruiser shone in his face, and he tried to block the light from his eyes. The officer sat in the car for a moment and then exited his vehicle.

Officer Robert Smalls was ironically a big portly fellow with an unfriendly disposition. He was mean and surly and didn't take too kindly to visitors in his small town.

"Identify yourself," the young officer said.

"John Summers."

"Do you have proper identification, John Summers?"

"Yes, hold on."

"WHAT ARE YOU REACHIN' FER?" Officer Smalls cried, reaching for his holstered weapon.

"Whoa, sir, I'm just reaching for my wallet."

"Did I tell you to reach fer yer wallet, son?"

"No, I guess you didn't."

"You *guess*?"

"No, you didn't say that."

"That's right, son, I didn't. Now reach fer yer wallet very slowly," Smalls said unlatching his sidearm but keeping it holstered.

John did as instructed and handed the officer his wallet with his other hand in the air. As soon as the officer took it, his other hand shot to the sky. John had never had an incident like this in New York City, ever. Even as a black man he was never harassed by the local law enforcement, which some of his peers couldn't say.   Luckily his father had taught him how to deal with a quick-tempered policeman if he ever encountered one.

"Where are you headed, John Summers?"

"Into town, sir."

"Are you tryin' to be slick with me? I can see yer tryin' to git in'a town. Where are you headin'?"

"I ah I'm—"

There was a chirp on a walkie-talkie that interrupted John's answer, and a voice came through.

"Smalls, where are you? You should've been back with the gas for Mrs. Ferder's generator."

"I'm on the way; I just saw me some city slicker just strollin' inta town, and he looks spusisious . . . supusisious . . ."

"Suspicious," John added.

"Shut yer mouth." Officer Smalls glared at him.

"Excuse me! Who do you think you're talking to?" came a stern voice from the other end of the radio.

"I'm sorry, sir. Not'chu. I was referin' to this suspeck' . . . he looks guilty of sumptin'."

"Did you catch him doing anything?"

"No, but I—"

"Look, just bring him in. Mrs. Ferder is going to have a conniption if you don't hurry back with that gas. Now get back here."

"Yes sir, right away, sir."

"I'll just be going," John said trying to slip away.

"Don't move. Turn aroun'."

John did as the officer instructed, and he was promptly handcuffed and stuffed in the back of the police cruiser. Officer Smalls drove John the rest of the way into town. Past the bar, the church, and the family-owned convenience stores before arriving at Mrs. Ferder's home. Mrs. Ferder was an old widow who lived alone. All of her children had families of their own and had moved to bigger cities after graduating college. Her home was experiencing a blackout, and it was getting dark. A very old tree, already on its last legs, had crashed into a power line.

When Officer Smalls pulled in he rushed out of the car with the five gallons of gas for Mrs. Ferder's generator. That would give her enough power until a tree removal company arrived in the morning. John saw Officer Smalls being reprimanded by a short slender man in a police uniform. The short gentleman put his finger in the chest of the tall, rotund man and then pointed toward the squad car. After he was done scolding Smalls, he walked toward the car and opened the car door. He let John out of the car and took off his cuffs.

"I'm sorry about Officer Smalls, he is . . . overzealous but means well. I'm Sergeant Thomas Goodwin, but you can call me Tommy; that's what my friends call me."

"We're friends?"

"Sure we are, John; any friend of God is a friend of mine. I know this sounds weird, but I've been expecting you for almost a week now. As soon as we're done here, I'll take you to my place for a nice dinner."

John raised his eyebrow and gave Sergeant Thomas a strange look.

"My wife's making meatloaf."

Both men laughed.

When the police had done all they could do for the old widow, they began to leave. John sat on the passenger side of Sergeant Thomas Goodwins cruiser as he drove home. Tommy didn't live too far away from the widow's home, so any attempt at an in-depth conversation was useless. Tommy pulled into his driveway, welcomed John into his home, and greeted his lovely wife of fifteen years. They were both in Andrea's graduation class and were family friends too.

Tommy introduced John to his wife, Kelly, and their three children, Thomas II, Brittney, and baby Derek. Tommy's sister Sally would also be staying the night because her house was affected by the downed power line as well. After the meal was over, Tommy and John went out to the porch with a couple of sodas to talk. Kelly and Sally stayed inside to get the kids ready for bed.

"So Thomas is named after me of course, Britt is named after Kelly's little sister who died from lupus, and Derek is named after the famous baseball player," Thomas said.

"You like the Yanks?"

"No, my dad does. He loves them but he grew up in the glory days of the team with Babe, DiMaggio, and Gehrig. I liked the Met—"

"No way, don't even say it. That's just sad," John laughed. "Are you from New York?"

"No my dad was; my mom is from here. They met in New York, though. They went to college in Syracuse. Fell in love and lived in the city for a while. My grandfather got sick, and they moved back down to Kansas to care for him. Then Mom had my sister and me here, but Dad raised us on New York baseball."

"And you chose Queens over the Bronx?" John laughed.

"Yeah, my dad wasn't thrilled about that either."

"I'm sure he wasn't. I'm not thrilled about it."

"You like the 'Evil Empire'?" Tommy joked.

"Ha! The 'Evil Empire.' Yes I do, like a *true* New Yorker."

"So it is you then?"

"I'm sorry?" John asked still smiling.

"Kelly . . . She dreams a lot. Sometimes those dreams are premonitions. She's sort of a prophet. Anyway, she had a dream about a stranger coming into town every night this week. But she can tell it better than I can."

Tommy called for Kelly and she came down, leaving Sally to finish bathing the kids. When she came down she saw the two men having drinks and waiting for her arrival. She was a short, blond woman with beautiful blue eyes. She had been really pretty as a young woman and had aged gracefully over the years. She sensed Tom wanted her to share her dreams with the young man and so she spared the pleasantries and got right to it.

"John . . ." Kelly Goodwin said, "I often receive dreams from the Lord; some are pretty clear and others require interpretation. The dream I had about you was the latter. In it, I see you and I know your name. You are standing with one of the biggest angels I've ever seen, shadowing you like a silhouette, the two of you moving as one. I've never seen anything like it before. You have one hand on a burden, and the other is free. I see God standing on one end, asking for the burden you carry, but you won't give it to him. You walk with the burden, and you come across a fire woman who burns without burning. But a dark, hooded figure appears, and you try to fight it.

"He starts to pull your free hand and it looks like you are about to be ripped in half. God is begging you to let go so you can fight the demon, but you don't and the demon rips your arm from your shoulder. When you finally let go of the burden the demon vanishes, and you find yourself in a meadow. However there is only a single rose growing in the field, and the flower itself is the face of a woman. . . . It is our friend Andrea and her flower has three poisonous thorns on the stem that choke out the flower and it dies. After the thorns destroy the flower, they begin growing and causing devastation to the field . . . but then I wake up."

"Wow . . . that's some dream," John said softly.

"I've had that dream for three nights in a row. . . . Does any of that mean anything to you?"

"Truthfully, no. I don't even really know what to make of it. The only thing that sounds familiar is the fact that I am looking for a woman, but I have no clue why she'd be on fire."

"It's a warning, John. What I saw is going to come true very soon. Make sure that there is no sin in your life, or whatever is going on with you is going to end very badly."

When John heard this he was taken aback. He had just met this woman and she was overstepping her boundaries, giving him warnings and talking about his private life. He didn't care whether she was a prophet of God or not, he felt that she was being rude, and his pride wouldn't let him receive another word, whether true or not. Truth was he didn't know her and although that shouldn't stop him from hearing a word from the Lord, he felt judged. Whether she intended that or not, she had offended him.

"Excuse me? Lady, don't talk to me about my sins, you don't even know me."

"I'm sorry. That's not how I meant it. I don't mean to upset you, but you need to hear this."

"Kelly . . . ," Tommy interrupted.

"No, I don't." John began walking off the property, but before he could make it off the porch she called out to him.

"Wait, this is so much bigger than you! The Lord has such a mighty hand on your life right now, and you can't even see how great you are going to be. You are going to protect all of God's entire creation. Not just earth but even planets in other galaxies of the universe. The things you will see, the things you will do, you can't even begin to comprehend. But first you must defeat your worst enemy."

"Oh yeah? And who is that?" John asked.

"You."

John softened his position, but he still wasn't ready to break bread and have a clichéd hug and crying session. He simply took the words for what they were. He knew that he should believe what she was saying and repent for the lifestyle that he had accidently slipped into, but his pride convinced him that whatever he and Camilla were doing was right because they loved each other and felt married, in their own eyes anyway. Who was this woman to question him about sin in his life like she was the consummate idea of a Christian?

John left the Goodwins standing on the front porch as he walked off seeking some alone time. He walked and thought about Camilla, what she might be doing, where she might be, what she might be wearing. He truly loved her, and it wasn't a love that was clouded by animalistic lust but a true mentally, emotionally, and spiritually connected love. If he was being honest with himself, he had loved her since he met her on that summer night at Lake George. Of course his young mind didn't interpret those feelings as love, but as he grew older he realized that he had always had those feelings. He wanted to talk to her, to see how her day went. She had never left his mind since he left her.

As he walked, he came upon Mrs. Ferder's home. He saw the tree on the ground atop the downed power line. He couldn't fix the power lines without the necessary equipment, but at least he could move the tree. So he approached the big oak tree and got a good grip. He lifted the big tree with complete ease from one end until both ends were off the ground.

When he had complete control of the tree he tossed it high into the midnight sky, and it flew several miles. Due to the darkness, he lost sight of the tree, but he heard a very faint thud. He had clearly thrown the tree farther than he anticipated. Getting used to all of his new abilities was very challenging and, according to Kelly Goodwin, he hadn't even tapped in to his full potential.

He kept walking. Thinking about everything that she said and his subsequent reaction, he wondered how he could have handled it better. He couldn't tell if it was his own indignant pride that kept him from doing what he knew he should or if it was the fear of disappointing The One after he gave him this wonderful gift and opportunity to do things that he had only read about in the Bible. His thoughts raced and shifted between what Kelly said and what Camilla was doing. He was clearly not paying attention to where he was going and had walked halfway out of town before realizing it. He stopped in the middle of the road and was turning around when something began happening in the spiritual realm that made him stay. John began seeing things in the spirit world as if he were reading a chronicle.

He began seeing shadows of a past event that had occurred recently. As he stood in the middle of the road he saw headlights heading toward him and a hooded figure standing next to him. As the car kept coming it swerved out of the way and hit a light pole. The car door was kicked off its hinges, and John saw a woman stumble out of the car.

After a brief conversation between the woman and the man, the woman changed into an angel with fiery hair. John knew this was the "fire woman who burned without burning" that Kelly had told him about and, according to Gabriel, her name was Sophia. He was thrilled to discover his first lead and patiently watched the events develop.

He watched the battle unfold. He saw everything from their brief conversation to Sophia's fire being extinguished. He even saw her being dismembered. The entire scene made his blood boil at the being that was obviously a demon. A demon named Ornias, and he was on the top of John's hit list. John watched Ornias stuff Sophia in the back of his car, and he followed the car back toward town.

The car stopped at the bar, and Oscar stepped out to talk with a woman named Andrea. By watching these shadows, John discovered who Sophia and Andrea were and where they had disappeared. Yet he didn't know their current locations and finding them could prove to be difficult. Even though he didn't know exactly where they were, he knew where to begin searching. This was a much needed break in a case that he didn't have a whole lot of time to solve.

It had been about an hour and a half since John had been gone, and the couple was beginning to worry. They hoped he wasn't lost or hadn't had another run-in with Officer Smalls. Tommy and Kelly were in their living room talking about her approach in dealing with the stranger who was supposed to be a guest in their home. Tommy was getting dressed, preparing to look for him.

"Honey, all I'm saying is that we don't know the young man," Tommy said, putting on his sneakers. "All you know is that some stranger was coming into town and that he was on an important mission from God. But we don't know anything about him."

"Baby, you know I didn't mean to offend him; frankly I'm surprised he was."

"Really, baby? You basically told him to get his life right. And even though I know the Lord truly speaks to you, it came off as a little judgmental."

"Well, that wasn't my intention. It's just the Father revealed so many things to me about him, and I wanted him to hear it all . . . to prepare him for what is ahead. . . . Look, I'm sorry.

"You don't have to apologize to me or to him; just be careful what you reveal and how you reveal it, that's all." He hugged her.

"Go and find him; I'll get his bed ready."

"I will, honey. I love you."

"I love you too, babe."

Just then John walked in, and he saw Tommy and Kelly hugging.

"Hey . . . ," John said.

"Hey, I was just going to look for you," Tommy answered.

"Sorry about that."

"No, no worries, sometimes you have to clear your head and do some soul searching."

"Did you find what you were looking for?" Kelly asked.

"I'm not sure, but something definitely found me. . . . I know where Sophia and Andrea are."

"Where is she?" Sally asked, coming down the stairs and getting ready to light a cigarette.

"She is in Missouri; both of them are."

"What do you mean she's in Missouri?" Sally cried. "She's supposed to be in California by now . . . something isn't right; I haven't spoken to her since she left."

"We've all been trying to contact her, but have heard nothing . . . ," Tommy added.

"Almost like she disappeared off the face of the planet," Kelly said.

"And that's not like her at all," Sally said beginning to cry, and her brother hugged her while she did. "I'm just so worried; she's closer to me than my own sisters, and I just don't know what to do. Please find her . . . and bring her back home."

"I will do what I can. I promise."

That was all that John could offer. He wasn't in the habit of making promises he wasn't sure he could keep, but here he promised Gabriel the safe return of

Sophia, Camilla the safe return of himself, and Sally the safe return of Andrea in a matter of one day. Any more promises and he'd have to start making a list. He truly didn't know how each situation would pan out, but he would try his best to make good on all three. However, before he could do that, he would require sleep. If all went according to plan, he would find both women tomorrow and return home to Camilla no later than the next day. And he was confident he could accomplish this personal goal.

CHAPTER 7

Andrea woke up to a surprisingly empty suite. She had gotten used to Oscar waking up either beside her or enjoying a warm drink on the balcony. Oscar would be waiting to surprise her with another marvelous day, or they would spend the day locked away in physical embrace. But today was different; he was nowhere to be found. She wondered where Oscar had gone.

The only clue to his whereabouts was a letter he wrote to her assuring his return after he met with his business partner. Andrea woke around 10:00 a.m. and waited for Oscar to return. While she waited she began experiencing slight cramps that annoyed her more than anything else but otherwise she felt fine. She waited to hear from him for three hours before calling him.

Usually whenever she called Oscar, he would answer right away. But his phone rang a bit then went to voicemail, then straight to voicemail, until finally an automated service informed her that his phone had been disconnected. After five hours of calling, she was worried beyond measure.

She worried about where he might be and wondered if something had happened to him. Then she worried about how she would manage without him. He had been financially responsible for their lavish lifestyle. Although she was technically not far from where she lived, only one state over, she was still alone in a strange town and most of her personal possessions were in her old Wilsonton home.

The only thing she traveled with was her wallet, which had her ID and a few credit cards. However, there was no trace of Oscar. He hadn't left his phone, any money, or a way to get in contact with him. She was alone. Andrea remained in the hotel suite all day, ordering room service and awaiting word from Oscar. She was worried sick until she fell asleep.

Stomach cramps woke her at two o'clock in the morning, according to the alarm clock in her hotel suite. They were the worst cramps she had ever had. She was late on her monthly cycle and normally cramps were a sign that it had arrived, but these cramps were otherworldly. She had no idea where they were coming from. She just knew it was the most unbearable pain, and it brought her to tears.

Andrea rolled over and reached for the phone to dial 911. She could barely speak, but the operator promised that an EMS unit would arrive shortly. When an ambulance finally arrived, they strapped her to the gurney and carted her to their vehicle. They sped through every stop sign with the sirens blaring to get her to the hospital as soon as possible. Andrea was sedated on the way to help ease her pain and once they arrived, she was wheeled straight into an emergency room.

A doctor finally arrived and after looking at Andrea's chart, she decided to perform an ultrasound. When the doctor finished scanning, Andrea was wheeled to a recovery room and allowed to rest. Andrea slept, no longer worrying about Oscar's well-being and whereabouts.

That morning at the Goodwins', everyone was sleeping. Everyone but Sally, who had awakened for her customary cigarette. Not being allowed to smoke inside her brother's home, she was forced to go outside. She lit up and took a long drag, playing with the smoke as she inhaled before blowing a smoke ring. It was a perfect circle that eventually lost shape as it made its way upward. The smoke traveled up and rose to the second floor of the humble home. It seeped into John's room as he slept peacefully and crept into his nostrils. When he took a breath, he woke coughing and gagging. His sense of smell was so powerful that it felt like smoke from a three-alarm fire.

His body, for all its glory, still hadn't fully learned how to control its new abilities, but he was being very patient with it. He woke and sat up in bed. The sun shone in his face, and he smiled at its warm embrace. He thanked the Lord for waking him up and being gracious enough to allow him to see another day, but his mind was on the task at hand. Today was his big day. He was going to find and rescue Sophia and Andrea and be home tonight to see Camilla—all in a day's work. Waking up this early just helped him get a good start to what was surely going to be a memorable day. He dressed and headed downstairs to meet the other early riser; much to his surprise it was Sally.

"Well, you're up early," Sally said.

"The smoke woke me."

"I'm sorry, I didn't mean to," Sally replied.

"Oh don't worry about it; I was planning on being up early anyway."

"Yeah, that's right, you're some kind of . . . special Christian agent guy or something like that," she said with a laugh.

"I don't really know what I am, but perhaps that's the most accurate."

"You're gonna try and find Andrea and another lady named Sophia, right?"

"Yeah, that's the plan."

"I think I met Sophia once. She came to my bar and then struck up a conversation with 'Drea."

"Do you know what she looked like?" John asked.

"Yeah, how could I forget . . . she was a gorgeous ginger . . . certainly my type—" Sally tried to finish her sentence but began violently coughing and spat greenish black sputum on the asphalt pathway. "Excuse me. I'm sorry."

"You have lung cancer . . . ," John said.

"Excuse me? How do you know that?"

"I can smell it in the phlegm. It's stage 4 . . . isn't it?"

Sally only nodded her confirmation.

"Judging by the color and the stench, you should already be dead . . . in fact, you have lived a month longer than you were supposed to already." John continued.

"How do you know all this?" Sally asked, stunned at the revelation.

"I don't know. I can just tell from looking at you I guess."

"What else can you see?" Sally desperately wanted to know.

So John reached out and took Sally's hands in an attempt to delve deeper into her illness.

"Your body is telling me that it has undergone and rejected various rounds of chemotherapy. It's been trying to grow your hair again and replicate healthier cells, which was proving very difficult until recently . . . your lungs have even begun slightly healing themselves but very slightly, and I suppose the next question is why?" John assessed.

"I . . . I don't know what it could be," Sally said bewildered.

"Think, Sally . . . I get the sense that there is something new around you that is causing these slight changes," he pressed.

"Oh, I think I might know . . . about a month ago I bought a feather and honestly everything in my home began changing for the better."

"A feather?"

"I know it sounds stupid but it's the most unique thing I've ever owned . . . and I'm not the only one. Other people who bought these feathers have experienced all kinds of, I guess you can call them, blessings."

"Where is it?" John asked.

"It's at my house. I don't know if the power is on, but the sun is out and that should give us enough light . . . You want to see it?" she wondered.

"Absolutely."

Sally drove John to her home and although the power hadn't been restored, the power company and the tree removal company were both there. Clearly the tree removal company was a bit peeved at having driven from the next town over to find no tree to be removed. John only smiled. Sally pulled into her driveway and invited John into her small home.

"Here it is," she said. "I keep it in this glass case because it's brought me good luck. Let me tell you the story of this feather. About a month ago, the sheriff and deputies found two of the biggest wings any of them had ever seen. Smalls came running into town telling us all about it. So naturally everybody went down the road to see for ourselves. Tommy was so pissed at Smalls that he almost fired him on the spot.

"Anyhoo, I'm front and center and lemme tell ya, these wings were the most beautiful and majestic wings any of us had ever seen. I feel sorry for the poor bird they belonged too because something had ripped the wings clear off of its body. There was even blood on parts of the wings, it was kind of sad truthfully.

"I'd hate to meet the animal that did it, though, because whatever it was had to be bigger and more dangerous. Well, the police didn't know what to do with them. And I guess they were planning on burning them, but someone said that they wanted a feather and in a town that's only so big, it's a whole lot of '*monkey see, monkey do.*'

"Before you knew it everybody wanted one, but there wasn't enough feathers for everyone. So they decided they would auction them off. One feather per buyer. Something in me just knew I had to have one . . . Something nice before I die, ya know? I bought the first feather sold for $687.24. That was everything I had in my bank account, but it was well worth it."

"Was it?" John asked as he inspected the case and then took the feather in his hands.

"It sure was. I started noticing small things like . . . not running out of food for one thing, and I always struggled with my bills. In fact, I owed $23,000 in credit card debt and was being harassed by debt collectors and then one day they called me and told me that a glitch in their system had them chasing the wrong Sally Goodwin. And they restored my credit . . . believe me, I remember spending every dollar I owed on those cards . . . and I guess the fact that I've been feeling better ever since the moment I touched it.

"I've been sleeping better, and my teeth and face have gotten healthier. I don't cough as often, despite what you saw this morning, and I don't even smoke as much . . . but I'm not the only one. Everyone, and I mean everyone, that bought one of these magic feathers has had similar stories . . . not everyone got one before they sold out, but Tom and Kelly didn't even want one. As if they needed it. They're always blessed."

"I know why Kelly didn't want one."

"She said it was not from this world, but not alien either . . . she's nice but a bit of a weirdo if you ask me."

"It belongs to Sophia; it's a feather from her wings," John said with a straight face.

"C'mon, I was born at night just not last night," Sally scoffed, lighting up another morning cigarette.

"Last night I went for a walk and saw her wings get ripped from her body."

"And what do you think dun it?"

"A demon."

"Ya see, this is where you lose me. When you start talking 'bout angels and demons."

"How else do you explain how well you've been doing this past month? Do you think it is more reasonable to believe it is magic rather than spiritual?" John asked, but Sally only looked at him a little bewildered.

"There are many talents and gifts that angels possess, but all of their power is drawn from God's Holy Spirit, as is everything in heaven. So even though having this object in your home has blessed you, it's really the Holy Spirit that empowers it that has blessed you . . . ," John tried to explain.

"Well, I don't care where it came from, it works."

"If you don't mind I would like to keep this, it will help me find Sophia."

"Well wait a minute, you can't have it. What am I gonna do without it?" Sally began panicking.

"Do you want to live?" John asked.

"Of course I do but that feather is my only chance to live longer."

"No, it's not. I can heal you if you want to be healed."

"Oh yeah, how on earth are you gonna do that? The doctor gave me seven months to live eight months ago. . . . If you take that with you, I'll probably die tonight. . . . And I'm . . . terrified . . . Can you really help me?" Sally confessed her fear.

"The same power that has been healing you this past month is more than able to do it for the rest of your life—if you are willing to take a leap of faith. . . . Are you willing to jump?" John asked.

"Yes . . . ," Sally said quietly and then once more sure of her decision.

John Summers approached Sally and placed his hands on her chest, right where the tumor was located, and began praying. The prayer wasn't long and drawn out. It was actually quite short and sweet, a few sentences at most. That heartfelt prayer, coupled with Sally's own faith and willingness to be healed, led to the miracle she experienced in her home. When John finished his prayer he finished with, "In Jesus' name, Amen." Sally felt instantly better and removed the cigarette from her mouth. She looked at John in a most astonished way, as if she knew she had been healed. Her eyes said it all as they welled up with tears.

"Who are you? Really."

"What do you mean?"

"I've gone to all kinds of doctors, been through four different rounds of chemo, and I've even tried faith healers. I've seen psychics and witch doctors, and even Kelly herself has prayed for me many times. What is different about you?"

"But he was wounded for our transgressions, he was bruised for our iniquities: the chastisement of our peace was upon him; and with his stripes we are healed," John said.

"Wow . . . that was beautiful . . . did you write that?" Sally asked.

"Ha, no I didn't. A prophet named Isaiah wrote it a few thousand years ago. It basically means that because Jesus went through all that physical punishment on his way to dying on a cross for all of mankind, we can be healed if we believe it. You believed in his power, that's why you were healed."

"I believe it and I believe Jesus is with you, and I want him to be with me too."

"If you believe that he is, then he is."

"Really, that simple?"

"Absolutely, if you confess with your mouth that Jesus is Lord and believe in your heart that God raised him from the dead, you will be saved."

"I believe," Sally said with tears streaming down her eyes.

"Go see your brother and sister and tell them what has happened to you, sin no more, and love the Lord with all of your heart, soul, mind, and strength."

John began heading out.

"Where are you going?" Sally asked.

"To find Sophia and Andrea of course. I'll be back when they are safely returned home."

"Okay, and you can keep the feather, I don't need it anymore."

"Thank you."

"No, thank *you*," Sally said.

After John healed Sally and she had accepted Jesus as her Lord and Savior, he left her home with the feather in his hand. He sniffed it to find the distinct scent of the angel and then searched the air. It was too faint for him to tell, but he knew that the angel was somewhere in Missouri so heading that way was the best start. John bent his legs and jumped into flight as Sally watched from her door. She watched as John got smaller and smaller and then vanished completely. She took her keys in hand and headed toward her car to tell her family the good news about her healing and lifestyle change.

Anzu's black feathery wings beat against the hellish ether. For days he hadn't been able to shake the feeling he had after he questioned Ornias. Other demons would be able to let it go, but not him. It was simply not in his nature to do so. Every question had an answer. If no suitable answer was given, he could not, would not, accept it.

He flew over the Ottocom Desert where Ornias and Lilith were last seen. He had to. Not because he wanted to either. He could have satisfied his thirst for an answer at the chronicles, but both of their chronicles went black after they entered the desert. They clearly didn't want anyone to see what they were up to, and a simple spell could make that possible.

Anzu knew they were looking for something, but what? With his amazing vision he could see if there was a disturbance in the sands from even more than a mile above the desert, but he found no such evidence. This was not a suitable answer.

He kept flying until he saw the mouth of Lilith's cavernous home. He began his descent, landed softly, folded his big black wings over his shoulders and chest, and walked in.

There was not much for Kenneth to do most days beside sleep and think. He dreamt about Andrea when he slept and daydreamed about her when he was awake. Hopefully she would believe his message and forgive him. He truly was sorry and paid dearly for his physical abuse. But if the two angels were really able to put in a good word for him, then maybe he could go to heaven. Or better yet, possibly be allowed to go back to earth to try and be a better husband to Andrea this time around.

When he wasn't thinking about her, he played with the creatures. Some were grazing animals, others were fierce animals of prey, but none of them resembled any animals that exist on earth. Kuyel was an enormous herbivore with horns and a black pelt. She was his favorite. She tended to her offspring quite a bit, and he felt the safest around her. But there were also predatory animals as well, and none bigger than Shaziel, who slept most of the day. The 13-foot-long, 1,100-pound beast had razor-sharp, protruding teeth that it couldn't hide and claws that weren't retractable. They could dismember a demon with one swipe. Shaziel was a powerful creature with deep orange, leathery, purple-spotted skin; she and her kind were among hell's deadliest creatures. No telling what she could do to a human. This creature was Lilith's favorite.

One day Kenneth heard noises coming from outside the chambers and went up to investigate. He heard banging and clanging and thought Lilith and Ornias were back. He ran to the door, excited that they were back, and cracked the door slightly. But what he saw scared him to death. It was neither Lilith nor Ornias. It was another demon searching her cave. The big hulking demon, dressed in a black, tattered robe with black raven-like wings, swung his sword smashing things, looking for all kinds of clues that he could possibly use against her.

Kenneth closed the door behind him and backed up, but he backed too far and fell from thirty feet to the dirt floor below and yelped. Anzu heard the cry, immediately ran to the door, and kicked it open.

"Who is here? Show yourself."

Kenneth didn't answer. If he were caught he would be beaten and taken back to his punishment, but even worse, he'd never escape this place. Anzu walked down the grassy walkway admiring the beautiful flowers and the brightly burning, sun-like fireball.

"I know you are in here . . . I can smell you. Come out . . . and I will make this quick."

When the demon reached the main grassy ground, Kenneth slid behind a big rock.

"I promise . . . I won't hurt you . . . much."

Kenneth moved from his hiding place as Anzu approached, slithering to a tree where he came upon Kuyel. She looked at him and cooed. Kenneth tried to shush her but to no avail. The demon hadn't seen anyone behind the rock but heard the animal in the background. He slowly made his way to the sound.

"I can hear your heart beating through your chest. You are afraid as well you should be. You are going to pay dearly for playing this game with me . . . although I must admit it is quite fun."

Kenneth tried to hide behind Kuyel who was walking slowly away from the trespasser. Anzu saw the big beast and noticed the four-legged animal had six; he smiled generously knowing that he had found whatever it was he was looking for. He jogged, which quickly turned into an all-out sprint. But just as he was about to reach the huge beefy beast, Shaziel jumped from the bushes and attacked him. Anzu was thrown to the ground and lost his sword when it fell into the bottom of the pond.

The demon fell flat on his back and Shaziel jumped toward him. He rolled backward till he was on his feet and jumped straight into the air, landing on the top of the grassy walkway and transforming his facial appearance into a menacing raven. Shaziel looked at her prey from down below, unafraid of the new form, and ran toward the walkway, sprinting toward the invader.

The demon went through the door slamming it behind him and pushing against it. The predator rammed the door and moved the invader every time she slammed against it. The trespasser reached for a metal pole and stuck it between the door handles. He backed away, thinking that maybe this would hold the beast. Shaziel rammed once, twice. There was a lull and finally the creature rammed a third time and broke through the door.

Shaziel roared and leapt toward Anzu, but he rolled out of the way trying to make his way toward the entrance of the cave. But Shaziel blocked his only way out. The beast jumped on Anzu pinning him against the wall, her claw sliced a portion of the demon's wing. Anzu struggled free and dodged the beast's mighty jaws chomping at his head. Shaziel swiped wildly with both paws and clipped Anzu in the ribs, making him scream.

Anzu could not waste time fighting this creature because he would surely lose. So he pushed the mammoth beast off with all his strength and when she lunged again, Anzu formed a fireball and hit Shaziel. It slowed her down, but she kept coming. Anzu summoned more fireballs and kept bombing the beast until it was severely burned and had no choice but to back down.

Anzu seized his window to run as fast as he could with Shaziel close on his heels. She chased the demon all the way out of the mouth of the cave and when the demon had gathered enough speed, he jumped high into the air and flew off, grabbing at his side where the beast had slashed him. Any closer and he would have surely been done for. Part of his wing had been taken from him, which made flying extremely difficult. When Anzu believed he was safe enough, he landed on the outskirts of the desert next to the boiling Sea of Fire. He was covered in filthy red sediment from rolling around on the floor with the mangy beast in Lilith's cave. But even though his wounds were substantial, they were still able to be totally healed with a day's rest. Anzu was lucky to be alive and he knew it. But he also knew that his ordeal was worth it. All that resistance was proof that Ornias and Lilith were indeed hiding something. This was a suitable answer.

Ornias sat in his chair thinking about Andrea, wondering where she was, what she was feeling. She never left his mind, which was the strangest feeling his dark heart ever felt. He looked at the time and rose from his seat. He grabbed the empty bucket and headed out of the cabin and toward the stream. It was a beautiful sunny day with minimal clouds in the sky. When he arrived at the stream he filled the water to the top of the bucket and walked back to the cabin. When he was back inside he approached the fireplace and pushed in the secret brick and a series of sliding units brought out Sophia, still chained and a bit damp. It was about that time for her "shower," which she hated. She couldn't wait to burn this place to the ground. She was so angry that she even thought about setting the lush woods on fire as well, but there would be no way she'd be able to explain that to The One, no matter how angry she was. Sophia stared at him. Ornias looked at Sophia and neither of them said a word, but they were saying so much in the silence. They were reading each other like books. Finally, she broke the silence.

"You look unsettled, old friend."

"You still consider me a friend?"

"We've never stopped being friends."

"How noble of you."

"It is, isn't it. . . . What's troubling you?"

"Nothing that you would understand."

"Is love something I wouldn't understand?"

"What do you know about love?"

"Love is patient, love is kind—"

"Oh shut up Sophia. . . you have no idea of what I'm feeling. To care about someone other than yourself. To love someone and only want the best for them. I never thought that I could feel that way about anyone . . . Andrea was just supposed to be a mark. A target. I was supposed to impregnate her and leave before she even realized what happened to her . . . but something happened to me. With each passing moment that I spent with her, the longer I looked into her eyes or smelled her fragrance or held her hands, the more I became blinded by her. It is her beauty as a being that makes it impossible for me to get her out of my spirit. There is a fire that burns deep inside me for her. I love her and she loves me. That is love."

"Aww, that is really sweet. I would clap my hands for you if I could."

The statement was wet with sarcasm and Ornias drank in every sour word and became angry.

"You must think this is a game?"

"No, *you* must think this is a game. You are a fool to think that she would fall for such a filthy creature if she knew who you really were. You do not love her. If you loved her, you would not have deceived her. You would not have carried out your plans. You would have risked your own spiritual being to protect her. But you could not possibly love her. You are a vile, disgusting demon who cares only about himself.

"If you love her so much, why don't you go to her and tell her who you really are? She will reject you and hate you more than you hate yourself for what you've done to her. You are filled with hate, and there is no good thing in you. But I, too, have a fire that burns deep inside of me for you and it is my desire to show you."

As Sophia spoke to him she began steaming and her eyes began turning red. Ornias, noticing what was happening, took the bucket of water and splashed her with the contents, which cooled her off immediately.

"You would be foolish to think that I will allow you to escape so easily."

"Enjoy it while it lasts," she said, soaked from head to toe.

The words Sophia said about Ornias struck him deep in his heart. He thought about what he had intentionally done to Andrea, and if he was being honest with himself, could he really say he loved her? But he fell for her before he slept with her and what happened between them was only a natural and logical outcome for two people in love to take.

Yet those words stabbed him and burned him as if someone put salt in his wound. Sophia was right. If he loved her like he said he did, then he must see her. Tell her the truth of who and what he is. Apologize and see if she truly loves him enough to forgive him.

"You are right. I must see her. I must confess my sins against her."

"She hates you and will turn you away."

Ornias backhanded Sophia, but no blood came from her mouth.

"You would do well to mind your tongue."

Sophia looked at him with vengeance in her eyes.

Ornias looked at the clock on the fireplace mantel; it was almost a quarter to five. He decided that he would go to the hotel and reveal himself to Andrea. Ornias pushed the key brick and Sophia disappeared behind the fireplace, convulsing and screaming, and he walked out of the door into the cool afternoon air.

He flew into the air toward the hotel, which was about an hour away from the cabin. When he finally arrived, he realized that she was no longer there. He had a retrocognition and saw that she had been taken away to the hospital. And he was on his way.

Andrea lay in her hospital bed asleep. Her pain had subsided, thanks to the drugs the hospital staff supplied, allowing her to achieve that sweet peace that eluded her earlier. There was no dreaming, no slumbering, only sleep that resembled death. She would have slept longer if Doctor Lillian had not awakened her.

Doctor Lillian walked into the recovery room holding Andrea's charts while she slept, checking on her IV and other equipment that helped her remain in stable condition. Dr. Lillian looked around to see if anyone was watching her, and when she realized she was alone, she kicked Andrea's recovery bed to rouse the sleeping beauty. Andrea was startled and sat up quickly.

"I'm so sorry to wake you," Doctor Lillian said. "I can be such a klutz sometimes."

"It's okay . . . it's fine."

"Please don't be upset with me."

"I said it was fine . . . How long have I been out?"

"Fifteen hours. It's almost five in the evening."

"Oh my god, I can't believe I've been out that long."

"Yeah, there was actually an office pool about when you might wake up . . . I said noon." Doctor Lillian smiled.

"I see. Did you guys find out what is wrong with me?"

"Oh yeah, of course. I actually have your chart right here. And it says . . . are you ready for this?"

"Please just tell me what's wrong."

"Why, nothing is wrong, Mrs. Rose. Congratulations . . . You're pregnant."

Andrea swore.

"I'm sorry, Mrs. Rose . . . is this not a good thing?"

"Miss."

"Excuse me."

"It's *Miss*. . . . I'm not married anymore."

"I see. Is everything alright? As your attending physician, there is patient confidentiality. You can tell me anything."

Andrea began to tear. Doctor Lillian closed the door to give them privacy and pulled up a chair next to her bed.

"You can tell me anything."

Andrea gathered herself and told Doctor Lillian about her inability to have a child and now that she had finally become pregnant again, she couldn't find her future baby's daddy. Oscar was nowhere to be found, and he should have called by now, or at least have returned to the suite. There, the staff would have informed him that she had been taken to the hospital. He could have easily found her if he cared; if he truly cared and had not been feeding her a load of bull that she ate up like a homeless person at a Thanksgiving feast.

She was hurt and angry. Angry at him for his apparent disappearing act, but angrier at herself for believing some strange man would swoop into town and give an aging wannabe model a chance to fulfill her dreams.

Doctor Lillian hugged her as if she, too, had been duped by the devilishly handsome womanizer.

"Thank you for listening to me. I must sound like a crazy person," Andrea said between sniffles.

"Oh no, no, dear. If I were in your position, I doubt I would react any differently."

"Really?"

"Yes, please don't worry about it."

"I need to get out of here and get back to the hotel."

"Sure, of course you do. Look, here is my personal number in case you need something. Anything. Please call me."

"Are you sure?"

"Never been surer about anything."

"Okay. Thank you. I will."

Doctor Lillian left the room, and Andrea got dressed and made her way to the front desk to check out. There, one of the medical billing assistants explained her bill.

"Ma'am, we ran you're insurance card, but they won't cover the bill because you are out of your coverage network."

"Okay, well then how much is it?"

"The total is $1,153.83."

"One thousand one hundred fifty-three!" she exclaimed. "I don't have 1,153 dollars . . ."

"Do you have a credit card, ma'am?"

"No . . . I don't, I didn't exactly have time to grab my purse when you guys rushed me to the hospital, you know?"

"Well, ma'am, we're going to have to . . ."

"Miss Rose, is there a problem?"

All of a sudden Doctor Lillian was there and came to her rescue.

"Yes, my bill is $1,153, my insurance won't cover it, and I don't have that money."

"Kathy, we're going to comp the bill."

"Yes, ma'am."

"There you go, Andrea, you're all set."

"Wow, thank you . . . thank you so much."

"Listen, you have my number, If you need anything . . . use it."

Andrea thanked the kind doctor and hugged her again. She didn't know Doctor Lillian, but she seemed so sincere, and she really listened to her story without judgment. And at this moment she was the closet person who acted as a friend.

Andrea left the hospital and walked to the hotel, which was within walking distance. All of her personal information was in the suite—driver license, maxed out credit cards, keys to her car and home. She kept those things out of familiarity. She racked her brain thinking about where Oscar was. Why had he deserted her? Was he totally lying to her to charm his way into her pants? Was she nothing but a challenge that he saw and conquered? *Some challenge I was,* she thought.

When she had finally arrived at the hotel, she was called to the front desk before she made it to her suite. She secretly hoped it was news from Oscar.

"Hello, Mrs. Rose, there was a problem with your room."

"What do you mean?"

"Well, the card that was on file has been canceled. And we cannot process the payment."

"Canceled? How . . . I . . . well, have you run it again?"

"We've run it several times, ma'am, but I'm sorry. It just keeps getting declined."

"Oh my god. Well, how much is it a night?"

"Well, that suite is $4,000 a night, Mrs. Rose."

"Four thousand dollars a night? Unreal. I do not have $4,000!"

"We know!"

"Excuse me?" Andrea stared down the front-desk clerk.

"Nothing."

"How much is your cheapest room?"

"Well, most of our rooms are booked and the least expensive room we have available is $439."

"Four hundred thirty-nine fu—" Andrea caught herself. "$439?"

"It's actually being discounted right now."

"I . . . can't afford that, you really have nothing else available?"

"No, Mrs. Rose, we don't.

"Miss . . . *Miss* Rose."

"Okay . . ."

"Listen, the entire stay here was being paid for by the man I was with, Oscar . . . God, I don't even know his last name."

"Miss Rose, there is no card on file for a man named Oscar. The card we have on file is in your name."

"What?"

"Miss Rose, I have other people waiting to check-in. I really must end this conversation."

"Wait. I don't understand."

"You'll find that all of your belongings are being held by security. We were waiting for you to come back to tell you, but you were away most of the day."

"Wait, *please*! Can't I just stay one more night and leave in the morning? I don't have any place else to go."

"No, Miss Rose, you cannot. We've already booked that suite tonight. Now if you don't mind, I must attend to other *paying* guests."

"Wait, you can't do this. I've been staying here for nearly four weeks."

"And we thank you for choosing The Grand Marquis Hotel, but you can either escort yourself or we can have security escort you out; the choice is yours."

Andrea cursed the young woman and kept swearing until she grabbed her luggage and left the hotel. All she could do was walk. She didn't know where she was walking to. She was alone. She had no one to turn to and, and to add insult to injury, her phone was dead. Thankfully, she wasn't too far from home so she could call Sally—the one constant in her life she clung to, She spoke to Sally every day she was in Missouri, but she couldn't call her now and that was killing her. Andrea was slowly being driven beyond tears. She was close to a breakdown and she would have had one right then on the corner if Doctor Lillian had not driven by at that very moment.

"Andrea?" she yelled across the street in her red Corvette Stingray. "Andrea, are you okay?" she yelled again before making a U-turn and pulling up beside her.

"Andrea, what are you doing out here with all of your belongings?"

Andrea tried to form words to answer her but she was too overwhelmed and no sound came, only tears and a quivering mouth.

"Oh no, c'mon get in."

Doctor Lillian escorted her into the luxury sports car, luggage and all. They sped off in the direction of the doctor's home.

Meanwhile, Andrea kept thinking of Oscar. She felt betrayed, alone, and hurt. The one man she had chosen to fall for since she lost Kenneth had abandoned her, and she was pregnant with his baby.

She hadn't seen him or heard from him, but what she didn't know was that he was watching her more closely now than he did when he was with her. His heart ached because he knew what she was feeling, but he was powerless to comfort her. He watched as long as he could and then flew back to his post in a pain he never knew his black heart could feel.

John landed just outside of a cabin he spotted from his aerial view. The scent of the feather had led him here, and he knew that Sophia was in the cabin, or at least in the surrounding area. The woods were still green and he could smell every pine. It wasn't overpowering; it was light but amazing. If he wasn't on such an important mission, he would have stayed there for hours. But it was getting late, the sun was going down, and he still had to find Sophia. He ran into the cabin, but it was empty. He looked around and nothing appeared out of the ordinary. It looked occupied, but he sensed nothing unusual about it.

He walked outside again to see if there was something he was missing. He walked all around the cabin and began kicking things and looking for trapdoors around the outside. When he found none, he walked back into the cabin. He searched all over the house and all of the bedrooms upstairs. When he came back downstairs, he sighed heavily. Then he threw a "hello" into the air hoping whoever was nearby would catch it and answer him. He lingered there and then a faint subtle reply came to him through the walls. He repeated his hello and moved closer to the walls to hear where the replies were coming from. As he moved closer to the fireplace, they became a bit louder.

"Hello? Sophia?"

"Who are you?"

"My name is John. I mean Seraph. Are you alright?"

"Yes, I'm fine."

"I'm gonna get you out of here."

He started knocking items off the shelves and kicking the fireplace, hoping that he would stumble upon the key to freeing her.

"You don't know what you're doing, do you?"

"No. I don't."

"Press on the bricks. I don't know which one it is, so push them all."

John did so and pushed in the correct brick after several attempts and out came Sophia—a bit damp but healed from all her injuries. Aside from being kidnapped and held against her will, she was actually okay.

"Are you here to kill me?"

"No, I just released you. Why would I kill you?"

"Because the enemy is a tricky one, and I do not know you."

"Right. Gabriel sent me to rescue you."

"Gabriel? Who are you?"

"I'm a friend," John said while attempting to break the shackles that bound her. But his strength could not remove them.

"How did you find me?"

John pulled out the feather he used to track Sophia down.

"I believe this belongs to you."

"A feather from my wings?"

"You don't look like any angel I've ever seen, ya know."

"I am in human form, but when I am dry enough I will transform from this flesh and blood that imprisons my true nature."

"Well, I would love to see that if I can break these chains off you."

"You said your name is Seraph?"

"Yes."

"There are rumors of Ahadiel, our brother, being trapped inside a human. I assume you are that human."

"Yes, the rumors are true. He's in here . . . somewhere," John said while trying to use heavy objects to break the chains.

"Incredible . . . how did it happen?"

Just then, as John worked on freeing Sophia, he could hear a whirling sound and instinctively swayed out of the way as a short battle sword whizzed by his head and got stuck in the wood of the cabin. When John turned around he saw Ornias. It was the same demon that he had seen in the retrocognition shadows the night before.

"Quite simple really. I put him there," Ornias said, appearing in his demonic form and ready for battle.

"You."

"Me." Ornias grinned.

CHAPTER 8

John grabbed the sword from the wall and flung it back toward Ornias, who was surprised at how quickly the object came traveling toward his head. He barely got his shield up in time to block it. The sword clanged off the shield and flew into the dark woods that were only lit by a pink twilight sky. Before Ornias could blink or recover, John used his super speed and kicked him, sending him flying and landing next to his sword. John stood in the door of the cabin.

"Sophia?"

"Go, I'll be fine," she said as she struggled to break free from her chains.

John stepped from the cabin and tried to use the power of his will to activate his suit but nothing happened. To his surprise his suit had not sorted itself out, and he had not changed into the hulking intimidating being that was supposed to protect the world. He tried concentrating harder, but he soon realized that he was going to have to do this alone. He didn't know how this would play out, but he would do his best. Ornias was getting up and grinning.

"You seem to be taking well to the gift I gave you."

"Suppose I should thank you?" John said walking down the stairs and onto level ground with the demon.

"You have no idea what you have gotten yourself into you filthy human!"

"Filthy? Do you not know what you smell like?" John said, smiling.

"Humor, a sign of weakness."

"Humor is a sign of weakness," John said in a mocking tone. "Blah, blah, blah, we gonna do this or not?"

"I am going to skin you alive and then take your soul down to the depths of hell."

Ornias screamed before charging John who just stood there and waited. Ornias swung his sword high at an angle and John ducked, grabbed the demon's legs, and lifted him high into the air before bringing him down in a most powerful slam. At that moment Ornias knew he was in trouble. He tried to crawl away from John, but John grabbed his foot as he tried to escape and swung him like a baseball bat into a tree. Ornias hollered in agony.

John ran to his opponent, picked him up by his throat, and pounded his ribs with his free fist. Then he threw the demon onto the ground about twenty or so feet away. Ornias, though a capable fighter, wasn't a warrior by any stretch of the imagination and that was being proven every moment he fought John. Ornias had been in a few angelic scuffles before. However, this fight was anything but angelic. Angels fight with a certain fluidity and grace, but John was very raw, powerful, and instinctive. And it made Ornias extremely uncomfortable.

Ornias stood up but was promptly kicked in the face, which lifted him off his feet once more. There was just no way that he could get the upper hand. After landing on his back, he slowly stood up. John was approaching and Ornias threw several attacks his way, striking with everything that was inside of him, but it wasn't even close to being enough. John evaded and dodged every attack. When Ornias threw another punch, John caught his hand and struck him with his own fist. John gained confidence, but wasn't cocky. He knew he was quite handily winning the fight.

Meanwhile inside of the cabin, Sophia was still chained to the fireplace when she began heating up. This time there was no one with a bucket of water to stop her from catching fire. She wasn't quite there, but with every passing minute she was getting closer to being free. Sophia was glowing and although she had not quite transformed, her illumination and warmth could be felt outside.

After being thrown into another tree, Ornias fell to the ground. John jumped Ornias and pounded him as if he were an MMA fighter. He pounded away, but suddenly he felt heat and noticed light emitting from the cabin. Distracted, he stopped his assault to see what could possibly be happening inside. Ornias reached for anything he could get his hands on and found a fistful of dirt with one hand and a rock with the other.

When John looked down, Ornias threw the dirt into John's eyes with one hand and smashed him in the face with the rock in the other. This was a tactic that would have proven futile if John were wearing his armor, but he wasn't. And this was exactly what Ornias needed.

John got up and rubbed his eyes while he walked away, bleeding from his temple. He was completely defenseless. Ornias took a moment, gathering whatever strength he had left, and rose to his feet, smashing John in the back of the head with his shield. John was flattened. Ornias went to pick up his sword as John rose to his feet. The sun had completely set. The only light came from the cabin, but the specks of dirt in John's eyes made seeing impossible.

Ornias approached John, who swung on the demon but missed terribly. John swung once more, but Ornias moved his shield in the way of the oncoming fist. John's fist dented the shield, but Ornias stabbed him in the stomach.

By this time Sophia was completely ready to transform and she caught fire as if she were bathed in gasoline. She laughed almost maniacally because nothing stood in her way. She focused on the manacles that held her down and began heating up to a degree that began slowly melting the chains away.

John clutched his stomach, but refused to give up, and swung again, but this time Ornias swung the sword at the incoming fist and chopped his hand clean off at the wrist. John howled like a wolf in the night. Ornias shoved John against the tree and stabbed him in the shoulder. The blade went straight through John's shoulder and into the tree, pinning him. John was in such excruciating pain that he fainted and hung on the tree.

Ornias knew that he was lucky to have escaped this battle with his life. He never thought that trapping Ahadiel in the body of this human would be a problem. And the human hadn't even become that big of a problem, yet. But Ornias was determined to make sure the human would never become one.

"John? Johnny Boy? Look at you now. Where are all your jokes now, Johnny Boy? I know you can't hear me, but I'm going to tell you this anyway," he said, growing his talons and raising his hand in the air while preparing to savagely attack John. "I'm going to make good on my promise to skin you alive."

While Ornias was dealing with John he didn't realize that the cabin was in total flames and burning to the ground. By the time he realized his mistake, it was too late. Sophia had transformed into her angelic form and stood where the fireplace used to be, burning like a six-foot pillar of fire. Ornias looked at Sophia and before he could say her name, she threw a fireball at him that sent him crashing into the woods. In the darkness all Sophia could see was a figure on fire fleeing into the woods.

Sophia cooled herself down. Only her hair was aflame. She extinguished the fire in the cabin before it devoured the forest. She approached John, who was still unconscious and hanging on the tree. She removed the sword and caught him as he fell into her arms. Sophia carried him, as a husband carries a wife over the threshold, and flew into the air until she disappeared. To anyone watching the night sky, she appeared to be a vanishing star in the cool night air.

⚞⚟

The light from The One shone throughout the entire city of Zion, the capital city of heaven, where the physical presence of God dwelt in the midst of his people. Hundreds of millions of souls sat in the middle of the city to commune with him, billions more came and went as they pleased. Some would stay for hours, while others stayed for months, yet others had been in his presence for centuries. The longer one spent in his presence, the more irrelevant time became in a place where time didn't really seem to exist at all.

This was what Sophia saw as she carried the unconscious warrior through a gateway from earth into the heavenly realm. This was the place of the safest haven. She landed on the edge of the city. She passed through the middle of the three gates on the eastern wall. Zion had four walls with three very large, wide entrances on every side.

When she entered the city it was quite busy, much like the most popular cities on earth put together, but it wasn't overpopulated. The pedestrian traffic moved freely and smoothly at all times. While most of heaven's citizens lived in one of the six heavens, many also lived in Zion. And although seeing angels going to and fro was a part of daily life, seeing one frantically running with an injured human was something entirely different.

Sophia ran as fast as she could until she finally reached the angelic sector. This area housed angelic homes, recreation, chronicles, and an infirmary, which was where she was heading. Humans and angels interacted in heaven frequently and daily, but there were certain places where both appreciated their privacy. It wasn't an uncomfortable hostility, just a simple and necessary separation; humans were humans that needed human comfort and amenities, and angels were angels with angelic needs.

She finally made it to the infirmary and laid John on the first open bed she could find. The archangel of healing, Raphael, was attending to other wounded angels when Sophia came bursting in.

"Sophia, what is this?" she asked.

"Forgive me, it is an emergency."

"I have many emergencies. Who is this?"

"John Summers."

"A human?"

Sophia nodded.

"The humans have their own infirmaries. You should take him there."

"Raphael, please help him. . . . He saved me . . ."

"Saved you? From whom?"

"It's a long story and I promise to explain later, but for now please just do whatever you can for him."

Sophia started to leave.

"Where are you going?"

"I must find Gabriel."

Sophia turned to leave but ran right into the chest of Gabriel, who had just arrived.

"Gabriel? Hallelu Yahuah. I was just going to find you."

They greeted each other by touching their foreheads together.

"I was meditating on the roof of my quarters when I saw you gate in. I saw that John was injured. I rushed here as soon as I could. Is he okay?"

"He will be."

"Sophia, how did this happen?" Raphael asked.

She was dressing John's wounds and trying to use her spiritual energy to heal him; however, the extent of John's injuries was causing complications. Her only other alternative was to place John in a healing chamber. Healing chambers were used for angels that had suffered serious battle-related injuries. This chamber was made for the anatomy of angels and not humans, but it would have to do.

"Ornias did this to him."

"What? Why?"

"Lilith and Ornias are working together. They captured and imprisoned me. John found me. Set me free."

"I'm glad he was able to find you," said Gabriel.

Sophia was visibly upset and felt this was all her fault.

"I did this to him . . . I shouldn't have allowed myself to be captured."

"Sophia, you are no warrior, you are a messenger and a great one. There is no way you could have stopped this from happening."

Sophia was silent.

"You know the Father has a reason for everything that he allows to happen. The reason was probably to spy on their plans. Did you learn anything?"

"Yes, Andrea Rose is an intricate pawn in their plans. . . . Her son, David, should be here."

"I agree. Uriel, summon David and have him brought here. Hopefully by that time, John Summers will be awake," Gabriel said, heading toward the door.

"Where are you going, sir?" Sophia wondered.

"The One will want to hear what you have to say."

"I'll come with you."

"No, I want Raphael to have a look at you. And it will be good for John to see you when he wakes."

Lillian pulled up to the gorgeous home surrounded by a forest. She remembered every little thing about the property. Something wasn't the same way she had left it. It looked as if there had been a struggle of some kind and evidence of a fire, but she didn't have time to delve into any investigations with Andrea around.

Lillian helped Andrea with her luggage and up the stairs to the guest room, where Andrea wasted no time flopping onto the bed. Andrea was emotionally and physically drained, and fell into the deepest sleep of her life. Lillian stayed and stood over Andrea, placing her hands on Andrea's stomach. She began chanting and Andrea's belly began growing. Her belly's growth accelerated from four weeks to twelve weeks.

Lillian wanted the gift child out of the woman as soon as possible. And stimulating the growth was the best way. When she finished chanting she left the room. Her plans were going so smoothly and nothing was standing in her way. Just as she was beginning to fantasize about her soon-to-be-new position in the ranks of hell, there was a loud banging on the door.

When she went to the door she wondered who could be so foolish and unlucky as to bang on her door at this time of night. She was going to make this soul suffer. She opened the door as Lilith, in her supernatural demonic form, preparing to scare this being into eternity. But when she opened it, there was Ornias, lying on the steps and smoking!

"Ornias! What happened here?"

"Mistress," he struggled to answer. "Mistress, they . . . have . . . escaped."

"You pathetic imbecile! One thing I command and you cannot even do that! I assume that is why the cabin looks partially burned down, hmm?"

"She . . . had help, mistress."

"Who?"

Ornias was in too much pain to answer her.

"Well, who was it? Do not make me ask you again or your bad night will get much worse."

"J-J-John . . . Summers."

"John Summers . . . who the hell is that? I do not remember an angel by the name of John Summers."

"Not . . . angel . . . human."

"A *human* did this to you? How in the hell did—" And then it hit her.

She remembered when Ornias told her he had imprisoned an angel inside a human.

"So . . . it *has* backfired on you after all. . . . He must be exceptionally strong."

"He has . . . no weakness."

"Everyone has a weakness . . . you only have to find it."

"Me?! If I meet him in battle again, he will surely kill me."

"I wished that he killed you this time. But no, not you . . . perhaps me, though."

"I'm lost, mistress."

"As always. I've seduced many of the earth's mightiest warriors since the beginning of time. He will be no different."

"Mistress, I—"

"Silence. Once again I am forced to fix another one of your idiotic mistakes. But we will see how strong he really is."

Lilith walked inside the cabin and Ornias followed her. She took a seat on her couch and began concocting a plan of attack.

"Is . . . is she okay?" Ornias asked.

Lilith ceased thinking and shot him a look that would burn a man alive. "You have almost single-handedly sabotaged us, and yet you wonder about the well-being of that insignificant wench? Have you lost your mind? Were she not sleeping soundly in the guest room, I would peel the flesh from your body."

"Mistress . . . please. Forgive me."

"I do not want you here by the rise of the sun. I trust I don't have to explain what will happen if she sees you?"

"But where must I go?"

"To hell for all I care . . ."

Ornias was truly dejected. Knowing that he had failed his master. Knowing that Andrea was so close yet so far away. Knowing that there was nothing he could do about it.

"Now keep quiet, I have much thinking to do."

Days and nights passed in the beautiful home surrounded by the gorgeous wooded landscape that Lilith used as her base of operations. With each passing day Lilith, masquerading as Lillian, was very kind and gentle to the pregnant Andrea. She prepared meals, listened to her life story, and to her ramblings about Oscar. She closed the blinds when Andrea expressed a fear of being watched in her sleep.

Andrea said she would sometimes wake up in the middle of the night and see two red glowing eyes staring at her from the trees. At night Lilith would work her true plan. She would steal away into Andrea's room and speak the same enchantment over her belly.

Andrea began losing her grip on reality when she started to notice that her stomach was growing at an alarming rate. She appeared to be five months pregnant after just a few days. And the normal symbiotic relationship between mother and fetus was now parasitic in nature. Her child drained her of vital nutrients, leaving just enough energy to keep supplying it with food.

The once stunning Andrea, with her glowing skin and voluptuous figure, was being reduced to pale skin and bones with all the baby weight protruding from her belly, making her look horribly abnormal. She felt so ghastly that she began to see herself as the bride of death itself. In two weeks' time she felt ten months pregnant and long overdue. Distraught, depressed, desperate to give birth and remove the demon seed growing inside her, she cursed herself, the day she was born, Oscar, and the baby.

One day, at about nine o'clock at night, Andrea phoned Sally as she always did. Sally and Lillian were her true friends and when she wasn't speaking to one, she was speaking to the other. Andrea called her friend and waited for her customary greeting.

"Hey, honey."

"Sal . . ."

"Are ya feeling any better?"

"No, everyday gets worse. I look like I'm about to give birth any day now . . . I can't do nine months of this. I wish you were here to take me back home. This thing is eating me from the inside out. I look a mess and my hair is falling out . . . just this morning a whole wad of my hair came out."

"Oh, Andrea, stop. I miss you too, but you must be living the dream with Oscar by now."

"Sal, are you listening to me? I haven't seen him. I don't know where he is. All I know is he played me for a damn fool."

"At any rate I'm sure he's better than that other idiot, Kenny."

"What did you say?"

"Oh nothing, don't mind me."

Andrea let out a whimper as the baby kicked and moved inside of her.

"You alright over there, princess?" she said in a sarcastic tone.

"No, Sal, I feel like I'm dying over here . . . Can you come get me?"

"Come get you? You know you've got some nerve? For the last week and a half all I've heard is you moaning and grumbling about being a little pregnant. Which I can't understand because for as long as I've known you, you've been tryna get pregnant. And now that you are, you're complaining about a little bit of baby pains. If I were you, I'd be grateful just to be pregnant."

"SAL . . ."

"And another thing, what makes you think that I'd just drop whatever I was doing to come and 'rescue' you? I've got my own problems; have you even stopped to ask me how I'm doing? Or what about my girlfriend? You haven't even asked about her. You've always been jealous about our relationship."

"SAL, HOW ON EARTH DID THIS BECOME ABOUT YOU?"

"WHY CAN'T IT BE ABOUT ME? WHY IS IT ALWAYS ABOUT YOU? YOU SPOILED, PRETENTIOUS, LITTLE WANNABE BEAUTY QUEEN!"

That was the nail in the coffin. Andrea broke down in tears over the phone.

"Who are you?" Andrea sobbed through tears.

"Someone who's tired of your bull crap."

With that last statement Sally hung up and Andrea was so hysterical at the way her best friend of over thirty years had just talked to her that she could not physically take it. She began vomiting violently in bed and all over herself.

Dealing with this rejection of epic proportions had dragged her down to a state worse than any physical beating that Kenny could have given her. The rejection, combined with dealing with this wholly unnatural pregnancy alone, drove her to her feet and out of her room. As if she were a woman possessed by insanity itself, she looked at the balcony separating her floor from the main floor, ran to it, jumped over the guardrail, and landed on a glass coffee table in the middle of the living room.

When Andrea crashed in the middle of the living room she realized she was not in a beautiful cabin but in an old ratty one. The new luxurious furniture that she had been accustomed to was old, moth-eaten, and replaced with dusty sofas and chairs. She could hardly believe her eyes. Whatever it was that blinded her from seeing the old cabin for its true nature had been undone. Perhaps it was the fall.

The loud crash brought Lillian from her room into the living room where she saw Andrea lying on her stomach in pain. Shards of glass cut into her face, hands, and belly. Lillian rolled her over and called out.

"ORNIAS, GET IN HERE NOW!"

Ornias came through the door and saw Andrea on the floor bleeding profusely, but still conscious. Andrea looked over at the man who burst through the door and was surprised to see that it was Oscar. The look of confusion on her face threw her into a conniption. Still in human form, Ornias ran over to the injured woman and tried to console her, but to no avail.

"WHO ARE YOU? WHAT ARE YOU DOING HERE?"

Oscar tried to explain and apologize, but Lillian put a stop to that.

"You . . . left me," Andrea repeated, weeping and struggling against both Lillian and Oscar.

"He was never yours to begin with. He is mine!"

"YOU'RE SLEEPING WITH HER?"

"Don't be ridiculous. You stupid human." And with those words Doctor Lillian transformed into her natural state and reintroduced herself as Lilith.

"I am Lilith, the first of all women and your mother. Oscar, as you know him, is my slave Ornias."

Oscar changed into his demonic form with much hesitation. His feelings for Andrea were strong, and he didn't want to hurt her more than he already had, but obviously the damage done was irreparable.

Andrea was incensed, betrayed, and deeply wounded. She regretted not trusting Sophia when they met; she regretted not giving her heart to the Lord when Tom and Kelly Goodwin witnessed to her. Most of all, she lamented not being able to have another chance because she knew that no matter what happened, this was her last few moments of life.

Lilith took her sword and cut into Andrea's stomach, making her cry out. Lilith was preparing to deliver the gift child, but what she saw stunned her completely.

John woke up in a dark room. He wasn't quite sure where he was, but fear was the furthest thing from his heart. He felt love so immense that it could be held, almost as if it wasn't oxygen he was breathing but love itself. He remembered feeling this sensation once before. He rose from the bed he slept on. His hand was completely healed, and he walked to a tinted window to try and confirm his assumption about his location. When he thought about wishing it was lighter in the room, the lights came on. He could see all over the room and out the window and knew that he was in heaven once again, but he was in some sort of hospital, which he thought was very strange.

John could almost see the whole city of Zion, which he had never seen before. The last time he was here, he wasn't allowed in. Jesus said he would never want to leave and he wasn't kidding. John was already dreading the moment when he'd be told he had to go back to earth.

The door to his room opened and a group of people poured in: The One, Gabriel, Sophia, Raphael, and David.

"Lord." John saw The One and bowed.

"Are you okay?" The One asked, pulling him to his feet.

"Yeah, I think so."

"I heard about your hand. How does it feel?"

John flexed his hand a bit.

"Good as new."

"You did well."

"*Well?*"

"Yes . . ."

"How long have I been out?"

"An hour and a half," Raphael answered.

"Oh, that's it?"

"That's *our* time. On earth you've been gone nearly two weeks. I'm David by the way." David extended his hand and John customarily shook it.

"TWO WEEKS? Oh my god . . ."

"Yes?" Jesus joked.

"Not you," he smiled. "I can't believe I've been gone that long . . . I've got to get back."

"You will soon enough but we must talk about what happened. Sophia, you can tell us what you know now," Gabriel responded.

Sophia stepped up and addressed the small crowd.

"I have reason to believe Lilith and Ornias have set in motion a series of events to bring about the Antichrist that John prophesized over 2,000 years ago."

"Lilith?" David asked. "I've observed this demon in my mother's chronicles."

"Who is she then?" John asked.

"Well . . . she was the first woman," David said, looking toward The One.

"Lord?" John questioned.

"On the sixth day we created man in our image. Male and female, we created them. There was a dispute between her and Adam and she called out to us. She used our holy name and transformed from a woman to something else. Adam asked us to return her to him. So we dispatched three angels and commanded that she go back to Adam as his wife or be cursed to remain in the abominable state forever. She chose the latter."

"But I thought Eve was the first woman."

"Eve came later."

"So what is she? A demon?"

"Now she is a succubus. She has perverted and defiled herself with the lust of men."

"Whoa . . . that's insane . . . how come we don't know about this?"

"There are many secrets the people of earth will never be ready to hear until they have made heaven their home. Here is where all secrets will be made known."

John seemed overwhelmed by this new information.

"Okay, okay, so Lilith and Ornias made plans to bring about the Antichrist?"

"Yes, Lilith told me the night I was captured. . . . Ornias confirmed it. He slept with the woman, and I believe she is now pregnant with his child. Their plans are well underway," Sophia said.

"The woman?" David asked. "You mean my mother?"

"Afraid so, David. I'm sorry. When the woman . . . *Andrea* gives birth they will present him to Satan as a gift. In hopes that he'll later preside over the earth as a king."

"As a god is more likely," Gabriel added.

"I've read some of the Book of Revelation, but I don't think their plan is going to work is it, Lord?" John asked. "I mean this cannot be possible, right?"

The One remained quiet.

"If it's possible that this child will be the Antichrist, then I must stop them. Should I kill him?" John continued.

"No. You cannot kill an innocent child."

"Innocent? If this child is who we think he's going to be then he's already guilty."

"Everything that my Father has said is going to happen will happen, and there is no way around that. You killing this child will do nothing to change the future. And he is but a child, he must grow to make his own choice to become what is prophesied or not."

"Choice? I thought the Antichrist had no choice."

"There have been many chosen by the Evil One to become the Antichrist. All those 'chosen' so far have rejected the offer . . . everyone has a choice."

"I'm sorry . . . I just don't know what I should do."

"If you all will excuse me, I will talk to John privately."

Everyone gathered to leave, but David lingered a bit longer and approached both The One and John.

"I've done some research on human and angel hybrids. This creature will not be the birth of the Antichrist," David said.

"How can you be so sure?" John asked.

"Are you kidding me? Haven't you read the Bible?"

"Yeah . . . but I might have missed this day when they brought it up in Sunday school."

"Are you being funny?" David asked in a serious tone.

"Apparently not," John answered.

David walked to the window and looked at the beautiful golden city that had been his home since he was six months old and continued.

"Genesis, chapter 6, 'And it came to pass, when men began to multiply on the face of the earth, and daughters were born unto them, That the sons of God saw the daughters of men that they were beautiful; and they took them wives of all which they chose. And the Lord said, My spirit shall not always strive with man, for that he also is flesh: yet his days shall be an hundred and twenty years. There were giants in the earth in those days; and also after that, when the sons of God came in unto the daughters of men, and they bear children to them, the same became mighty men which were of old, men of renown.' . . . Giants."

"Giants? You're not serious, are you?"

"Why wouldn't I be serious? My mother's life is at stake here." David turned toward The One, who listened intently to David trying to educate John on matters of the spirit. "Master, Friend . . . please don't let my mother die in her sins. She's a good woman whose been dealt a bad hand."

"David, can you by worrying add a single hour to your life?" The One asked. "No, but seek first his kingdom and his righteousness, and all these things will be given to you as well."

"You're right . . . I should pray to the Father."

"Yes, but remember that we are patient and do not want any to perish but to come to repentance."

"John . . ." David turned to him.

"Yeah?"

"Help her."

"I will. I promise."

David reached the door but before he left, he addressed John once more.

"John."

"What's up?"

"When all this is over, if you really want to fulfill your destiny . . . you're going to have to get into the Word."

Before John could respond, David left with the purpose of heading into the middle of the city to seek the Father for comfort and guidance. He couldn't physically help his mother, but he could at least help her spiritually. At this time it was just Jesus and John alone.

"I could have stopped them already, but there is something wrong with my suit."

"Let us go for a walk, shall we?"

"Yeah . . . sure, Lord."

John blinked his eyes instinctively and when he opened them, the sky was black with stars off in the distance. He and Jesus were alone on a planetoid that was bare but had many craters and no wind. John's mind was blown as he looked around and saw earth in the distance.

"We're . . . we're on the moon?" John said with tears welling in his eyes.

"What can you see?"

" . . . Home . . ."

"You know what I see? I see a planet that I gave my life blood for. I see a planet filled with people that let evil into their lives with no regard as to how it affects them or the others around them. I love them. Every single one of them. Some love me, others hate me, and the rest simply don't care."

Tears began to come to the Savior's eyes as he held his hand up, the round earth visible through the hole in his hand.

"What I wish most for every soul on earth is for them to know that we are not some 'out of touch' Supreme Beings waiting to punish them at a moment's notice. We do not wish for their demise. Satan roams the earth freely seeking to steal their joy, kill their dreams, and destroy their lives, but my father and I only want them to live the most abundant life and live it eternally. Their sins were forgiven before the foundations of the earth for I am the Lamb of God who was slain before it was made."

Jesus had placed his hand upon John's chest in the middle of his speech and when he withdrew it, John's suit was fully powered and operational. John looked down at his body and saw that he was not only forgiven, but still in The One's good graces. He was not abandoned for falling into a lifestyle of sin. He felt reenergized and ready to fulfill his destiny and destroy every barrier the enemy set in his path.

"Now go. Lilith and Ornias are bringing their plans to pass at the old cabin. Andrea is going to die. Tell her I love her and David is waiting for her."

Seraph hugged Jesus, stepped back, and was gone.

Seraph flew into the black sky, blasting off the moon like a small rocket. The silence in the vastness of space was eerie. Seraph flew as fast as he could until he felt gravity beginning to pull him toward the earth. He was coming in so fast that he caught on fire reentering the earth's atmosphere. He was high above the gray clouds on the dark side of the planet.

He fell through his first cloud and saw millions of city lights from his aerial view. Seraph appeared to be a falling star that wasn't consumed by the atmosphere. Free-falling and gliding his way to the small cabin that he could see from more than 11,000 feet. He had reached a top speed of more than 400 miles per hour, tracking the cabin. As he approached the cabin, he slowed his descent so as not to cause a small crater, but when he landed there was a huge thud that scattered the birds in the surrounding trees.

Lilith was shocked at the reality of what she was looking at. Andrea had not been carrying one child but three. The first child Lilith delivered was a boy weighing twenty-four pounds, a girl was next weighing nineteen pounds, but the last baby boy was the heaviest, coming in at a whopping twenty-nine pounds. All three babies cried loudly. They were big, healthy babies.

Andrea was slipping in and out of consciousness when Lilith pulled each demon seed from her body. She looked at the monsters that had caused her so much pain and anguish, disfiguring her and eventually leading to her death. She was relieved that they were finally removed. Andrea stared down Ornias, who was present, and she was filled with a deep hatred as she stared at him.

"You . . . hurt . . . me."

"I'm sorry, Andrea, I didn't mean to . . . I love you."

"I HATE YOU!" Andrea screamed almost cutting him off.

Ornias couldn't bear to even look her in the eyes. When Lilith had all three babies she cleaned them, swaddled them, and cooed them to sleep.

Andrea sobbed as loud as she could with her remaining strength.

"I am all alone. I am all alone. What did I ever do to you to deserve this? God has deserted me, Sally has deserted me. I am all alone," she cried bitterly.

When Lilith heard this she stopped.

"You deserve everything that has ever happened to you. You deserve more pain, more misery, more torture, and you will have it. You are weak and only fit for punishment. You are going to die because you are a spoiled, pretentious, little, wannabe beauty queen!" Lilith spoke those last words in Sally's voice.

Andrea was so drained that she couldn't even respond emotionally. How much more could she take? Lilith clearly hated her for reasons that were beyond fathoming. She hated her so much that she schemed this horrid plan and even played on her emotions to send her into a tailspin that she could never recover from.

Andrea sought death and had lost her will to live.

"Yes, you are going to die but it will not stop there," Lilith seethed. "I will welcome you to my home in the Ottocom Desert in the bowels of hell. There you will spend an eternity imprisoned in a dark coffin, but that is not all. Someone in hell misses you. Wishes to reunite with you. In fact he led us to you in a way. Kenneth Rose. Your deceased husband. He misses you so much and when you arrive, I will see to it that you two are reunited. Sharing in each other's torment forever. So enjoy these few moments on earth, my child, for as unpleasant as they seem, they shall soon become fond memories." Lilith laughed.

" . . . Who are you really?"

"I am Lilith, mother of all earth's inhabitants, the first human woman, created from the same dust as Adam and I—"

Before Lilith could finish her sentence there was a very loud thud, as if something had just landed outside of the cabin.

"Ornias, find out what that is."

"Yes, mistress."

Ornias ran to the door and what he saw bewildered him. He didn't know what to make of what he saw, nor did he know who this figure was.

"Mistress . . . I . . . uh . . . you should see this."

Lilith left the young woman to die, assuring her that she would be reunited with her to continue her torture in the next life. When she arrived at the door she saw the figure dressed in a bluish white suit and standing but twenty feet from the old cabin steps.

"Who is that, Ornias?"

"Mistress, I am unsure . . . I have never seen anything like this before."

Seraph stood there looking at the two demons, still smoking from his reentry into earth's atmosphere. The suit offered marvelous protection and had already proved its usefulness.

"Are you friend or foe?" asked Ornias.

Seraph didn't answer, but chose a dramatic gesture instead. By the power of his thoughts he powered down his helmet, but not the whole suit, allowing for Ornias to get a good look.

"You!" Ornias said, powering up his battle armor.

"Me!" Seraph said, activating his helmet again.

"Who?" Lilith chimed in and then realized that this figure must be the John Summers who Ornias had told her about a couple weeks back.

She couldn't wait to see what was going to happen. Was John Summers as dangerous as Ornias had led her to believe? How much of a real threat was he? She was about to find out what they were up against, and she eagerly waited for it all to unfold.

CHAPTER 9

This is exhilarating," Lilith admitted and couldn't help but smile.

Seraph and Ornias stared each other down so intensely that their hatred for each other was palpable. Ornias clearly hated Seraph and was quite sure he had never hated anyone as much as he hated him. This was their third encounter, and Ornias was going to make sure that it was their last.

"Well don't just stand there, do something." Lilith instigated.

Ornias unsheathed his sword and calmly walked down the cabin porch steps and then charged Seraph, his hands clasping the handle high above his head, while letting out a demonic war cry. Seraph stood there— waiting patiently, unmoving. Ornias reached Seraph and brought down the sword upon him with all the strength that he had. Seraph clapped his hands around the blade, stopping it in midair. Snapping the blade off halfway between the sword's tip and handle, in one continuous motion, he stabbed Ornias in the throat.

The shock on Ornias's face spoke more than any words his mouth could have shaped, more than his voice could utter. The disbelief was written all over his face, and he slowly fell to the ground with his hand sliding down the powerful warrior's arm. His hand held Seraph's hand and when he could not fall anymore, Seraph simply shook it off. Ornias's body withered away and blew off into the wind as dust.

"Outstanding," Lilith whispered.

Seraph turned his attention to the powerful demoness and charged her at super speed, but she jumped from the porch, flipping and twisting in midair, landing in the spot where Seraph had been just a moment ago. Her landing was so soft and graceful that the babies never even made so much as a peep, sleeping soundly in the sheet that she carried them in. Seraph started down the stairs, but Lilith addressed him, stopping him in his tracks.

"Stop!"

"Who are you?"

"That is not important right now."

"What else is?"

"You do not have much time left."

"What are you talking about?"

"You can choose to let me lead you on a merry chase or you can be the hero and save the life that is seconds away from death."

"Andrea."

"Yes."

"Where is she?"

"In the cabin behind you."

Seraph turned and walked toward the door. Lilith opened a portal behind her.

"Predictable," she said, a bit disappointed.

Without turning around, John spoke to her.

"If I were you, I'd pray we do not meet again."

Lilith smiled and walked through the portal with the three sleeping babies. Seraph burst through the doors of the old, rickety cabin and found Andrea lying on the floor amidst broken glass and wood. She was a bloody mess. She was barely conscious and only had enough strength to whisper. Seraph ran to her side, but was afraid to move her. She was so fragile at this point that with any major movement her spirit would surely leave her, but he picked her up as softly as he could.

"Andrea . . ."

" . . . Who are you . . . ," she whispered.

Seraph deactivated his helmet. "John," he said.

"What . . . what do y . . . you want?"

"I want to help you. I'm going to try to heal you."

John placed his hands over her and Andrea began to heal, but the pain was so intense that she stopped him.

"N-no please stop . . . It is my time . . ." Andrea began to softly cry. "Li . . . Lilith is w-w-waiting for . . . me in hell."

"That is a lie. Jesus told me to personally tell you that he and David are waiting to welcome you home."

"Wh-what?"

"Jesus loves you. He's forgiven you of all your sins and tonight you will dine in heaven."

"H-how?"

"All you have to do is believe. Do you believe that?"

Andrea's face took on the look of someone perplexed, but she did have the hope in her to believe what John said was true. One month ago she would not have believed him, but in this past month she had met an angel, heard she had a son living in heaven, and met two demons.

John's words didn't need much convincing, and they were far from foolish. The truth is she did believe. She believed that there were demons in hell that had plotted against her and used her to bring evil into the world, but she believed even more that Jesus did love her and had a place prepared for her, where her son was also waiting, and all she had to do was say "Yes."

"Yes . . . I . . . believe . . ."

Andrea smiled slightly, closed her eyes, and died in John's arms. Tears fell from John's eyes. Even though this was their first official meeting, John honestly felt like he knew her. But what he saw next blew his mind. His spiritual eyesight was opened and he could see Andrea's soul rising from her body.

She was dressed in an all-white robe, looked at him and thanked him, and blew him a kiss. Just then an angel came down from heaven in a fiery chariot and personally escorted Andrea to her eternal home. John rose to his feet and ran outside. He watched Andrea and the chariot rise into a white light until they vanished.

John knew that something was coming, but he couldn't place his finger on it. All he could do now was grab the body, and head back to the Goodwins and deliver the bittersweet news.

Lilith walked out of the deep red portal and into her personal chambers carrying the three sleeping babies. She was both intrigued and distraught, but tried to hide her true emotions. Her sidekick for over ten millennia was gone. She had no idea when he would come back. For now, he would float in outer darkness without a physical body, which was a fate as bad as being in the Sea of Fire. In order for spirits to feel complete and keep their sanity, they needed a body, and a spirit without a body would surely go insane if they couldn't find one to possess or generate one of their own. Both tasks were extremely difficult. Ornias could be gone for a very long time, and there was no telling what state he would be in when he did come back.

Lilith was so upset at the loss of her comrade that the wreckage in her cave hadn't immediately caught her attention, but when she did notice she felt a deep knot in her stomach. It looked like a rather intense struggle had taken place, and she wondered who could have been involved. She walked around the ruins and could see foot and paw prints. Shaziel must have gotten loose, but she couldn't tell if the footprints were human or demonic.

Had Kenneth been the victim of Shaziel's uncontrollable rage? If so, then it saved her the trouble of having to get rid of him herself. She kept examining the wreckage and stepped into soft mud; she bent and picked it up. A liquid substance had caused it to harden and become clay. She toyed with it in her hands; it was blood. Demon blood.

The knot in her stomach grew, and she ran to the doors that were no longer erect and screamed Kenneth's name. She went to the edge of the walkway and jumped off, landing on the soft fertile ground below, the babies still undisturbed.

"Kenneth . . ."

There was no answer. There was no telling the kind of trouble she'd be in if Lord Satan caught her harboring a human soul. There would be no explanation, no trial, no jury, only punishment.

"Shaziel!"

The large beast limped out with a bandage on her paw. Greeting Lilith and toting a large lengthy bundle, Kenneth walked at her side.

"Mistress Lilith."

"What happened here?"

"We were attacked by a large demon."

"A demon? Where is he?"

"He left . . . Shaziel chased him away."

"She looks hurt, is she okay?"

Lilith let the babies down and rushed to the beast, petting it and kissing it on the snout.

"The demon burned her with fireballs from his hand, but he fled after that."

Lilith was livid and wanted to find out who it was and seek revenge. Who would dare enter her boundaries, let alone her home? She could eliminate Satan; he went where he pleased in this realm, and Shaziel wouldn't have dared attack him. She couldn't conceive of a general or other high-ranking officials wasting their time on raiding her place, though she couldn't rule it out completely.

"Who was it?" Lilith said seething.

"I . . . I don't know, but he did drop this at the bottom of the pond . . . and I got it back."

Kenneth handed her the bundle. She unwrapped it and held out the hefty sword. Demonic calligraphy was on the side. The symbol of the black raven belonged to one demon.

"Anzu, I should have known. Ornias told me he was sticking his beak where it didn't belong. He is going to pay dearly when I find him."

"Speaking of the devil, where is he?"

"He spends most of his time in his throne room."

"Why would Ornias be in the throne room?"

"He isn't, that is where the devil is."

Kenneth realized his poor choice of words.

"Right, forgive me. I meant where is Ornias?"

"I don't want to talk about it."

Just then one baby cried loudly and another followed in a raucous duet. Lilith rose and saw to the crying babies. Two babies were crying, but the third, the boy whom she had delivered first, simply looked at her with his wide black eyes. Eyes blackened from the pupil to the iris and even the sclera. They looked as black as the Sea of Fire itself, and Lilith thought they were the most beautiful things in all of hell.

"Babies? What are babies doing here?"

Lilith ignored him completely. Shaziel limped to her side, sniffed, and licked the babes. Kenneth walked closer to get a better look.

"Where did they come from?"

"Earth."

"Where's their mother?"

"The woman who gave birth to them is not their mother. *I* am their mother."

"Who gave birth to them?"

"You should know the answer to that question."

Kenneth looked puzzled.

"How should I know?"

"Because you helped us find her."

"Andrea? Wait a minute, where is she? What did you do to her?"

Lilith turned to face Kenneth and shoved him lightly.

"Why do you care so much?"

"Because I love her!"

"Love? Ha!" she said, shoving him again. "You could not love her—you don't love anyone. Not even yourself. You claim to love her, but you beat her mercilessly, cursed her, and stopped her from being the one thing she wanted to be most, a mother. *I* gave that to her. *I* cared for her. *I* loved her more than you ever could, even in my hatred for her. If you truly loved her, you wouldn't have helped us find her. She is no longer in the land of the living thanks to you."

Kenneth began to cry loudly.

"No . . . NO!"

"Yes! Oh don't worry. Her suffering is over now, but it is time for you to begin yours once again."

"I thought you were here to save me?"

"Oh come now, naivety is so unattractive."

Kenneth fell to his knees and cried profusely, begging not to go back to the coffin in the desert.

"Please . . . please don't s-send me . . . back to the d-d-desert."

"No, I wouldn't dream of sending you back there. You have not outlived your usefulness. My children will need a steady diet if they are to grow big and strong."

"W-what?"

"Shaziel."

Shaziel roared and mauled Kenneth, shredding him to pieces. Kenneth screamed and tried to get away, but he was powerless to fend off the mammoth beast. Shaziel ripped him open as if he were a rag doll, but she did not eat him. Kenneth was a disfigured, bloody mess by the end of the vicious attack.

Lilith called off Shaziel and walked to the body with the three babies crawling behind her.

"W-w-why?" Kenneth whispered.

"Because this place is hell and there is no escape." She spoke to her children without looking at them, "Eat my children. You must grow big and strong if you are to avenge your father."

The three Nephilim spawn crawled to the open body and ate Kenneth's flesh, muscles, and even his bones. They ate as much as they could, devouring every part of him. Kenneth was in so much anguish that he would've screamed if his vocal chords had been intact. But they weren't. Hell's ritual of torture and pain had begun again, and Kenneth was the sacrifice.

Lilith's plans had changed and if she played her hand right, she could be nearly unstoppable. The potential of these babies was limitless. She was going to train them to be the most fearsome warriors in all of hell and when they were ready, they would carry out her vengeance.

She walked up the grassy walkway, leaving her children to devour Kenneth. She looked at her vandalized cave. The only thing left intact was her throne of bones. She sat upon it and thought about Ornias, her companion for nearly 10,000 years. She put her hands on her head and wept bitterly for her fallen friend.

The rain fell endlessly on the oak-finished coffin of Andrea Lewis-Rose. Most of the small town of Wilsonton were in attendance and paid their respects to a beloved friend. No one knew how she died or why her body was slightly disfigured, save for the Goodwins and Sally. The rumor floating through town was that she was in a head-on collision. The mortician believed she suffered that fate, and the family thought it wise to let him believe, neither confirming nor denying it.

Black umbrellas, a sea of them, protected the heartbroken crowd from the elements, save one man standing in the back in a black trench coat. The rain fell on his brown face as he looked on in a blank stare with warm brown eyes, listening intently to the preacher's comforting words.

"Friends, family . . . we gather here not to mourn the loss, but to celebrate the life of our very special daughter, Andrea Lewis-Rose. To see her light snuffed out so soon is indeed a moment in life when we begin to reflect on our own mortality. Many of us are not only the same age as Andrea but also went to school with her.

"This tragic event touches us all so deeply, but I don't believe that Andrea would want us to mourn for her in sadness alone. She would want us to rejoice in the fact that she was a good person. A person who touched all of our lives in extremely special ways. She gave what she could to charity and volunteered her time at out-of-town soup kitchens. She loved children and they loved her. She was a fantastic daughter to her parents, Paul and Ruby Lewis, whom she will now reunite with in God's great heaven. As we mourn, the earth mourns with us."

After he finished his short eulogy, he ended with a simple prayer that he read directly from the *Book of Common Prayer.*

"Forasmuch as it hath pleased almighty God of his great mercy to take unto himself the soul of our dear sister here departed: we therefore commit her body to the ground; earth to earth, ashes to ashes, dust to dust, in sure and certain hope of resurrection to eternal life, through our Lord Jesus Christ, who shall change our vile body that it may be like to his glorious body, according to the mighty working, whereby he is able to subdue all things to himself. Amen."

After the prayer, attendees threw flowers on the casket as it was lowered into the ground and eventually dispersed, hugging family members as they left. Eventually all that was left were the Goodwins: Tommy, Kelly, and Sally. And the only other remaining soul was John, soaked from head to toe, letting the rain fall upon him as if he wanted it to wash his soul clean.

"John, thank you for everything," Tommy said through tears.

"I wish I could have done more."

"No . . . no it's exactly how it should be," Kelly added. "For as long as I can remember I've been praying that she find Jesus as her own personal savior, and yes it's tragic that it happened this way, but we know that God is always at work for the good of everyone who loves him. God used you to bring our long lost sister into the kingdom of heaven, and we will forever be grateful . . . if there is anything that we can do for you, just ask."

Tommy and Kelly hugged him and then walked off holding back tears, heading to their car to go on home.

Sally kept quiet and was still in tears. She felt partially responsible because she advised Andrea to go. Though she knew it was foolish of her to feel that way, she simply couldn't help it. John approached the grave where Sally stood crying.

"I-I just can't stop thinking that this is all my fault."

"Sal, what are you talking about?"

"I-I told h-her she should go with that . . . demon."

"Oh, Sally, there is no way you could've known what was going to happen. . . . They plotted against her soul since day one."

"I thank you for keeping your promise to us . . ."

John looked at Sally.

" . . . You brought her home."

John was silent.

"I . . . I just wish I could see her again."

"You will."

"I know I'm new to this Christian walk thing, but I just can't shake the feeling that all this was for nothing. . . . Why did they do this?"

"They're demons, do they need a reason? They're evil."

"Yeah, but *why*?"

John looked a little lost.

"I just can't help but think that something big is coming, and you need to be ready."

"I will be."

"Damn right you will. I can't do much, but I'm learning how to talk to God . . . and I'll talk to him about you."

Sally gave John a big hug and walked to her car where Officer Smalls was waiting. Andrea was buried and everyone was gone. John stood alone.

He knew that Sally was right. Something was coming. David gave him a hint, and Sally gave him confirmation. He knew that whatever test was coming he needed to be prayed up and physically ready to take on the second part of Lilith's plan.

"Andrea . . . I'm glad to have met you," John said. "Heaven gained a strong warrior, and I gained a sister. The enemy plotted against you and stole your life, but I'm going to make them pay. I promise."

The rain soaked his black trench coat and drenched his head. Tears mixed with rain. John bent his knees and flew high into the air. Through the pain. Through the rain. Through the clouds into the bright beaming sunlight that shone above them and flew home.

By the time John arrived at his rooftop, it was well into the night. He was unaware of what was going on in New York (at his job that he was sure he had lost by now) or with Camilla. He was completely out of the loop and knew that she was going to give him an earful when he saw her.

He opened the roof door and walked down the stairs to his apartment. He stuck his key into the keyhole and opened the door. Home sweet home. He missed the familiarity, his coffee table, his kitchen, his television that was being watched by Camilla.

She looked at him, angry but relieved. He looked at her and she at him, but she didn't say a word. John looked at her, sensing he was in hot water with the mixed beauty. He walked to his closet and hung up his trench coat and when he turned around she was behind him. How she moved without him hearing so much as a creek in the floor escaped him.

John formed his lips to speak, but he was interrupted before he could utter a sound.

"Two weeks. You've been gone for two weeks without so much as a phone call. I've been worrying about you nonstop. You're all over the news . . . they don't know it's you, but I know that all the weird stuff has to be you."

"Weird stuff?"

"Yeah, like a kid being found next to a tree that fell on her kidnapper, there weren't any trees around. The little girl says it fell from the sky. There's even footage of a 'bright light' shooting into the night sky and disappearing from the woods in Missouri . . . was that you?"

"I can explain."

John didn't right away, which prompted Camilla to roll her eyes and fold her arms over her chest.

"I'm waiting."

John led her to the couch and told her the entire story, sparing no details.

"Unbelievable."

"Tell me about it."

"Is your hand better?"

She grabbed and inspected his hand.

"Yeah, it's like I never lost it."

"That's some story . . . I'm sorry to give you attitude; I just missed you so much."

"I missed you too . . . more than you can even imagine."

"What is heaven like?"

"It's indescribable . . . but I don't really know because I was only there for an hour and a half, and I was asleep for most of it."

"An hour and a half?"

"Yeah . . . *their* time, but for the little time that I was awake, I can tell you that it was the most magnificent place I've ever seen or experienced."

"Really?"

"Yeah, I didn't want to come back to earth."

"Is that so?"

"Yeah . . . There is so much love there, almost like that's what you breathe instead of oxygen."

"Well, I may not be an angel, but I can give you a few reasons to come back to earth."

Camilla kissed John passionately. Her lips were soft and as sweet as the caramel her complexion resembled. He kissed her like he'd never see her again and almost got lost in her embrace.

"Wait." John pulled away.

"What's wrong?"

"We can't do this?"

"What are you talking about?"

"We can't have sex again."

"What?"

"We have to wait."

"John, I don't understand."

"We have to wait or my powers won't work."

"I'm sorry? What the heck are you talking about?"

"My powers, they don't work if I sin."

"That doesn't make any sense. What . . . you have to be perfect now?"

"No, no I can't keep sinning. If I do, I'll lose my power. That's how I got hurt."

"So you're trying to say that to keep your precious little power you can't be with me anymore."

"Yeah, you get it?"

"Oh yeah, I get it. I'm in the way and you don't want to be with me."

"Yeah . . . NO! That's not what I'm saying at all."

"No, I understand. You're a real piece of work, John. I give you the most sacred part of me, the part of me I was saving for my husband, the man I hoped would be *you,* and you come up with this cockamamie story about how you can't protect the world if you aren't single, after you've already taken my most prized possession . . . I can't believe you would do that to me!"

"No, Camilla, let me explain."

"No, I've heard enough. Screw you, John."

It was too late. Camilla heard what she heard and was too hurt to comprehend or listen to any explanation John could offer. She took some of her things, said she would be back for the rest later, slammed the door, and left John's apartment with tears streaming down her beautiful face. John held his face in his hands and collapsed in his chair. He considered chasing her but didn't know whether he should or whether he should just let her go. This was their first fight, and he really didn't know how to handle the situation.

John was starving but had lost his appetite. Coupled with his extreme physical and mental exhaustion, he decided the best course of action would be to go to sleep. He'd deal with Camilla when he had the energy for it. Even though sleep wouldn't come easy, it was the right choice.

John had been asleep for nearly two hours after struggling most of the night, but when he finally fell asleep he slept soundly until the beautiful Camilla woke him. He saw her face, heard her voice, and felt her soft touch. They kissed each other passionately. John found himself doing exactly what he told Camilla he shouldn't be doing until he realized something was wrong.

"Camilla, what are you doing here? I told you we can't do this, not like this."

"Oh, John, you're so sexy when you resist me."

"What are you doing? Get off!"

"Just relax, baby, I'll make you feel good."

"Stop . . . no . . . ," he whispered.

"C'mon . . ."

"I said NO!"

He woke. John lay in bed, sweating and wondering what had just happened. He got out of bed and got a glass of water. It was one o'clock.

When John went back to bed he was asleep again in minutes, yet he had another visitor. It was the gorgeous Andrea Lewis-Rose, and this visit was more vivid than the first. He could feel her golden hair on his flesh and he even tasted her lips. Her thighs were wrapped around his body, and he was in utter confusion as to what was happening.

"Andrea?"

"John," she said with a seductive smile

"What are you doing here?"

"I just want to thank you for rescuing me."

"You already did."

"No, I want to *really* thank you."

She kissed him deeply and John was confused. Why was she here? They had no mutual attraction for each other. He loved Camilla. Andrea put her hands on his body and began reaching down.

"Don't. No. Stop."

"Don't you mean, 'No, don't stop'?" She giggled.

"STOP!"

Again he woke up. John was sweating even more now; that dream was more vivid than the first. He lay in bed but realized that he had to go to the bathroom, so he answered nature's call, splashed some water on his tired face, and went back to bed. Two o'clock.

Once again he found himself asleep and once again he had another visit, this time with the angelic Sophia. This dream was more graphic than the first two. He could smell her and feel the heat of her fire. He touched her and she touched him. Their bodies became a tangled mess.

"Yes, John, take me."

"Sophia?"

"Shhh . . ."

"What is this trickery?"

"This isn't a trick."

"Have *you* been doing this to me?"

"Yes . . ."

"Why?"

"I didn't know if you would take me in my actual form, so I visited you as Camilla and Andrea."

"Why in the world would you do this to me?"

"I've never been in love before . . ."

"Love? You don't love me. I don't love you in that way."

"Don't you think I'm beautiful? You want your whore, Camilla?"

John realized this most certainly was not Sophia. How can an angel of the Lord speak against those whom she has sworn to protect in service to the Father?

"I don't know who you are, but I command you to leave. You just wait until I speak with Jesus about what you have done. Get out."

"But wait, John . . ."

"I said GET OUT!"

He woke up again. Three o'clock. John was beside himself; what kind of attack was this? This was definitely not a coincidence. John called out to God with his eyes still closed.

"Jesus, give me peace."

"How about a piece of me?"

John opened his eyes and there was Lilith straddling him as he lay in bed.

"Lilith . . . Lilith."

"That's my name don't wear it out or I'll make you get me a new one."

"What are you doing here?"

"You intrigue me. . . . I've never seen quite a man like you throughout the whole earth. I just want to get another look at you. . . . You're gorgeous."

"So are you . . . but I know that you are a demon appearing as a woman."

"John, I do not *appear* as a woman . . . I am a woman. The first in fact."

"Eve was first. She was fashioned from Adam's rib after God put him to sleep."

"That's not the whole truth. Doesn't it say that on the sixth day God made man *and* woman, but according to your scriptures, Eve was created from Adam's rib?"

"I know all about you."

"Oh come now, I am a product of almighty God's hand. I, too, was made from the dust of the earth."

"What do you want, Lilith?"

"I want what every woman wants . . . someone who is worthy of her submission. Do you know why Adam and I never worked? He was weak. How could I submit myself to a weak man? But *you*, you are far from weak. You destroyed a very powerful demon with no effort at all. You are someone I could submit to . . . rule with . . . give my all to."

Lilith still straddled John as she leaned forward and licked his lips and kissed him deeply. Her aroma was a lavender field, her skin was soft and toned, she had perfect breasts, and John could tell her butt was also very shapely.

This was no amateur; Lilith invented the art of seduction and had been teaching harlots since the beginning of time. This is how you please a man, this is how you control him, this is how you look at a man you want, and this is how you look at a man you don't want. She was the master, and in ten thousand years she could count the men on one hand who were able to resist her.

This was John's most important test yet. To give into her was not only to reject God's call on his life, but to become a servant of the most powerful succubus in the known universe. John fought through his arousal and grabbed Lilith by her throat and squeezed.

"Ooo harder, I like it rough."

John threw Lilith off him and she crashed into the dresser; his mirror fell from the wall and crashed around her and onto the floor. Lilith became enraged and jumped on him. They wrestled with each other for the upper hand, each choking the other.

Most demons would revert to a menacing figure in order to intimidate their enemy, but not Lilith. This *was* who she was. A beauty beyond words that was just as lovely, even when she was angry.

"You are a fool to resist me!"

With her free hand, she dug her nails deep into John's stomach. He winced from pain, but didn't scream.

"I'd be an even bigger fool to be seduced by you!"

"You think you are so special, don't you? I've seen men like you before and I have conquered them, David, Solomon, and even the great Samson. All men are weak and you will be mine!"

"I will never be yours. I belong to Jesus and he said to the Father, 'I did not lose a single one of those you have given me.' You are just another demon cursed to the fires of hell, and he has also given me authority over all the power of the enemy; I will not be harmed by trampling over snakes and scorpions, but I don't rejoice because evil spirits will obey me. No, I rejoice because my name is written in the *Lamb's Book of Life*."

Lilith screamed and convulsed upon hearing the Word of God.

"Now in the name of Jesus Christ, who is my savior, GO TO HELL!"

John let go of Lilith's neck and she grabbed her head with both hands, as if she were trying to block out the command that she must obey. She looked deep into John's eyes.

"This is not the end."

John sat up quickly and when he did, Lilith was gone. He was once again in his bedroom all alone. He couldn't tell if what he had just experienced had really happened. He looked at his dresser and the mirror, and they were still intact. Nothing was out of place. Everything was as it was when he went to sleep. He remembered she had dug her nails into his ribs and he went to check his injury. There wasn't a cut, but as he inspected a little closer there was blood on his hand. His body must have healed, but the blood was all the evidence he needed to realize that this attack was definitely not a dream.

John plopped back into his bed spiritually exhausted. When his head hit the pillow, he was fast asleep. The last sight his eyes beheld was his alarm clock. Four o'clock.

When angels and demons summon gates to travel through dimensions, it is a painless experience that they control. They know where they are going and how to get there. Spirits of the recently deceased travel through different vortexes, one for the innocent (which is a beautiful process full of peace and serenity) and another for the guilty (which is an absolutely horrid and fearful experience).

However, the gate that is worse than that is strictly for the devil and his angels, and can only be activated by a child of the Most High God.

When a child of God calls on the name of Jesus to rebuke a demon, they are sent on a devastating vortex that rips them apart at a spiritual and molecular level. Thunder and lightning live there and feed off the spirit trapped like a fly inside a Venus flytrap. Insanity, death, and fear all seem to exist in this place all at once.

Lilith was careening into a deep orange-red vortex that pulsated with electricity and collided with the edges of the small tube that seemed to get smaller the more she free-fell. The abyss seemed bottomless. Her essence was stretched and mutilated as it finally passed through a tiny hole at the end of the portal. She landed on the dark side of hell, the part of hell that never sees the hellish sun, called the Island of Darkness. She landed disfigured, wings and bones broken, blood oozing from her entire body.

The Island of Darkness was a place of perpetual night, hence the name. It was colder than the coldest night on the furthest planet in the solar system. There was no snowfall, just a freezing wind. The hellish sun never shone here, and the poor unfortunate souls that lay buried beneath the solid ice saw no relief from the worst hypothermia and freezer burn in the universe.

If she did not hurry she would freeze into the surface and be lost there a very long time.

Demons hated dropping souls here, for the chances of them getting caught in the maelstrom was extremely high. Many demons had been lost in times past, so they adopted a new way of bringing in lost souls and that was air-dropping them from more than 20,000 feet above the surface.

Lilith's wings were slowly being iced, but she was able to pull them from the surface before they totally froze. She struggled to walk, but she pushed on, coaxing herself forward. She was dreaming of being in her warm cave surrounded by her children. But what really drove her on was revenge. How dare that impudent human invoke the holy name of God to rebuke her! How dare he refuse her advances! She had seduced kings and a few queens, the wealthy and the poor were the same to her. Just who does he think he is? She was livid and that rage was the true motivation to get back to her cave. With each passing thought about the destruction of John, Seraph, or whatever it was he was calling himself, she gained steadier footing.

As she trudged on, her plan was to scale the nearest mountain and find a launching point and fly the rest of the way home. Hopefully, by the time she reached it, she'd be completely healed. And even though her situation would have certainly claimed a lesser devil, she was Lilith. Crafted from the dust by God's almighty hands themselves, albeit from filth and sediment, unlike Adam who had been made from the finest minerals and dust that Eden had to offer, she was no less than anyone. She *will* make it, she will get back to her home, and she will have her revenge.

⚮

Camilla Adams cried herself to little sleep. She prided herself on being a virgin into her late twenties. Her body was not to be shared with any and every one. She knew many men found her completely desirable, and she was proud of that fact. She dressed sexily on many occasions, but never slutty. There is a fine line and she purposefully toed it. This only helped boost her ego and made her guard her gift like a lioness protecting her cubs. To her, it was her most precious gift because of her strong moral character, and it was a gift she was saving for the man who she would marry. She was certain the man was Jonathan Michael Gabriel Summers. But after what he just told her, she felt as if she had squandered it.

Camilla was embarrassed by the way she had been acting the past month with John, living with him like husband and wife when no vows were said before God. Her mother warned her about this kind of behavior, and she beat herself up over it. *You deserve to cry these tears for acting like a whore.* She was brokenhearted and felt lied to. *He never loved you.* And what did God think? *He thinks you're a whore too, Jezebel.* Religion.

What happened? What really happened in the two weeks she hadn't seen him? Had he drunk from the waters of another well? Doubtful, John wasn't that type of man, at least that's what she thought. But why lie? If he didn't love her and didn't want her any more, he could just tell her. She was a big girl. She could handle it. He didn't have to treat her like Amnon treated Tamar.

Wait a moment, *I am being so irrational.* But it didn't change the fact that her heart was scarred, and right or wrong, she felt how she felt. Forgiving John would have to come later, forgiving herself would have to come next. But first Jesus needed to forgive her. *He already has, over 2,000 years ago.* Relationship.

CHAPTER 10

Five long hell years went by. Revenge, rage and bitterness had consumed her dark heart and had given birth to murderous hatred. Murderous hatred led her to breed the most evil offspring that she could. Lilith raised her Nephilim on Kenneth's regenerating carcass and chemaworms—a truly disgusting meal that they ate as if it were a five-star dinner. They grew big, nasty, and evil. She trained them every day and if hell rotated, she would have trained them all night too. They became sharp, extremely dangerous, and volatile. The lone planet in outer darkness revolved around the lone red dwarf star five times. Lilith evaluated her children as she prepared them for the coming assault.

Emim was the baby but the biggest of the siblings. He towered at 8'10" and weighed 680 pounds. He was built like an offensive lineman and loved to eat. He wasn't the smartest, but what he lacked in intelligence, he overcompensated for by being the most aggressive of the three.

Emim loved to eat. It was his favorite thing. He loved to scavenge for his own food, even though Kenneth and the chemaworms were readily available.

Kenneth was his absolute favorite. He loved the sweet taste of roasted human meat and had eaten Kenneth to the bone on more than one occasion—leaving very little, if any, for his older brother and sister. Soon they forced him to search for his own food if he was still hungry after meals. And search he did.

The Ottocom Desert had been his feeding grounds for the past year. He'd dig up the caskets of the tortured souls and pry them open with his bare hands. He'd pull the soul from the casket and wait for it to regenerate, which took a few hours, and then he'd devour it. Soul and all.

He was never bothered after the first set of demons crossed his path. A new pair of demons, Ghan and Taziel, had replaced Nicor and Raum on patrol and had approached the four-year-old Nephilim and was never heard from again. After about four days when Ghan and Taziel failed to report to General Deviat, he sent yet another replacement patrol. Ubriel and Qa, who were a bit sharper than their predecessors, decided not to approach whatever was out there but monitor the action from the sky.

They hovered above and saw Emim eating a human soul, and they could hear the screams over the howling desert wind. Ubriel and Qa watched the beast, code-named him Soul Eater, and followed him back to Lilith's cave. Afterward, they reported all that they saw to General Deviat. Deviat was shocked to learn of the hybrid walking about hell, but decided that since the creature wasn't freeing souls but eating them, they should not interfere until he decided its fate. Deviat was surprised, however, that a Nephilim lived with Lilith. She was a known troublemaker and an outcast, but this was high treason.

In the year that General Deviat knew of Soul Eater, he did nothing, allowing Emim to eat his fill of human flesh and souls in peace. As was his routine, Emim walked alone in the hot hellish sun, salivating about his upcoming feast. He walked until he came across someplace new where he'd begin to dig. He had never been to this area of the desert. He decided that he'd dig here and wondered what kind of savory human he'd find to satiate his ravenous hunger. He knelt and scooped massive heaps of sand with his hands rather quickly, thanks to a technique he developed. This allowed him to conserve energy while still being able to haul loads of sand. Emim would typically dig some six to nine feet to retrieve a coffin.

Emim kept digging until he got to the eighth foot and came across something hard, but neither metal nor hollow, which was what the coffins typically were. This object was solid and thick. It matched the sand and even shared a rough sandpaper or gravel texture. Emim stomped on the object and used his massive weight to crack the surface, but when he did, it shook violently.

The sand rumbled and caved in at certain places and moved in other places. There was clearly something inside the sand, and Emim figured it was a serpent of some kind. He stumbled backward away from the commotion, and then suddenly, out shot a mother giant chemaworm.

Her name was Chema Maw. She was sand-colored with a hooded, pointed head that made it easier for her to travel under the sands like a spear through the air. Chema didn't have teeth but had no use for them; she swallowed her victims whole, and the deadly acid in her digestive system killed her prey within a few hours. She screeched and shrieked over eighty feet into the air before sliding back into the sand. Emim was unsure of what to do as the enormous Maw circled him while he stood there. Suddenly it stopped.

Out came the worm from a distance of about twenty feet away, and it launched right at Emim and dove deep into the sand, taking the young Nephilim with her. Emim rode on the tip of her head and held on for dear life until she shot back into the air. He lost his grip on the 100-foot-long worm and fell from more than sixty feet onto the sand. The worm's forward momentum carried her into the depths of the sand.

Emim tried to regain his poise and prepare for another assault, which he knew was coming but didn't know from where. Once again Chema Maw blasted through the sand, but Emim lost his balance and fell to the ground while trying to avoid being carried into the air again. However, he quickly rose to his feet and jumped on the worm's tail, but as Chema Maw began to nose-dive deep into the sands, her tail flipped the giant more than a mile into the air. Her strength was truly immense.

He stabilized himself as he free-fell back to the Ottocom Desert, but Chema Maw shot out from the sands like an anti-air missile. Preparing to devour her prey whole, she opened her gullet. Emim dove to increase his terminal velocity, and they collided in midair. Emim was in the belly of the beast with no apparent way out. He had a few hours before the acid would begin to have its effect on him.

Chema Maw slinked back into her hole, satisfied in the demise of her prey. But before Chema Maw could savor her victory, she rose back to the surface and began dry heaving onto the deep orangey dunes. The only thing that came out was a little blood but no giant. She tried to spew out Emim, but after a few minutes she passed out. She lay there incapacitated and eventually the impression of Emim's hand and foot could be seen on her giant belly.

Suddenly a small wound appeared on the belly, and it gradually got bigger, piece by piece, until Emim began ripping open the giant chemaworm. Emim fell forward and landed on his hands and knees, trying to catch his breath. He was covered in blood and guts, and had bits and pieces of worm flesh in his mouth.

When he had gathered enough strength, he stood and looked at the worm once more. He put his hand deep into the body of the giant chemaworm. Feeling his way around, he finally smiled, as if he had found what he was looking for and pulled it out. He held it at the handle and kept pulling until it was out. It was a six-foot-long hammer covered in blood and entrails.

The long staff of the hammer weighed close to eighteen pounds, and the hammerhead weighed twenty-three pounds. It was a powerful and heavy hammer that once belonged to a warrior demon that had obviously fallen victim to the once mighty worm. Emim took it and began his long journey home. His only regret was that he didn't have a bigger stomach to devour the rest of the fallen Maw.

General Deviat bided his time for a whole year until it was the perfect opportunity to strike. Information traveled well in the underbelly of hell, and rumor was that Anzu was waiting for an opportunity to bring Lilith down. Anzu was not a patient demon, but he had no choice. He was but one demon and didn't have the cachet to demand an audience with Lord Satan. Only generals or very old, wise, and terrible demons could request such a petition and have it granted. And since he was neither, there was no way he could make a case against Lilith without certain proof—proof that was nearly impossible to come by.

When General Deviat got wind of Anzu's ambition, he met with him in his private chambers in the city of Sheol.

"General, you do me a great honor by stepping foot in my humble home."

"Yes, I do."

Anzu bowed low and the general sat in Anzu's personal chair. Deviat's two personal bodyguards took the other seats, leaving Anzu no other place to sit.

"Sir, would you and your servants like something to drink?"

"No, I'm fine. So are they."

"Perhaps something to eat then?"

"Listen very carefully," the general said. "We are not equals. I only eat and drink with Lord Satan and other generals. Do you really think I would allow myself to be seen being entertained by the likes of you?"

"N-No, sir," Anzu said, barely above a whisper.

"Good, you are wise to know that. I did not come here to be entertained. Now dispense with the pleasantries and let's get down to business."

"Yes, sir."

"So I hear that you are looking for a way to bring down Lilith. Is this true?"

"Yes, sir, it is."

"Why?"

"She is sneaky, my lord. Planning something I know it . . . bordering on treason."

"Anzuuu . . . That is an extreme allegation. Even for one held in as little regard as she."

"I know it is but . . ."

"But do you have *proof*. That is the only thing that I care about. Furthermore, if you go to Lord Satan with nothing but your charm and accusations he will surely throw you into the Sea of Fire as a reward for wasting his time . . . I've seen it happen."

"Sir . . . I have nothing else."

"What if I told you that *I* have proof?"

"Sir?"

"Yes, Lilith has been raising a Nephilim for the past five years."

"A giant? Well, what in the world for?"

"That is what I will find out."

"I beg your pardon, my lord, but don't you mean 'we'?"

"What did you hear me say?"

" . . . *You* will find out."

"And that is exactly what I meant."

"Yes, my lord . . . do you have a plan?"

"I will go and see Lilith with a dozen of my best servants, and we will capture this abomination and bring her to Lord Satan for sentencing."

"That is a most excellent plan, sir."

"Of course it is."

"What do I do in the meantime?"

"You wait till I send word to you."

The general turned to his bodyguards.

"We're leaving. I will summon you to my manor in two days."

They all rose in unison and headed toward the door, but Anzu asked them one last question before they left.

"My lord?"

"What?" Deviat said halfway out the door.

"When she is captured, please don't forget to mention me to Lord Satan."

General Deviat kept walking but assured him he would be promoted for his assistance.

General Deviat headed to his palatial estate for the night and left for the Ottocom Desert with twelve of his best warrior demons first thing in the morning. They departed from the Forest of Deviance, named after the general, for the Ottocom Desert. The desert was a part of his official jurisdiction, but he left Lilith alone as part of an unspoken peace treaty.

They arrived just outside the mouth of the cave and waltzed in like they owned it. Lilith had no time to hide her beloved children as they all sat around a stone table, eating a meal of chemaworms and Kenneth.

"Lilith!"

The general walked in like her cave was simply an extension of his own home.

"Deviat," Lilith said in a surprised tone.

"You will address him as *General* Deviat," said Roth who was the captain of the guard.

"It's alright, Roth. We can't expect manners from this wench."

When General Deviat insulted Lilith, the three Nephilim grunted as if preparing to make him pay for his disrespect.

"Easy, my children. Eat your dinner."

"*Heeelllp . . . mmeeee,*" came a voice from the stone slab. It was Kenneth. But Anakim shut him up immediately by smashing a fist into his face, and Kenneth was no longer able to speak, see, or hear.

"Well, well, well, you have been busy."

"I have."

"I thought you had one abomination, but as it is you have three. Lord Satan will be pleased to have this brought to his attention."

"No, sir, please don't."

"I didn't think you would wench."

"That's two," said Rapha.

"That's two?"

"That is the second time you have insulted my mother, and there will not be a third."

"Rapha!" Lilith said sharply.

"She is feisty . . . she must get that from you . . . I wish to sit."

"I don't have an extra chair."

"Don't bother. I wasn't speaking to you."

Roth looked at one of the armed guards and made a notion with his head, and the guard got on his hands and knees at the stone table and Deviat sat on him.

"I like this one. What is your name?"

"She is but a child . . ."

"I didn't ask you Lilith. Now what is your name, child?"

"Rapha."

Rapha was the middle child and the only girl. She wasn't nearly as depraved as her brothers, and she was by far the most intelligent. She was also extremely beautiful and resembled her birth mother Andrea, but with deep black and brown hair. She had learned the art of manipulation and seduction from Lilith and was trained to not only use her fighting skills to overcome enemies, but to outthink and conquer them. She stood 8' tall, but her weight was kept a secret.

"You are very beautiful, Rapha."

She said nothing.

"Are you a virgin, Rapha?"

"General . . . ," Lilith said quietly.

Deviat shot Lilith a look.

Deviat used to be an angel of love and decency, but when he decided to join Lucifer in the great war of heaven, he changed his name to Deviat. He perverted himself and became the demon that inspired molestation and deviance—hence his name. He was a very beautiful angel, but he had changed since his fall and had become a very fat and ugly demon. Once stirring romantic love, he now motivated lust.

"Have you ever pleased a man?"

"No," Rapha answered quietly.

"Do you want to?"

"General. Please," Lilith said quieter still.

"Lilith, I will not have you interrupt me again."

"Anakim, Rapha, Emim. Leave us."

The Nephilim rose at the behest of their mother.

"Rapha stays," Deviant said. "They can leave."

Both of her strong boys looked at their mother as she reluctantly nodded her approval, and they left. They headed for the private chambers, and once they were gone only the general, his royal guard, Lilith, and Rapha were left.

"Sir, is it not enough that I give myself to you as payment for the land that I graciously and humbly live on?"

"Let me educate you on the parameters of our relationship. I am as the mortals say the 'landlord.' And you are the . . . the . . ."

"'Tenant' is the word I believe, sir."

"Thank you, Roth. 'Tenant.' You are the tenant and whatever payment you were offering to live here in a desert that was given to me by Lord Satan himself has just increased. . . . Do not forget your place. You are at my mercy. What you are doing here with these . . . these abominations is treason of the highest order, or have you forgotten all the trouble the Nephilim caused nearly 9,000 years ago? Perhaps I should tell Lord Satan of all you have done here?"

"No," she whispered.

"So then we have an understanding?"

Lilith said nothing.

" . . . I will have her. One way or another."

A single tear fell from Lilith's face for she had waited millennia upon millennia to be a mother, and for the past five hell years, she was one. She fought to protect her children from the likes of many demons, making many disappear over the past few years, but here she was dealing with a demon that she couldn't just kill. This was a *general*, a demon that walked and talked with the Evil One. If he went missing, there would be a search party.

Lilith couldn't protect the sanctity of her daughter and that burned a hole in her heart. She may be a demon now, but there was a time when she was once a human with all the emotions, complexity, love, and beauty that all women who exist today possess. This simultaneously made her one of the most emotional and complex demons in all of hell, but the love she held for these three creatures made her powerless.

"Mother . . . ," Rapha said. "Mother, do not cry. I will do this . . . I want to."

"You don't have to do this."

"Yes, she does."

Lilith begged the general with her eyes, but he would not be moved. Lilith kissed Rapha on the forehead while fighting back tears. She rose and went to her private chambers. She couldn't bear to see her baby walking off with the father of deviance.

"Good, it is settled then. We leave at once."

General Deviat stood up as the two brothers were walking out of their private chambers. They eyeballed Deviat with murderous intent.

He felt a cold chill going up his spine and wanted to leave as soon as he could.

"Get up—ahem," he cleared his throat as his nerves formed a knot that made it hard to speak.

"Get up," he said clearly to the demon that was exhausted from holding up the massive weight of the portly general for the length of the conversation. But he either would not or could not move; in either case, General Deviat was in no mood to wait. Emim and Anakim closed in on the drained demon that had collapsed on the floor.

"Leave him."

Roth ordered the other eleven guards to exit the cave, and they did so with General Deviat, Rapha walking behind him with nothing but her dark brown, hooded cloak. The two brothers viciously attacked the tired demon before the company left. His screams made the general and his demons leave even faster. Rapha smiled.

General Deviat and his company gated to a spot about a mile away from his luxurious castle. There they climbed into a carriage being pulled by two enormous beasts that resembled Kuyel. They would ride the rest of the way through the Forest of Deviance. Rapha had barely explored hell. She knew how unsafe it was for her and her brothers, knowing they could end up in the same situation she found herself in right now or worse, even though being in this situation was not any fault of her own but due to Emim's gluttony. Rapha had told her brother on many occasions that his overindulgence was going to bring danger to the family, and so far she was right.

Her whole existence for the past five years had been that of training. Training to kill a being named Seraph and avenge the death of her father, Ornias. But here she was wasting her time entertaining a general because he liked virgins. *What is a virgin anyway?* She pondered. *I don't know, but when I find out what it is, I will kill it.*

"Do you like the view?"

Rapha looked up and saw the forest.

"Beautiful, isn't it?"

She continued to look and suddenly the forest's beauty showed its true hideous nature. Men and women of all kinds were buried deep in the trees as if they were a part of the bark. What Rapha believed to be the wind howling was actually the guilty, moaning in unison and buried deep within the trees. They were being eaten alive by worms and demonic ravens, and some were being hacked by demons trying to build their strength, every second of every hour of every day.

She reached out of the carriage and grabbed a chemaworm. It squirmed in her hands, and she ate it in front of the general, who was slightly disgusted. They continued riding and she noticed souls also hanging from the trees—by their feet, necks, arms, and even their waists. Some were being eaten by gigantic black ravens. Others were healing and growing new bones, body tissue, muscle, and tendons, just waiting to be completely healed so that they could once again offer themselves as a daily sacrifice.

"Do you know why they are here?"

"No."

"Aha, she does speak. Would you like to guess?"

She said nothing.

"They are here because of the sins they are guilty of committing on earth. . . . Well, that is not entirely true. Every soul in hell ends up here because they have chosen to reject the salvation our Father has provided through his son, Jesus."

She hadn't heard these stories about The One. Lilith had only told her that they were the creator of all she saw, and if she was ever blessed enough to meet them, she should show them the utmost respect and reverence. For whatever reason, her mother hadn't told her any stories, so General Deviat had her undivided attention.

"Really?"

"Yes, there are two books. The first is Torah and the other is the Lamb's Book of Life. And in this book is written every name of every soul who has been forgiven by the blood of the Lamb, but all of those souls are with The One in heaven."

"Who is the Lamb?"

"It is another name for The One. Jesus, in particular."

"Is your name in this book?"

"No . . . my name is in another book. That book is only for humans."

"What happens if a name is not written in the book?"

"I was just getting to that. If your name is not in the Book of Life then you are judged by the Torah."

"What is Torah?"

"Torah is the instructions or the Divine Law of the Creator. Instructions by which all mankind should live."

"And . . . if they don't keep this Torah, these...instructions?"

"Then they come here to be judged by Lord Satan for their sins. We have a multitude of the guilty here. The sins of the guilty are as diverse as they are endless. Guilty of murder, stealing, lying, fornicating, and sexual perversions of all kinds, including homosexuality and bestiality or incest, those who eat the unclean and abominable thing, idol worshippers, Sabbath breakers and even Satan worshippers."

General Deviat laughed heartily at the irony of that one.

"What are these people guilty of?"

"I thought you'd never ask. These guilty have molested and raped other souls on earth. They are sentenced here because they gave into my temptations and committed deviant acts against other men, women, and even children. All of their victims were powerless to defend themselves, and in turn they are molested by our chemaworms and these magnificent ravens, and now they are powerless to defend themselves. Amazing, isn't it?"

She said nothing.

"Do you feel sorry for them?" the general asked.

"No, if what you say is true then they deserve their punishment."

"You see, here in hell everyone is guilty of something great or small, and the punishment always fits the crime."

"I see."

The carriage stopped at a black gold gate and behind it was the most magnificent palace she'd ever seen. It was a large sixteenth-century medieval castle with a drawbridge and moat filled with a portion of the Sea of Fire.

"We are here."

They walked from the carriage through the main gate and onto the drawbridge. Rapha stopped to look at the moat, and the slick, black, boiling oil popped, as if eagerly awaiting a victim.

"Careful not to fall," said Deviat with a chuckle.

She kept walking and then found herself in the middle of Deviat's courtyard. There must have been thirty demons, not including the royal guard that they traveled with. Deviat's castle was well fortified.

General Deviat escorted Rapha into his personal chambers. They were finally alone with only two of his elite guards standing watch outside his room. Rapha looked around the room; it had a lot of black gold everywhere, from the tables, to the chairs, to the mirrors, and the bed frame. The bed was a canopy with sheer burgundy coverings and black gold rope ties. It really was beautiful and she would have felt very comfortable if it weren't for the simple fact that Deviat was going to try to have sex with her. She noticed that he had many accomplishments by the number of gifts on his wall. The gift that caught her attention was the dual sword and shield set that hung over the bed frame.

There were big tall windows that showed a great view of the dark forest. Even the sky was beautiful. Deviat lived on a part of hell where it was a perpetual twilight, making the sky a wonderful orange pinkish color. It was quite peaceful until you realized that souls were in constant torture and pain just outside.

Deviat took off his sheathed sword, laid it against the stand, and climbed into bed.

"Rapha. Come."

Rapha turned to him and stood at the edge of the bed.

"Remove your cloak."

She had a nearly perfect body. She was very toned with an overall athletic look. She looked very strong, but still very sexy; her feminine features were present and accounted for. She wore a low-cut shabby gray halter top and tight dingy shorts, which is what she wore almost every day. There wasn't much of a selection of clothing for her to choose from.

"Wow . . . you are more stunning than your mother."

General Deviat's hefty frame lay resting on his bed and was only held up by pillows. With his finger he commanded her to approach and she did. She stood over him and began dancing, hoping that Deviat would continue to become increasingly more comfortable.

"Ah yes, now kiss me."

She kissed his lips, then his cheek, then moved to his neck, and bit a huge chunk out of it.

He hollered in excruciating pain, which made both of the guards outside his room rush in. Deviat grabbed his neck to try to stop the bleeding, but Rapha just sat there straddling him. With his skin still in her mouth and blood dripping down her neck, she looked behind her.

The demon guards were in shock. They were used to dealing with humans and were not afraid of them. But most demons hadn't seen Nephilim in over 9,000 years, and many more thought they were simply legend.

Rapha spit out the flesh and stood up, her back to the guards. She took possession of the two ceremonial short swords mounted on the wall and calmly stepped off the bed. Deviat rolled off the bed slowly, still holding his neck. He grabbed his sword and disappeared through a secret escape door.

The demons rushed her and attacked in unison, but Rapha was so graceful and so much stronger than they, that dispatching them was one of the easiest things she had ever done. She exited Deviat's private chambers and screamed his name to let him know that she was coming for him and his death was at hand.

More demons met her and she chopped them down. One by one, two by two, and even three by three. They stood no chance as she blocked, parried, and slashed her way through the lot. Many of the demons where utterly destroyed, some were badly injured. Wings were torn and limbs hacked.

Finally, the last demon fell at her hand. She looked down from the balcony and saw Roth and Deviat trying to leave. As he was being carried to safety, Deviat watched in horror with one arm over Roth's shoulder. They were by the main entrance leading to the courtyard, and their plan was to get Deviat safely over the drawbridge.

Rapha jumped from the balcony and looked at them; Roth stopped before they could make it out the door.

"Master, you need to make it over the bridge. I will hold her off."

"No, Roth, we can make it together."

"I must hold her off or she'll kill us both."

Deviat was truly afraid for his existence. He had lost thirty of his best men and now Roth was about to sacrifice himself. Or perhaps he could win, after all Roth was quite an accomplished warrior. He not only fought in the great war in heaven, but he was also involved with the Nephilim civil wars more than 9,000 years ago. He was strong, aggressive, and had been a wise first officer for countless millennia.

"Make it to Lord Satan and tell him of what you've seen here."

"Roth . . ."

"GO!"

Deviat stumbled out the door into the courtyard, barely able to move without the aid of his best friend. Roth stayed inside the main hall of the castle and closed the door behind him. He took out his sword and assumed a battle stance. Rapha could have ended it all by killing them both as they spoke, but she hated the idea of cheating herself out of testing her limits.

Roth cried, "Ok . . . monster, it is just you and me."

Rapha smiled. "No. It's just me."

Roth went on the offensive with a magnificent flurry-filled fury. Rapha didn't even break a sweat as she dodged most of his attacks. Roth misstepped and created an opening that Rapha took advantage of, backhanding him, and he flew across the floor and into a wall. Roth had been hit hard before but had never been hit *that* hard. However, he got up because he knew the longer he stood against her, the more time Deviat had to get away. So he would take as much punishment as he could.

When Roth was fully on his feet, Rapha was just a step away. He swung but she caught his fist in one hand and punched him in the gut with the other one. Then she punched him in his face and pummeled him until he spat blood. He futilely fought back, missing one attack and blocking the other. She hit him with her knees and massive legs, sending him flying from one place to the next. Roth was knocked into columns and beams and other various structures that held the house up.

Eventually the house began to crumble around them. Roth was exhausted and physically spent. This was definitely the worst beating he had ever received. As Roth lay there on the floor of the main hall, she grabbed his sword and stabbed him in the back. The sword went through his back and came out on the other side into the floor. He was stuck and could not move. Rapha's work here was done, but she still had unfinished business with Deviat. Before she could leave, Roth spoke to her.

"You and your brothers—" Roth had to pause, his body wracked by a terrible cough, "will suffer a fate worse than hell itself. You will die—" again painful coughing interrupted him, "like your people before you. You will destroy yourselves—" he coughed, "and when you die, you will be utterly destroyed. . . . Soulless abominations, there is no heaven or hell for you in which to find rest—" a final cough seized him, "or punishment. . . . Annihilation is your destiny."

"We have learned from the mistakes of our ancestors," Rapha said. "We will not destroy ourselves. We shall be fruitful and multiply, subdue the earth, and claim it as ours. The union of the sons of God and the daughters of men will once again reign upon the earth as the dominant race."

Rapha left the castle and it crumbled with Roth still inside. She walked with a purpose away from the destruction, never turning around as if she were afraid she would turn into a pillar of salt if she did. She followed the blood trail and noticed that the drawbridge had been lowered.

General Deviat was stopped in his tracks. He should have been long gone by now and would have been if Anakim had not been waiting on the other side of the drawbridge, daring him to cross. Anakim was the first born and most promising of his triplet siblings. He was 8'4" tall and 390 pounds of rock-solid muscle. A natural born leader, almost as smart as Rapha, and almost as dangerous as Emim, he was most certainly the best warrior. He was extremely overprotective of his siblings, and the need to protect was the reason he was standing before General Deviat now.

Deviat was in shock and dared not move. He turned around to see Rapha walking toward him.

"Please . . . please forgive me. Can't we work something out?"

Neither Rapha nor Anakim said a word.

"I will not tell Lord Satan of your existence. . . . I won't even tell him how my men were slaughtered or how my home was destroyed. . . . I will make sure you are left alone . . ."

Still no word.

"I will no longer harass Lilith."

"DON'T YOU EVER SAY HER NAME!" Rapha screamed.

Anakim grabbed General Deviat's sword and sheath, and Rapha stabbed him in his heart and chopped his head off his body. General Deviat fell to his death over the drawbridge and into the Sea of Fire moat.

"What are you doing here?" Rapha asked her brother.

"I could not stay home knowing that this fat slob could be violating you."

"Thank you, but I can take care of myself."

"Clearly."

"Did mother send you?"

"She did not . . . come now we must get back. This much devastation will not go unnoticed."

"Then let us leave this place."

On the morning of the second day, Anzu left his humble home in the city of Sheol and set out toward General Deviat's estate in the dark Forest of Deviance. He walked to the outside of the city limits and gated to the dark forest. When he arrived he saw a pillar of smoke rising into the sky and his black heart dropped. He sprinted and when he reached the gate he could see that the extravagant estate was no more. It had crumbled to the ground with various fires that needed to be put out. *Lilith.* She had always been seen as a recluse, but she wasn't considered a betrayer. She had clearly become a traitor and was planning sedition. Brazenly attacking a high general in this manner was crossing the line, even for her. Once Lord Satan finds out about this there will be literal hell to pay. The only problem was that he had to prove that Lilith was somehow connected to all this. Without actual proof of her involvement, it could be explained away as a human rebellion. Human uprisings were not uncommon in hell. Though the demons were clearly more powerful, they were outnumbered fifty to one. Every now and then a human would free himself and incite a rebellion. Each time, however, they were crushed.

Anzu walked all over the estate and looked for any evidence that would lead to Lilith's involvement. He poured over the footsteps. There was indeed a struggle here, but not nearly enough footprints to suggest a human uprising. There were demonic footprints and prints of one or two others, neither belonged to Lilith. *Dead end.* Not willing to give up so easily, he bent down and inspected the prints more closely. Dipping his finger into the bloody mud, he noticed that red dirt was mixed in with the fertile ground of General Deviat's estate. He had encountered this red dirt in one other place: Lilith's cave. *I've got you.* He knew it was a stretch, and not nearly what he would call evidence to present to Lord Satan, but it was a viable lead in his mind. Anzu knew what he had to do to find more concrete evidence. He had to go see her. He flapped his massive raven-like wings and rose off the ground. Higher and higher he rose until he was well on his way to the Ottocom Desert.

"YOU DID WHAT?" Lilith yelled pacing back and forth while her brood sat at their table.

"We . . ."

"I heard you . . . I just didn't want to believe that you both could be so stupid."

"Mother . . ."

"Quiet, Rapha. . . . Have you the slightest clue of the danger you have put us all in? Deviat wasn't just some insignificant low-level demon. He was a general. One of Lord Satan's best. He will send a battalion to come looking for him, and when they find out what we've done, Lord Satan will surely throw us all into the Sea of Fire," she panicked.

"I think I speak for all of us when I say we do not fear him."

"Anakim, that is because you are too stupid to not know any better. . . . He is the vilest, most untrustworthy, and evil being in the entire universe . . ."

Silence.

"Do you not think that you should be careful how you speak about a being that tempted the Lord for forty days in the wilderness?"

More silence.

"Mother . . . You've always told us that we are the only ones of our kind and that we should protect each other. How could I just sit back and let that pervert violate my sister?"

Lilith had no answer for Anakim.

"Mother, tell us what we should do and we will do it," he asked.

"I . . . do not . . . know. I am certain that he will send his troops to march on us . . . millions . . . maybe even tens of millions."

"Then we do not just sit here and let them come for us."

"And where do you suggest we go? Plead our case to The One in heaven?" She laughed nervously.

"No, we go to earth."

"And do what, Rapha?"

"You told us that our people once ruled earth nine millennia ago. We should go and reclaim it as our ancestors once did."

"What Rapha says is good, Mother," Emim chimed in. "We can take it territory by territory. We will bring down their kings and generals, and crush their cities."

"Their men will be our slaves and their women shall bear our offspring," Anakim added.

Lilith thought about the plan and was genuinely impressed by it. She had surely trained them well and they obviously were amazing students.

"Mother, are you with us?" Anakim asked.

" . . . Yes, I am. That is truly a genius plan. I have been seducing the sons of Adam far too long. . . . It is time for them to become useful. . . . After you take the first city, I will lead a horde of incubi and succubae to help further our cause."

"Yes, Mother . . . ," Rapha agreed.

"Where shall we strike first?" asked Anakim.

"New York. There is a very powerful warrior there. His name is Seraph."

"Is he the one who killed our father?" Emim questioned.

"The very same. If we kill him first, then the rest of the world will offer little resistance."

"Then we will destroy him," Anakim confirmed.

As the four of them discussed plans to overtake the earth, Anzu walked into the cave and called out.

"LILITH!"

CHAPTER 11

LILITH!"

Anzu screamed out at the mouth of the cave. He marched into the dwelling as if he owned it. This personal vendetta against Lilith was about to come to a head. She was up to something and now was the time to find out what. He knew Lilith had something to do with the devastation he found at General Deviat's estate, he only needed to prove it. He could imagine the kind of reward Lord Satan had in store for him, finding a traitor in the midst. Maybe he'd be given a promotion, a grand home, or maybe his own territory where he would welcome the guilty daily.

But what he saw shocked him beyond belief. Not only did he find Lilith, but he also found something he was ill prepared to handle—giants, three of them. Anzu had only heard stories of the Nephilim in the old age. He heard they were big, nasty, and ferocious beings. However, no matter how many stories and legends one hears, there is nothing like finding out for one's self.

"Anzu . . . what a surprise," Lilith greeted him.

"What in the hell is this?" he said, stopping dead in his tracks.

"Anzu, your language," she giggled.

"Lilith . . . what have you done?"

"Why . . . whatever do you mean?"

" . . . Monsters . . . How . . . Why would you create these . . . monsters?"

"THEY ARE NOT MONSTERS . . . These are my children."

"Children? They are an abomination! Don't you remember what the Nephilim did all those years ago? Have you forgotten the devastation and the chaos their kind unleashed on the earth? This abomination is the reason for the Great Flood!"

"You shut your mouth, you filthy bird," Lilith screamed.

"I will not! I know that it was you who brought down General Deviat."

"Actually, it was me," Rapha said, rising to her feet.

"Ah yes, you will receive punishment worse than the deepest pit of hell."

Rapha smiled.

"Lord Satan will certainly learn of your treachery."

"Yes, Anzu, he will learn but only if you're alive to tell him. Kill him!" Lilith commanded.

Anzu started backing away, but never turned his back to Lilith and the Nephilim for fear that he would be cowardly attacked from behind. Anakim stepped forward, separating himself from his family, and gave chase to Anzu.

Anzu turned around and broke into a full sprint. He ran as fast as he could, made it outside, spread his wings, and flew into the air. He rose forty feet in the air faster than he ever had in his entire existence, but just when he thought he had escaped, Anakim landed on his back and they began free-falling.

They fell uncontrollably, and Anakim was on the offensive during the whole fall. Anakim head-butted Anzu and ripped off a wing, and then they crashed into the sand with Anakim landing on top. Anakim picked up Anzu and threw him as if he were a rag doll. Anzu tried to recover, but he was grossly outmatched and badly wounded.

His swings were futile, and even when they landed, they were ineffective. Anakim, however, proved that he was indeed the better warrior. He crushed

Anzu with bone-jarring blows to the head and body. When Anzu got desperate, he shot fireballs from his sword. Anakim didn't even bat an eye as he took out the sword he stole from the long-gone general and deflected them. When Anakim grew tired off the "fight," he decided he would end it in style.

Anzu, bloody and battered, attempted a halfhearted swing, partly because giving up was against his nature, but he was simply exhausted. However, to Anakim battle was battle and Lilith had taught him to make his enemy pay for all their mistakes. Anakim chopped Anzu's arm off. Anzu backed away screaming at the top of his lungs. Anakim threw the sword at Anzu and it sank deep into the demon's chest. Anakim rolled forward, grabbed the sword, and in one fluid motion spun around and sliced Anzu's face in half. The top half of Anzu's face flew off and landed in the sand, the rest of his body fell lifelessly to the floor. He was finished.

Lilith and his two younger siblings approached Anakim as he stood over his fallen adversary.

"You are all ready for the battle to come."

"We are," Anakim said.

"You must understand that Seraph will not be as easy as the weak demons you have faced here, but I have faith that you will destroy him and grind his bones into dust. Trust your training and trust each other."

"We will do it, Mother," Rapha added.

"Emim, take Anzu and throw his carcass into the sea, and we will leave for earth and claim it."

"Yes, Mother," Emim said.

They were ready to leave hell behind, to escape the inevitable punishment that they would all face if they stayed. However, this campaign to claim earth wasn't just to escape the devil's wrath. It was their chance to have a home where they could live and prosper. The only thing that stood in their way wasn't seven billion souls that posed little to no threat, but the one heavenly warrior who protected them.

Lilith opened a deep red portal and they all walked through it—ready for battle.

It had been three long earth months since John and Camilla had had a real conversation. They had barely seen each other at church and when they did, Camilla kept it moving, not allowing John an opportunity to communicate. Each Sunday was the same and today was no different, but this Sunday John was determined to speak with her. This situation had gone on far too long, and he was sick of it. He was several steps away from her and he was about to lose his opportunity.

"Camilla!" he yelled.

She kept walking toward the car where her parents were waiting.

"Camilla!"

"Hey, there's John." Her father waved.

"Wait." John fought past the crowed of churchgoers.

"I'll drive, Dad." Camilla took the keys from her father and started the car.

"But John's coming."

"Let's go, Dad," she said sternly.

"He looks like he really wants to talk."

"Daddy . . . ," she whined.

"Fine."

Richard Adams entered the car and before he could even put his seat belt on, Camilla sped off. John was literally a step too slow. Camilla left John to choke on exhaust fumes on the beautiful sunny day—not a cloud in the sky, and yet it was raining in his heart. John had spent three months calling and texting and even showing up at her job, only to be ignored. This was one of his best chances to talk to her, which had become too few and far between. His heart ached.

Camilla was no better, but she was just too hurt to deal with him. Even though three months did seem like enough time, she simply wasn't prepared to talk to him, although she knew she couldn't avoid him forever. She'd have to talk to him sooner than later, and it was closer to sooner.

"Camilla, what was that all about?" her mother said in a South African accent that had been weakened due to her permanent residency in the States.

"Yeah, you two were inseparable ever since you were kids and now we hardly see you together."

"Would you guys like something to eat?" Camilla asked. "I'm starving . . . Mom? Dad?"

"You can't avoid this conversation, Cammy. We're going to have it."

"Dad, please . . ."

"No, Camilla, your father is right. What is going on between you two?"

Camilla found a restaurant where they could eat and parked. They conversed further inside the diner.

"So, Cammy?"

"It's nothing. We don't have to be with each other all the time. . . . It's not like we're married or anything."

"Whoa . . . who said anything about marriage, baby girl?"

"Camilla, we know that you love the young man. . . ."

Camilla only looked at her mom.

"So why are you avoiding him now? He is such a sweet young man, and he is madly in love with you too."

"Yeah, honey, we can all see it."

"Who's *we*?"

Her father laughed.

"For starters anyone who's ever seen you two together."

Both her parents laughed at that comment.

"So tell us now, Camilla . . . what happened?"

Camilla let out a huge sigh.

" . . . Have you guys heard of the new superhero guy?"

"Yes, I have. Didn't he save the Freedom Tower about four to five months ago?"

"Yeah . . . that guy. . . . Well, that's John."

"For true?"

"Yes, Mom, for true."

"How did that happen?"

"Well, he has an angel living inside of him."

"What? When did this happen?"

"On his thirtieth birthday . . . sometime that night. He walked home one way and the next day he was . . . just . . . different."

"Oh . . . yes, he is different. I knew that body didn't come from going to the gym. He is very handsome now, right?"

Camilla could only blush and used her hands to cover her smile.

"Okay, that's enough drooling over the guy like he's a piece of meat."

"A piece of choice meat."

"Abri!" Robert laughed.

"Mom!" Camilla shared in her father's laughter.

"What, I must say? It is true." She joined them.

"You are something else."

"Oh, honey, you know you are the only man I have eyes for."

"Of course I know, *Apple*."

Apple was an affectionate name that he gave her for being the "apple of his eye." She kissed him.

"Oh lord." Camilla rolled her eyes.

"Camilla, your father and I have been married for thirty-two years, and we are still happily married in a world that tells you to quit when things get too hard. You should be proud of us."

"I am . . . I just wanted that too."

"Why do you say that like it won't happen? John wants to marry you."

"Yeah, back to him. What does his transformation have to do with anything? Has he changed?" Robert added.

"Other than physically, no. And I know it's going to make me sound shallow, but I was never attracted to John before he changed."

"Well, how could you? Those thick glasses and he was so tiny, he was. Not very handsome at all."

"Mom!"

"What, I must say? It is true."

"Yeah, but he was still so nice to me. That counts."

"Yes it does, sweetie. Has he changed?" her father asked.

"I guess . . . after he changed he was just . . . better but he was still the same guy. I just fell so deeply in love with him and . . . anyway we had sex and a lot of it. Then he went somewhere and got into a fight with a demon and got really hurt. And when he came back he told me he didn't want to be with me anymore."

"That doesn't sound right. I know John, I know how he feels about you, and I doubt he would say that to you. Are you sure that's how he meant it?"

"I am . . . and he didn't say that exactly, he just said we couldn't sleep together anymore. And I didn't want to stop, I still don't want to stop, but I was just so hurt. He was my first and I'm rambling." Camilla sighed deeply. " . . . Now I'm just so embarrassed for not talking to him about this sooner and . . ."

Just then her phone rang. It was John. She sent him to voice mail.

"Was that him?"

"Yeah . . ."

"You need to talk to him, Cammy . . ."

"What do I say, Daddy?"

"You tell him how much you love him . . . duh."

"Oh my lord, sweetheart. You are so smart and yet you are so silly," her mother added.

The phone rang again. John. She looked at it as it rang this time.

"Answer it, darling," Abri said.

She did, stepping away from the table and outside of the diner for privacy.

"John . . ."

"Cammy . . . I was beginning to lose hope.. . . we need to talk."

"I know. . . . Where are you?"

"By the church."

"Want to meet me in Central Park?"

"Yeah," he said surprised.

"Meet me by the castle."

"Sure. Okay."

She hung up and ran back inside, grabbing her belongings and telling her parents she was on her way to see him. They were both thrilled that she was going to repair what had been broken and wished her well.

She drove slightly faster than she should have, swerving through traffic like a New York City taxi driver. She thought about all she would say. She was going to declare her love again, forgive him, ask to be forgiven, and it was all going to be so magical. He was going to embrace her tightly, kiss her, and the sun would shine, wild unicorns would race, and a rainbow would make the reunion complete.

Camilla parked and was so excited to see him that she speed-walked. But when she got to the castle, she didn't see him. She searched and looked, but he wasn't there. Maybe he wasn't coming, or maybe she had scared him away. Maybe he had lost interest; after all, she hadn't talked to him in three months. Why was she always so nervous when it came to him?

Camilla prided herself on being level-headed, but something about John made her irrational. What was it? *Love.* She overlooked a lake that was at the bottom of the pavilion, connected to the castle by a beautiful walkway with marble guardrails. She was all alone until a man approached her from behind.

"Hey . . ."

Came the only voice that could calm her and make her heart beat at the same time. Camilla turned around with the brightest smile on her face. He was a sight for sore eyes, and she couldn't help but think that he had become more handsome since the last time she had seen him. Camilla greeted John with the biggest hug she'd ever given him and searched for the perfect words.

"You smell like heaven."

"What?" He laughed and cocked his head to the side.

"I'm so sorry that was really cheesy. I was trying to say something cute and that came out."

"It was cute, albeit very cheesy."

She laughed a little.

"I do miss that laugh, though . . ."

She smiled.

"And that smile . . ."

"I've missed you so much and I'm so sorry for reacting the way I did."

"No, I said it wrong. I could have handled it better than just springing that on you like that. It was very stupid of me."

"Well, it's over now and I just want us to start over."

"Me too. . . . I want us to be together again, and though it can't be like it was, I want you to know that I love you and want to be with you forever."

"I know."

"Oh do you, 'Han Solo'?" John said.

That elicited a great laugh from them both.

"You know, I know. You know I love you more than life itself. . . . I'm just glad that we're not fighting anymore. I couldn't take it. I was just so nervous to talk to you after a while . . . I was afraid."

"Afraid?"

"Yeah, that you'd be so mad that you wouldn't want me anymore or that you would think I may have overreacted. Which I did, I was just so emotional . . ."

"Cammy, you don't have to explain anymore. I have moved on from that and I only want to focus on a future that includes us together forever."

She kissed him passionately. A kiss that said, "I miss you, I love you, I want you."

"There's one more thing I want to talk to you about."

John stared deep into her eyes, reached into his pocket, and was about to bring something out, but suddenly there was a series of large explosions that seemed to come from the middle of Manhattan. Everyone in the park could hear it.

"My god, what was that?" Camilla said.

"I . . . I don't know."

There was a TV being played in the main lobby of the castle.

"TV in the castle, c'mon," John said.

When they made it to the lobby, the news was already on, and people were crowding around the big-screen television. There were already several helicopters on the scene and what they captured frightened everyone but John. There was a brave reporter who was first on the scene.

"My name is Gary Russo and I'm reporting live at the scene. At the heart of Times Square are what looks like three . . . giants and there is a woman who is next to them. . . . It looks as if she is leading them. I know it sounds unbelievable, but what you're seeing on your TV screens is indeed real . . . Oh my god. They're destroying everything in sight. As you can see, there are indeed dead bodies strewn throughout the streets, many of the bodies are police officers. They put up a good fight for a while, but these gigantic monsters are simply too much for them to handle. OH MY GOD, DID YOU SEE THAT? Jesus Christ. Excuse my language, America, but there was a very brave, but also very stupid, truck driver who tried to run over one of the giants, but it just stood there and took the head-on collision. The trailer flipped up and folded on itself. My god, I'm sure that guy is dead. . . . Oh man, now one of the 'copters seems to be getting too close and now the female giant. . . . What is she doing? WHOA! She just took a car and threw it like a missile into the aircraft . . . the carnage . . . Oh no . . . Sean, let's get out of here; the other one is looking at us. RUN, SEAN! . . . RUN! AAAAHH!"

Everyone in the lobby could see that the cameraman was running backward and still shooting the enormous giant chasing them down, and then static appeared on the screen. The news network returned the viewing audience to the news studios where an anchorwoman continued the broadcast.

" . . . I'm just speechless . . . poor Gary and Sean, our cameraman, . . . they've been working here for over fifteen years and were always the first on scene for many of New York's biggest tragedies such as 9/11 and Hurricane Sandy. They were truly the bravest of us all and will be missed, but now the question is, who are these creatures? Who is the mysterious woman? What do they want? Who will save us?"

The crowd in the lobby had grown during the broadcast. They were all terrified. Some were openly crying, others were praying, and some just stood there as though they were frozen in time. John led Camilla through the crowded lobby and back to the pavilion where they were before the attacks started. Tears welled in her eyes because she knew what was coming.

"Cammy, please don't cry. You're making this harder for me."

"Don't cry? What do you mean don't cry? Monsters are tearing up Times Square and you're going to face them, aren't you? . . . I'm not going to ask you why it has to be you because I know it has to be . . . just . . . just promise to come back to me."

"Can you get home from here?"

"Yeah, I think so."

"Run home and hide. You don't stop and talk, you run . . ."

"And hide. I got it."

"Step back."

"No! You promise me, John."

" . . . I promise I'll come back . . ."

They were afraid. Neither of them had ever seen anything on earth like this before. Their hearts raced and they kissed each other zealously.

"Protect the sheep; kill the wolves."

That was the last thing she said to him as she stepped away from him.

When John thought about his suit it powered on. Hues of blue and white engulfed him and John transformed into Seraph. Some people had rushed outside the lobby and stood with Camilla. Everyone marveled at catching a glimpse of New York's guardian angel. At first the people only stared at him, but then someone said, "Go get 'em," and then others began to join in with more encouraging words, and soon there was a chorus of cheers and applause. They weren't sure if he could win and didn't really know what to expect, but the mere fact that he was there to fight was good enough for them. Then he bent his knees and shot off into the sky.

The crowd dispersed and went back into the lobby. Camilla just stood there. A tear streamed down her face. She was so worried about him. How would he fair? Could they kill him? Could John die? But then the Lord spoke to her. *Can you add one extra hour to his life by worrying about him?* So she prayed.

"Jesus, please protect him. Give him the strength he needs to destroy these creatures. Send your angels to watch him and cover him with your precious blood. I have faith that you will see him through this and bring him to victory. In your mighty name I pray. Amen."

She felt much better but wondered if praying for him was enough. She knew it wasn't; after all, faith without action is useless. Even though John did tell her to run home and hide, she just had to do something. She was crazy about him; and they were both insane.

***

Seraph had flown over Times Square and could see the devastation from above. He saw Lilith and the three Nephilim wreaking havoc on the city. Seraph picked out a target to attack first. No talk, just action. He shot down like a bullet and geared for an attack. Emim was in his sights and totally unaware he was about to be hit by a supernatural missile. Emim held a car high above his head and was about to throw it into a building, but was hit with the force of a comet and tackled to the street. He left a trail of concrete more than twenty feet before he finally stopped. Emim looked around totally dazed, searching for the source of the attack. He got up slowly and dusted himself off. Lilith and her children looked at each other and wondered who would dare impede their destruction.

"I was beginning to think you wouldn't show."

"You didn't really, did you?" Seraph said.

"No. Not really."

"Go back to the hell hole you came from and take these . . . things with you!"

"Things? You don't recognize them, do you?"

"Should I?"

"You most certainly should. . . . You may not see it in my sons, but what about my daughter? She doesn't look familiar?"

Seraph looked closely and examined Rapha's face and then he saw the resemblance.

"Andrea? How . . . ?"

"Oh, don't be ridiculous. She does resemble the woman, doesn't she? I will tell you how though. . . . That simple little minx fell in love with a demon . . . A DEMON. She was so lonely and disgusting that she gave herself to him night and day, day and night for almost a month. Like a whore. Do you know what happens when angels and humans . . . do it?" She burst out into heavy laughter.

"Lilith . . . What have you done?" asked Seraph, sadness in his voice.

"I've watched you humans poison this world for more than 10,000 years. You fight each other over meaningless religions and traditions, land that you have no right to live on, and over different shades of skin color. Humans are a blight on this world. There was once a time when the Nephilim ruled this once glorious planet. It is time that they rule it once again."

Lilith opened a portal, preparing for her departure.

"And it came to pass, when men began to multiply on the face of the earth, and daughters were born unto them, that the sons of God saw the daughters of men that they were fair; and they took them wives of all which they chose. There were giants in the earth in those days; and also after that, when the sons of God came in unto the daughters of men, and they bear children to them, the same became mighty men which were of old, men of renown."

Lilith calmly backed into the portal, gracefully with a hint of sensuality that she was never without. And then it was just the four of them. Anakim stood across from Seraph, but sent his siblings in opposite directions. Emim and Rapha both hid in the tall buildings to confuse Seraph, a tactic that was totally lost on him. He was expecting to be surrounded. Something that he could deal with, all of them being in clear view, but now that Rapha and Emim were hiding, it was going to be a difficult experience.

Anakim stared down Seraph.

"C'MON!" Seraph yelled.

Anakim smiled from across the street and continued to stare Seraph down. Emim had snuck around Seraph and jumped high into the air behind him. He had his hammer in hand, preparing to crush Seraph, but Seraph turned around quickly and punched Emim in the face as he landed. He was not going to be taken by surprise. Emim was crushed and left a hole in the street. Seraph turned around to see Anakim running toward him, and he ran to meet him. However, before he could meet Anakim, Rapha speared him to a car on his right side. It was a blindside attack that split the car in half.

She pounded her fists into his face, then lifted him high above her head and threw him like a rag doll into a broken-down bus. Emim was waiting for him and peeled him from the bus, punching him in the gut and slamming him to the concrete ground. Emim took his great hammer and brought it down with such force that the ground split underneath them. He sought to do it again, but Seraph kicked Emim in the gut and jumped up. He tried to fly to create some space between them, but he was caught by Anakim, who proceeded to put him into a full nelson. Rapha approached and beat him in his midsection. Anakim lifted the hero up and viciously slammed him into the pavement. Emim rushed forward and punted Seraph more than 100 yards into a construction building.

When he landed, he tried to regain his equilibrium. *That was some beating.* Seraph stumbled his way to his feet and thanked God every moment that he had that armor. The blows did hurt and he felt every one of them, but he knew that without the armor he would have been obliterated. What were they? Could they die? He was getting ahead of himself; did they even bleed? How was he going to beat them? He obviously couldn't take them all on at the same time. Being outnumbered three to one, with no backup, and facing enemies that were just as strong or maybe stronger than he was, was going to be difficult. He had to separate them. Yes, divide and conquer, but how?

The giants were upon him now. But it was only Emim and Rapha. No Anakim and that worried him. Both giants had their weapons drawn and Seraph was also armed. He activated his shield, then reached down and grabbed his sword that was tucked neatly into the thigh of his suit. It radiated with the warm orange flame and then cooled to show its blue steel. He was ready.

Rapha went in first and swung with grace and extraordinary elegance. Seraph wasn't trained in the art of sword fighting, but he found himself not only keeping up with her, but besting her. This was certainly not him. And even when Emim joined the fray with his heavy weapon, Seraph blocked with his shield and dodged every blow as the hammer smashed into concrete and bent steel. Even though he was getting the upper hand, the combination of both of them was forcing him to retreat.

Emim brought the hammer down, but Seraph blocked it with his shield and sliced him along his fat belly. Emim fell back and grabbed his stomach. First blood had been drawn and the sight of it gave Seraph hope that he could defeat them. They were indeed flesh and blood. Rapha swung but was parried. Seraph pushed her away with his shield and flew through the cement ceilings until he made it to the roof where he could be alone and recuperate.

Rapha rushed to her wounded brother's side.

"Emim, are you alright?"

"I'm fine."

"You are bleeding. Stay here."

"No! I will be fine. I will end him," Emim said with rage.

"Then come, brother."

"Go, I will be there."

Rapha was the first to make it to the rooftop of the unfinished building, but there was no sign of Seraph. Rapha paced slowly, trying to use her senses to detect him.

"Hiding will only delay the inevitable."

No answer. She walked slowly.

"I know you are here. . . . I can smell you. . . . Come out and face me!"

Still nothing.

"It was torture being buried inside that weak wench . . . Andrea? My brothers and I ripped her apart. I only wish I could have known her today so I could eat her heart . . . But since that has escaped me, I will do this to the people of earth you seem to care about so much."

Seraph jumped from his hiding spot behind her with sword in hand, but she turned and blocked the attack and lost her footing a bit and dropped to a knee. Seraph kicked her in the head and tried to do it once more, but she swung her sword with her free hand and swiped at his waist. And though the strike did connect, it glanced right off his stomach. Seraph came down with his shield and knocked her on her back. Seraph brought down his sword to deliver a death blow to Rapha, but she moved and the sword got stuck in the roof floor. Rapha fought him from her back.

Seraph was surprised that even from this position she was far from defeated; in fact, she was just as dangerous on the ground. She put Seraph in an arm bar and would have completely ripped his arm from his body, but he summoned his strength and pulled Rapha up and power-slammed her. Rapha's head hit the cement roof and blood flowed from it like a river.

Emim climbed to the roof, unbeknownst to Seraph, and palmed Seraph's face, lifted him off Rapha, and slammed him to the floor. Emim brought down his fist, but Seraph moved and the fist went through the floor. He was stuck. From there Seraph got up and assaulted him with hit after hit. But when Emim finally mustered enough strength, he pushed Seraph away with one hand. He stopped just short of the roof's edge, but Rapha, who had recovered and was now on her feet, kicked Seraph in the side of his head and he fell off.

Seraph plummeted from the seventy-story construction building, and before he could gain his balance and fly back to the roof, Anakim came running from one of the lower levels and speared him while he was in the middle of free-falling into the nearby office building. Anakim rained down blow after blow. Seraph tried to block and dodge but to no avail. He went limp. As the giant beat him, they sank through the floor and into the ceiling of the floor below until it collapsed under the massive weight. Anakim finally stopped. Armor or no armor, Seraph was in trouble.

Camilla knew that she should have been heading home but could not, would not sit uselessly by watching John get killed on TV, or listen to it on the radio like everyone else as if it were a sporting event. This was the man she loved and she was going to do something. She got in her car and drove through the wrecked city to Times Square. She managed to arrive on 42nd Street just as Seraph was being escorted down the street in chains to where Lilith was waiting.

Camilla snuck up and found a place where she could hear what was happening. All around her were dead civilians and police officers. It was catastrophic. She picked up a dead cop's sidearm and stuck it between her back and skirt and placed her shirt over it. She didn't really know how to use a gun, but she knew the safety had to be off, point, then fire. *Simple enough.* From her vantage point, she saw two of the male giants and a woman, too short to be one of them, but clearly not from earth. However she couldn't find Rapha and that worried her.

"Mother, we present your fallen enemy to you," Anakim said.

"You have exceeded my expectations. He never stood a chance. Not so tough now are you, Seraph?"

"Still tougher than Ornias."

Lilith was enraged and smacked him in the face, but his helmet was still on so he didn't feel a thing.

"You hit like a girl."

"Defiant till the end. It is over, you fool."

"It ain't over yet."

"On the contrary . . . you have been beaten, you have lost. All I have to do is figure out how to separate you from your precious armor."

"You'll never get it off me."

"Oh, I will . . . even if I have to peel it off your cold dead body."

"Good luck with that."

Emim backhanded Seraph, but winced due to the cut on his stomach.

"Emim, my son, are you alright?"

"Yes, Mother, I am fine."

"No, you're hurt."

"It is but a flesh wound."

"Anakim, what about you? Are you alright?"

He simply nodded.

"Where is Rapha? RAPHA!"

"Right here, Mother."

Rapha appeared behind Lilith and was standing over Camilla. She picked her up and placed her hands behind Camilla's back and walked her over to where her brothers stood with Seraph.

"And who might you be?"

"Camilla . . ." Seraph's head dropped.

"I smelled her, and by the way she was looking at Seraph, I can only come to the conclusion that she cares for him."

"Is that so? Ah yes, of course, why else would you be here . . . Camilla?"

Camilla went down to help John, but instead she became a liability. She watched with dread as Lilith advanced toward her brandishing a dagger.

"I will cut right to the chase. If you do not remove your suit, I will make you watch as I kill her painfully . . . slowly . . ."

Seraph struggled in his chains, but Anakim kicked him in the back of his head. Camilla began tearing up. All she wanted to do was help, but by interfering she may have killed him. Maybe she should have listened to him and gone home. But it was too late for that now.

"Camilla, you have gorgeous eyes. . . . Shall I start there, John?"

"LILITH, PLEASE, DON'T!" John screamed.

Camilla looked at Seraph and mouthed the word, "No," and shook her head.

Seraph screamed and powered down his suit. Camilla burst into tears. John was going to die, and it was going to be all her fault. Lilith approached John with the dagger, but to John it felt as if she were walking in slow motion. There were so many things going on in his mind that he needed to try and calm his spirit. In the midst of this storm, he heard a small still voice repeating, *The Word of God is living and powerful. Living and powerful. Living. Powerful.*

John closed his eyes and meditated on that portion of scripture and just before Lilith could reach him to kill him, the sword shot straight to the ground where John's hands were. *Living.* He grabbed the sword and instantly transformed into Seraph. Before any of them knew what was happening, he cut his chains loose and in one smooth motion cut Emim in half— diagonally, from his legs all the way through to his shoulder blade. *Powerful.* Anakim fell back and Emim stepped back, grabbing his chest before his top half slid off his bottom half.

Lilith screamed in horror. Rapha was in awe of what she had just seen and couldn't believe her eyes. Camilla grabbed the gun from her back and shot Rapha in the foot, then the face, and gunned down Lilith. Lilith blocked each bullet with one hand and opened a vortex with the other and disappeared into it, leaving her children behind.

"Run, Camilla!"

"What?"

"RUN!" Seraph yelled.

Camilla ran as fast as she could with Rapha limping behind her. Seraph tried to get after her, but Anakim grabbed him and held him back. While they tussled, Rapha was on Camilla's heels. Rapha wasn't as fast as normal with a hole in her foot, and her eyesight was also diminished because the bullet that landed went through her jaw and eye socket.

Camilla took off her heels and ran as fast as her feet could take her. But she stepped on sharp metal and fell to the ground. Rapha kept limping as fast as she could while watching Camilla struggle to get through rubble and over busted cars. Finally Camilla reached a dead-end corner with nowhere to go: rock to her left, metal to her right and back, Rapha straight ahead.

Even though Rapha was drastically injured, there was no way Camilla was going to beat her in hand-to-hand combat, or any combat for that matter. Camilla took out the gun and squeezed the trigger, but it was empty. She could see Seraph trading blows with Anakim and thought there was no way that he'd be able to save her now.

"CAMILLA!" Seraph yelled as he watched Rapha closing in on her.

This slight loss in focus allowed Anakim to pin the inexperienced hero down and choke him. However Seraph reached out and grabbed a boulder and bashed the giant in the skull. The rock crumbled and Anakim lost consciousness. Seraph got up and raced over to Rapha and just as she raised her hand to smash Camilla, he caught it. He kicked Rapha in the back of the knee and grabbed her by her neck. Still trying to grab her, Rapha struggled and stared deeply into Camilla's eyes. Camilla stared back and in that moment it was almost as if time stood still for them both. Seraph snapped Rapha's neck and her lifeless body fell to the ground.

"Are you okay?"

"My foot. I hurt my foot, but I'm fine," Camilla said, hugging him tightly.

"I told you to go home. I had it all together."

"Sure you did, so getting chained up like that, was that Plan A or Plan B?"

"C. It was Plan C."

"I'd love to continue this lovely chat, but can we please get outta here?"

"Yeah, let's get you home."

"You were amazing, by the way."

"Not really, I was getting my butt kicked."

"True but it's your first real battle and look on the bright side."

"Bright side?"

"You didn't get yourself killed."

John powered down his suit and they both laughed at that joke and walked by the body of the fallen giant, but as they walked by him, his eyes opened and he sat up. When he stood up completely, he called out to Seraph.

"Seraph . . ."

John stopped dead in his tracks and turned around to see Anakim standing opposite him approximately thirty yards away.

"Leaving so soon?"

"It is finished. . . . You and your family have been defeated. Now go back to the pit you crawled out from."

"We will never be finished. You killed my father, my sister, and my brother. You think after all you've done to me that I would just let you walk away so easily? No, I am going to take from you what you have taken from me. The only way to stop me is to kill me. And after I kill you, I am going to eat the flesh from your bones."

"Is that all you got?"

"Not nearly, after I have killed you, I will repopulate earth with my people. Camilla, is it? Yes, she shall be the first to bear my offspring and they will split her open . . . just like Andrea."

When John heard this he knew there was only one way that this fight was going to end. He addressed Camilla without turning to her.

"Cammy . . . you best get out of here."

Camilla didn't protest but began limping away from the two warriors, because one of them was surely going to die today and anyone around them would become a victim of what was about to ensue.

John turned into Seraph and Anakim drew his sword.

"Let's finish this," Seraph said.

Seraph drew his sword and began walking toward him. Anakim started trotting, then he went into a sprint. Seraph ran to meet him. They swung their swords and when they clashed the shockwave from the collision blew out the windows on the entire avenue.

CHAPTER 12

Sunday morning had been pretty eventful for Sally and the Goodwins. The church's children's chorus had sung and there was even a praise dancer today. Kelly led a marvelous worship and Tom delivered a great sermon, as he did every Sunday. After the service let out, most stayed for the weekly potluck and watched football on the downstairs TV. Tom offered a quick prayer and turned on the TV, but instead of getting the local game, everyone in the room was shocked by the carnage in New York City.

Helicopters continued to shoot footage of the battle between Seraph and Anakim. Sally was the first to realize what was happening.

"Oh my god. It's John!"

"Jesus, Sally, it is him," Thomas confirmed.

Other church members were wondering who John was and what exactly was happening. Confusion and panic began to rise in the small basement. They watched as the two warriors struck each other and slammed each other into buildings and cars. The people were afraid.

"What's going on?" one member asked.

"Yeah, do you know that blue thing?" Officer Smalls asked.

"It's not a blue thing, handsome," Sally replied. "His name is John and he's family."

"John . . . John . . . Tommy id'n't that the young man—"

"Yes, Robby, that's him."

"Well, shucks I didn't know he was one of us . . . ," Robert said.

"Well, what in the world is that other thing?" Mrs. Ferder added.

"My kids are getting scared!"

"Kid's scared? *I'm* scared."

"Turn it off!" shouted another.

"Everyone calm down, panicking will not help. John is not only a friend of ours, but he is also a child of God and he is fighting on the Lord's side. I can vouch for that. We're not going to turn this off, but those with children are welcome to go home. However, I would ask the clergy and all other prayer warriors to stay. . . . This situation calls for some serious spiritual battle," Thomas said.

No one moved. Not even the women with children. The flock listened to their shepherd and decided that if their wise pastor needed them, they should not flee from this opportunity to help another believer. The whole community of believers prayed and their prayers filled the room. After a while Thomas stepped up and prayed aloud.

"Heavenly Father, we come to you right now asking you to hear our prayers. Forgive us of our sins and cleanse us from all unrighteousness. Right now, Lord, we bring our brother John to you. He is in serious need of your help. Cover him with your blood. Give him the strength he needs to endure and persevere. Let not his heart be filled with fear, but give him a mind that is sound and focused on battle. Send your angels to protect him and help him. Give him power . . . to kill that thing. Amen."

And the church said, "Amen."

Seraph and Anakim's swords clashed and clanged, they parried one another, and dodged blows. Anakim attacked Seraph with such ferocity and power that Seraph found it hard to keep up. Seraph's style was much more fluid and graceful. Though it, too, was powerful, the strength of Anakim was not to be matched.

Anakim brought down his heavy sword for a mighty blow and Seraph blocked it, but Anakim hit him with his free hand so hard that he lost his sword and flew into a wall. Anakim threw his sword in Seraph's direction, but he dodged to the side, and it missed. The sword plunged deep into the rock. Seraph ran toward Anakim who clotheslined him. Seraph flipped into the air and landed on his back. Anakim tried to stomp him, but he moved and threw a boulder in Anakim's face. That shot dazed Anakim, allowing Seraph to go on the offensive. He grabbed Anakim and flew into the air, banging him into buildings in midflight.

Anakim grabbed hold of the building wall. The momentum carried Seraph, face first, into the building's exterior. Anakim slammed Seraph's head into the wall repeatedly until he fell, but he flew back up. Anakim jumped down from his perch and caught Seraph in the air, they both started falling downward, fighting to avoid not being landed upon. They came crashing down with Seraph on the bottom. Anakim picked him up and threw him into a nearby garbage dump truck. He turned on the machine, and it began crunching Seraph.

"Do you see the futility of your fight? Earth is my inheritance, passed down from my ancestors long ago."

Anakim laughed, assuming victory was in his grasp, but the truck levitated and Seraph stood underneath, raising the vehicle above his head and smashing the hulking giant. He raised it again and brought it down. He did so once more, but Anakim caught it with one hand and got his balance and tackled him, landing on top. Seraph kicked up at his adversary, landing a few kicks, but Anakim caught a leg and swung him as if he was looking to medal in the hammer throw.

Seraph flew and smashed into the corner of a building and landed in the middle of the street.

"I admire your courage, but by now you must realize that you are going to die today?"

"You. Talk. Too. Much."

Anakim jumped high, following Seraph's trajectory, landing not far from Seraph. Anakim kicked him in the head and assaulted his body, but Seraph was able to block and punched Anakim in the kidney. Anakim spat blood. Then Seraph flip-kicked him. The menacing giant was lifted off his feet and fell flat on his back. When he got to his feet, Seraph grabbed a manhole and flung it like a Frisbee. It was a direct hit that sent the monster flying into an oncoming bus, but that did not slow the creature down. He literally ripped the bus in half and the passengers scattered, but not before Anakim attacked a few of them.

Seraph flew and stole Anakim from his next victim, flying about twenty feet in the air before power-punching him back to the ground. They slugged it out further down the street. They fought for blocks and avenues, through buildings and restaurants, construction sites, and abandoned warehouses. They raged on with Seraph putting forth a valiant effort in everything he did. However, Anakim was simply too strong for him, and he was losing hope of finding a way to beat him. To make matters worse, the people began pouring into the streets dissatisfied with watching the fight on TV. People watched as the two behemoths fought—one with a murderous intent, and the other trying heroically to save the people of the city. Camilla was among the people cheering Seraph on and praying for him.

Seraph was being overpowered and sought to create a little distance between them, but Anakim grabbed him and dropped him on his head and neck. Anakim stood over him and stomped him several times till Seraph's body created an imprint in the concrete. Seraph was too hurt to move, and Anakim began focusing on the people.

"Do you see your hero, people of earth?"

People looked at him with total fear and disbelief in their eyes.

"Is this your best? Is this the greatest one among you?"

Anakim grabbed his sword and started attacking the people. They all scattered, but some weren't lucky enough to get away. Then he saw her. Anakim and Camilla made eye contact, and she knew she was in trouble once again.

She ran as fast as her feet could carry her, but he caught her easily and lifted her by her throat above his head.

"You, as if I would let you get away."

Camilla gasped for air and coughed.

"Choking? I haven't even begun to choke you. I could snap you like a twig, but that would be too easy for you. Because of you, my sister is dead. No, I will not kill you. You shall be the first woman to bear my children."

"I will NEVER bear your children."

"As if you have a choice, wench."

"I would rather die!"

"In due time. You will."

In a last act of defiance, Camilla spat in Anakim's face. Anakim didn't wipe his face, but simply squeezed her throat a little tighter. Camilla struggled even more to breathe and get free, but she began losing consciousness.

"Where is your hero? Where is he now? He is defeated and you are mine."

Camilla almost blacked out but looked past Anakim to see Seraph in the air, coming down with his sword in hand. Anakim turned around just in time to see him, but too late to move. Seraph plunged the sword deep into the chest of the giant, and the blade came out the other side.

Anakim dropped Camilla, grabbed Seraph, and slammed him into the ground. Seraph, still weary from being stomped a few minutes earlier, was hurting and tried to catch his second wind. Anakim kicked Seraph in the side, and although it hurt, Seraph wasn't sent flying. The sword in his body really did some damage. Anakim pulled the sword from his chest and threw it to the ground. He grabbed Seraph and put him in a choke hold from behind.

"That was your last mistake, whelp. And now I will end this. I will squeeze the life out of you."

Seraph struggled to get free but couldn't. He wiggled as best he could but began losing consciousness. Camilla watched him and screamed for him to keep fighting.

"JOHN!!!"

"Do you see her? Take a long look. She will be the first mother of my children before she dies. And there is nothing that you can do to save her."

Seraph heard this and gathered up all his lingering strength and shot into the air with the giant still on his back. They kept flying past the clouds until the air became thinner, paper thin, and then it was no more. Silence.

Seraph had flown into the void of space with Anakim hanging on for dear life. Anakim could no longer breathe, although Seraph could thanks to his suit of armor. Anakim's grip loosened and then he fell. But as he fell he caught fire as he passed the Karman line. Seraph marveled at the view of space before he flew down and tackled Anakim in midfall. Both of them were scorching, and Anakim was burning alive, but Seraph hadn't even broken a sweat. Seraph drove Anakim past the clouds.

Back on the ground, Seraph's sword began to shake and then shot into the sky. The sword was going up as the two warriors were coming down. The sword went through Anakim's body, and Seraph caught it in his hands when it went all the way through. He drove the sword back into the chest of the giant once more and finally into the ground with such force that the shockwave shattered windows for miles.

Smoke and dust lived in the newly formed crater that was only twenty yards in diameter. People crowded around it, their curiosity getting the best of them even though the situation was extremely dangerous. As the dust began to settle, a figure walked out of the crater. It was Seraph.

The people cheered as he walked out. He looked around at everyone and at Camilla, who was standing with everyone else in awe. He bent his legs and flew high into the air until he disappeared into the sky.

As Seraph flew into the sky and away from the crowd, a bluish white, starry portal opened and he flew into it. He flew into the vortex. It was filled with love, joy, and peace. His suit peeled off as he traveled through it and was replaced by a white robe. Not only had his clothes changed, but he was also handcuffed to his friend Ahadiel who was on this journey with him.

They came out of the portal into the whitest white light, which no human eye could dare look into. On the other side was the throne room of heaven. Other angels and Jesus the Christ were waiting. There was a huge reception waiting for them. When they arrived they knelt down reverently, but Jesus greeted them both with a hug and had them stand up.

"Well done, my friends. Well done."

They couldn't hide their smiles after receiving praise from God.

"The Father is equally pleased with you both, and we have something for you."

Jesus lifted the gold chain that bound them and broke it. They were thrilled and hugged him at the same time. Then he continued.

"You two will no longer be bound together. I have plans for you both . . . Michael."

Michael walked up and presented Ahadiel with gold trimmings for Ahadiel's wings, which was a sign of promotion.

"Ahadiel, you have worked hard as an angel in the Lord's service. Fighting in our battles with the enemy and showing unwavering loyalty, but you have outdone yourself in your service and will be promoted to captain."

"Thank you, sir." He bowed slightly.

Jesus stepped up again.

"John, you have shown enormous courage in everything you've done. Not only did you discover a plot to destroy creation, but you stopped it. You also managed to help spiritually awaken millions of people on earth."

"That's awesome."

"It sure is and one of those millions wants to personally thank you."

Jesus turned to Gabriel. "Bring her in."

When he said these words, Andrea Lewis-Rose and David came in, along with a few others.

"ANDREA!" John exclaimed in genuine excitement.

They rushed to each other and tightly embraced.

"I am so glad to see you again," she began. "If it weren't for you, I would not be here. And what's better than that . . . you've given me the chance to get to know my children."

"Children? I thought you only had one son?"

"So did I . . . but I had two other miscarriages and they grew up here like David."

"Outstanding."

"This is Shar-el, my youngest son, and my daughter Rubiel."

"Wow. Those are interesting names."

"Yes, they were named by the angels that cared for them. . . . Shar-el means 'strength of God,' and Rubiel means 'one whom God loves.'"

"Shar-el, Rubiel, it is wonderful to meet you." John knelt down and hugged them both.

Both the children giggled and were excited to meet the man who helped bring their mom to heaven.

"Without you . . . I'd hate to think what could have happened to me. . . . Thank you again so much."

She hugged him again, bowed low before Jesus, and left.

The only ones that were left with John were Jesus and the heavenly hosts.

"Now if you all will excuse us, I want to talk to John alone."

The angelic beings left.

"Walk with me."

The throne room seemed to transform into a beautiful land where they walked and talked. The land was the most beautiful place John had ever seen— filled with green trees and grass, exotic flowers never seen on earth, the bluest water imaginable, and the most wondrous mountain ranges. They talked and walked past various animals, some that looked like animals of earth but others that were much stranger. John even witnessed dinosaur-like creatures of all kinds.

"Is this a part of heaven?"

"No . . . we are on a distant planet on the other side of the Milky Way galaxy called Nersa."

"Inhabited?"

"Certainly. My father and I created so many children that they cannot be counted. Children who worship us throughout our vast creation, including here."

"Are they like us?"

"What do you mean?"

"Do they look like us? Act like us?"

"There is a slight resemblance to your people, yes. Their planet is very similar to Earth, but there is no sin here on Nersa."

"No sin? Do they have a choice?"

"Yes, of course they do. All of my creation does. Free will is one of the most important gifts that I give to creation. Nersa has its own 'knowledge of good and evil' test. So far they have chosen to choose life."

"Wow."

"Most of the planets in the universe are like Nersa. Evil hasn't entered their world, and I commune with them daily. Only a handful of planets have turned out to be like Earth or worse."

"Worse?"

"Certainly. As fascinated as you seem to be with this place, this is not why I brought you here."

"Then why, Lord?"

"You have been brought here so that I may tell you that you will one day travel to distant worlds and face all manner of evil. Satan's reach extends far beyond Earth, and you will be a savior of sorts and help bring my lost children back to me. . . . But you must not be held back by your greatest enemy."

"Who?"

"You. You are going to be the greatest enemy that you will ever battle, so I am going to do something new in you. Something that I have never done for anyone, nor will ever do again . . ."

"What are you going to do to me?"

"I'm going to remove your flesh."

"My skin?"

"No." Jesus smiled. "Your flesh."

John still didn't quite understand what was about to happen.

"This is going to hurt a little . . . COME OUT!"

Jesus spoke those words, and John fell to the floor shaking and convulsing, screaming at the top of his lungs in sheer pain. The pain was unbearable, but Jesus kept calling for his flesh to come out. And almost as if there was a demon fleeing his body, evil John crawled out and fell to his knees.

"JESUS IS LORD! JESUS IS LORD!"

He shouted. Evil John was unkempt and disheveled. His eyes were bloodshot and his nails were filthy.

"Silence."

Jesus commanded the evil nature of John, and John's lips began melding together. Jesus raised his hands and thorns and thistles appeared and wrapped around the hands, feet, and neck of the being. The ground that held him was ripped from Nersa and catapulted into the sky, leading into a dark red vortex and disappearing.

John gathered himself and rested on his knees before standing.

"What was that?"

"That was you . . . your flesh. The part of you that I tell you to kill daily. . . . There are so many things that I will request of you, and you will need to be at full strength at all times in order to accomplish them."

" . . . Did you destroy him? Me? It?"

"No, to do that would destroy you too. Only citizens of heaven have their flesh completely destroyed when given their glorious body. I have given you the gift of having a glorious body while you are still an earthly resident."

"So where is it?"

"I've cast him into outer darkness, but far from the reach of Satan, who would seek him to torture him."

"I'm lost, my Lord."

"It's a lot to take in. Just know that you are free from the temptations of man."

"Free? Wait, what does that mean exactly? I get that what happened between Camilla and me was wrong, but I still love her . . . what does this mean for us? I mean, I want to marry her and have children one day."

"I know. I haven't removed that desire from you. You are like Adam when I first created him. Holy, perfect, innocent. You still have free will and a desire to love and be loved. Camilla is the special gift that I crafted for you, your helpmate in the most difficult times of your life. I have a vast plan for both of you, separately and jointly, and even plans for your son."

"Son?"

"I will send him to you when you are ready for him, but first things first."

Jesus and John had walked and talked and ended up on a dormant volcano. Jesus extended his hand, and the ground pushed up the purest diamond. It was flawless, the most spectacular stone, more phenomenal than the most beautiful diamond on Earth. Precious metal formed around the rock, and Jesus fashioned it into a ring.

"When you propose to her, use this."

He handed John the stone and enclosed his hand around it. He hugged John and told him how proud he was of him. John closed his eyes and embraced the Lord and when he opened them he was back at his apartment. In his bed.

What just happened? One moment he was in heaven, then a strange world, and the next moment he was in his bedroom. Had it all just been an elaborate dream? But it seemed so real. John felt something in his right palm and opened it. The diamond ring was in his hand. It was big but not gaudy. The sunlight snuck into his room through his blinds, and he looked at his clock: 8:37 a.m.

He knew Camilla would be at work, and he reached for his phone and called her. He was shocked to hear her ringtone coming from the other side of his bedroom door. He reached for some clothes, walked into his living room, and there was Camilla, looking more beautiful than he had ever seen her.

<hr/>

Evil John was stuck and there was no way free as he careened through the dark vortex, which was terrifying enough. He hit all sides of the portal and finally shot through into the red sky of hell. He fell and burned in the atmosphere like a meteor from space. His flight was in a part of hell that wasn't frequently traveled. He landed in some mountain ranges just off the coast of the volatile, slick black oily sea. When he landed, the rock broke apart and crumbled, loosening him from his thorny entrapments.

He looked up at the hellish sun; all he had was hate to keep him going. He hated what just happened to him, hated who did it to him, but he also hated giving in, and hated the idea of wasting away in these mountains. He would not die here. He would not die *here.* He stood up and began walking further into the mountains until he found an unoccupied cave. The cave looked like it belonged to a fallen angel, but whoever was once here had abandoned it a very long time ago.

This looked like as good a place as any to live until he could find his way back to earth. There was only one person who could make him complete, and he had just been ripped away from him. He was incomplete without him, and he was determined to get back to him. But what would he do once he found him? Would he try to reunite? No, that was probably impossible and furthermore, he liked having his own body to control. No longer fighting for control of one body, now he was the true master of his own destiny. All that was left to do was to concentrate on becoming as strong as he could be.

If he had finally found his other half and had gotten his hands on him, then that would be a victory in itself. He would relish seeping every last breath from him that he could, and he couldn't wait to do it too.

"One day . . . one day." He laughed maniacally.

Berith was building new altars of sacrifice as was commanded by his superior officer. He worked in a place that was rarely patrolled, but an expansion project had just begun. He had concentrated and built fourteen altars and was six away from his quota for the day. Just then, something shot from the sky and caught his attention. Berith was indeed intrigued and deserted his building to follow it.

What could it be? He flew into the air and kept a low profile. He followed in the direction it had landed, and once he reached the landing zone, he investigated the crash. He didn't recognize the thorns as anything that had originated on hell. He tasted the dirt that had been left behind and it definitely was an alien substance.

The dirt wasn't from earth or hell and now he would not stop until he found out what had caused the disturbance. He smelled the thorns and there was a trace of familiarity.

"Human!"

Berith was furious. How dare a human enter into hell without first being processed? He would find this human and bring him to justice. There will be no guilty on his watch that will go unjudged by Lord Satan, who was in the foulest mood lately after not being able to find and judge Lilith and the monsters that she created, but hopefully this would lighten his mood.

Berith tracked the human by his scent and his footsteps. They led him to a cave, and he was so thrilled at the possibility of finding one of the guilty that he began to salivate. Berith normally took the form of an old man with gaunt features and black leathery wings. He had another form in which he had the body of a warrior faun with the head of a cobra. A very menacing figure indeed, but he figured that form would be overkill in this situation. All he had to do was go in and capture the already frightened human and bring him before the devil. Simple.

When Berith arrived at the mouth of the cave, he heard laughing and was angered even more at the nerve of this insolent human. He entered the cave and walked right up to the figure who sat with his legs crossed, facing the cave wall.

"That laughter will soon be replaced by your cries."

He grabbed the human and dug his nails into his shoulder. The laughing only got louder. Berith dug his nails in deeper and drew blood. Evil John grabbed Berith's hand and flipped him over his shoulder with such force that it shook the cave. Berith was more than shocked and looked into the face of the immensely powerful creature.

Evil John grabbed the demon by his mouth and dragged him across the floor. He smashed Berith's face against the walls and pounded it. The attack was beyond vicious. It wasn't demonic and there was no way Berith could defend himself. John smashed Berith's face with rocks and bit him. He broke his limbs and didn't stop the assault.

This human was no ordinary human. He had the strength of a warrior angel and looked like a human, but didn't possess the good nature that could convince one to stop an attack. It seemed almost like there was no conscience to inhibit the evil that existed in the hearts of all mankind. No, this human had no conscience, no good side to contend with, and it showed in the way he fought.

Berith was slammed to the ground, and then the unthinkable happened. Evil John began eating Berith alive. He began eating his wings and other parts of his body. In Berith's many millennia of existence, he would have never pictured a human eating one of his kind; yet it was happening. Berith cried out in horror and tried to get away but could not.

"DID THE LORD SEND YOU HERE TO PUNISH US?"

"The Lord? No. I am not on the Lord's side."

"THEN WHOSE?"

"I am not for the Lord. I am not for Satan. I am for *me*."

Those were the last words that Berith would hear for a very long time for his time of torture as evil John's prisoner had just begun.

"Camilla, what are you doing here?"

Camilla ran to John and hugged him tightly.

"I was worried about you and couldn't sleep. So I came here. . . . Actually, Gabriel appeared to me and told me to wait for you here."

"I see."

"I was so worried about you during the fight. Everyone is looking for you. They all want to know who you are, what you are, where you're from. . . . The news is going crazy over you and those giants. You know they never found the bodies? There is even footage of a woman dressed in red making them disappear. Vanishing out of thin air and it's got everyone talking about it. And I—"

"Cammy . . . ," he interrupted. "I was so worried about you; you didn't go home. . . . When Rapha closed in on you, I . . ."

"You saved me. Like I knew you would. If I ever doubted your love for me, I was convinced after that."

"I don't ever want you to doubt that I love you. I would go through hell and rescue you from the devil himself if I had to."

"Wow, that's tough talk. Let's hope you never have to."

"You mean more to me than the next breath I take. The Bible says that 'He that finds a wife finds a good thing and obtains favor from the Lord.' . . . I have found my good thing. Will you marry me?"

John dropped to his knees and raised the ring. Camilla's eyes welled up with tears of joy and she nodded and voiced, "YES!" She kissed him, and he picked her up and twirled her around. At that moment, the world was perfect for them until he heard sirens from his apartment. Fire trucks raced toward a massive fire. John looked at Camilla. It was a look that said he needed to help.

"Go ahead." She smiled.

John and Camilla went to his roof as they had done so many times before. She stepped back and watched him transform into his familiar blue and white armored suit and fly into the sky. He was gone. She smiled and watched him get ready to save another day.

Printed in the USA
CPSIA information can be obtained
at www.ICGtesting.com
JSHW022326140824
68134JS00019B/1319

9 781630 474287